DARK MOTIVE

A CARSON BRAND NOVEL #2

CRAIG RAINEY

Craig Rainey Creative, LLC

AUSTIN, TEXAS

Craig Rainey/Craig Rainey Creative, LLC
Austin, TX USA
craigrainey.com

Publisher's Note: This is a work of fiction. Names, characters, places, and incidents are a product of the author's imagination. Locales and public names are sometimes used for atmospheric purposes. Any resemblance to actual people, living or dead, or to businesses, companies, events, institutions, or locales is completely coincidental.

Cover Design by Paramita Creative

Dark Motive/ Craig Rainey. -- 1st ed.
ISBN 978-1-7339867-6-2

OTHER BOOKS BY CRAIG RAINEY

The Carson Brand Series

Stolen Valor

Dark Motive

Reasonable Sin

Sovereign Rule

Nations Law

Western Fiction

Massacre at Agua Caliente

HOODOO WAR

Nonfiction

The Art of Professional Sales

Reviews
DARK MOTIVE

"Reading Dark Motive feels like watching an action movie in 3D display. The author's way of describing scenery and unfolding events is quite gripping and adds to the momentum, as the reader is left wondering with anxiousness about what is going to happen next. This book is a masterpiece and deserves the maximum stars!"

– I LOVE UNIQUEBOOKS REVIEW

Like Stolen Valor, the first novel in the series, this book holds your attention - you can't wait to read what happens next! The detailed narrative allows you to picture each scene in vivid detail. I can't wait for Book #3 - thank you for the great read, Craig!

– READER REVIEW

Action packed, exciting, well written. Brand ... Rough, tough, no-nonsense, ...Quite an accomplishment for a character involved in the horrors of the dark drug and human trafficking's underground. I am looking forward to the third Carson Brand book.

– READER REVIEW

For Louise – The Queen of Valhalla and a true friend

Under the loftiest monuments sleeps the dust of murder.
— ROBERT G. INGERSOLL

1

THE MORNING WAS BRIGHT. A COOL BREEZE carried a false promise of relief on a day when the heat index would again break records for the city of Houston. In the heart of the city's Theater District, the Bob Casey Federal Courthouse rose above the heavy traffic clogging the busy street in front of the modern building.

A large crowd milled about, filling the wide sidewalk in front of the glass-and-steel entrance to the courthouse.

A long black car pulled to the curb. Speaker of the House Franklin Cole stepped out from the back seat and onto the concrete sidewalk. He was immediately surrounded by his team of attorneys and a cadre of stern-faced Secret Service agents.

Tanner Morales slapped his cameraman on the shoulder and broke into a run. His cameraman, William, shouldered his way through the converging pack of journalists, keeping pace with Morales as they approached the Speaker's entourage.

William shouldered through the crowd beside him, camera balanced on one shoulder. Tanner valued him precisely because he was big enough to push through the crowd and tall enough to shoot over it if he couldn't get to the front.

Morales arrived with the first wave of reporters. He thrust his microphone forward and asked the first question.

"Good morning, Mr. Speaker. How high does this scandal go in Congress?"

"To the top," Cole replied flatly. "My intentions were the best, but I see now intentions alone weren't enough to protect this great country from the enemies working to destroy her."

A deafening rise of voices followed this admission from the famous congressman. Tanner Morales pressed closer, raising his voice above the cacophony of questions.

"Mr. Speaker, who are these enemies you say want to defeat America?"

Cole stopped abruptly, causing his entourage to stumble as they halted their momentum. The Speaker turned and looked directly at Tanner Morales.

"You are, sir," he replied heatedly. "The truth is right in front of your eyes."

He swept his gaze around the mass of journalists encircling him. His accusation silenced them.

"The enemy is no longer at the gates. The enemy is here among us. You people are supposed to be custodians of the truth, but you've become harbingers of the very evil you claim to revile.

"No matter what is said about me in the coming weeks, I took an oath to protect and serve this country. Somewhere along the way, I lost sight of that.

"That's enough," one of the attorneys ordered, gripping the Speaker's shoulder.

Cole shook off the hand, once more facing the stunned reporters.

"I will have my say," he continued. "I ask, for once, you act as the voice of the people rather than using your platform to amplify your own voices. To the people, I say: even if I have to bring the whole thing down around me, I will expose the evil threatening our very way of life. I will honor the oath I took so many years ago."

He glanced at the attorney, silently giving permission to move forward. The reporters' voices exploded into a chaotic frenzy of shouted questions as the entourage resumed their path toward the courthouse.

Tanner Morales looked behind him, searching for William. The tall cameraman met his gaze with a lanky smile and a nod—he had gotten it all. Tanner grabbed William's sleeve and pulled him away from the group, heading for a spot under one of the large trees near the congested street. He rotated until the courthouse was visible in the background.

"Roll, William," he instructed.

"Rolling, boss," William confirmed.

"This is Tanner Morales at the federal courthouse here in Houston, where Speaker of the House Franklin Cole is surrendering to authorities on charges of accepting bribes and conspiring to defraud the government. Additional charges are likely to include obstruction of justice and treason.

"After nearly a year of investigations and rumors of corruption surrounding the senior congressman, Speaker Cole announced yesterday he would surrender to the authorities this morning. Moments ago, he had this to say."

Tanner signaled for a pause.

"Insert," he directed to the camera. After a brief pause, he began again.

"The press has been barred from the courtroom. We anticipate a press conference after the hearing from the FBI and the Department of Justice. We'll bring you developments as they occur. This is Tanner Morales in Houston."

William rolled a short outro and pressed the stop button.

"We're out," he told Tanner.

2

HIS NAME WAS ACHMED AND HE WAITED in the front passenger seat of the idling Toyota Prius. The air conditioner labored to keep him cool beneath the long black pea coat and the shaped explosives strapped to his torso.

He tasted fear's rusty bitterness in his mouth. He knew the fear was no more than his body's natural reaction to what he must do for God. He learned to view fear, in the course of his service to the destruction of all false faiths—*at-Taaghoot*, merely as a blister to honest labor. Fear was natural, yet unimportant. His belief and training reduced his fear to nothing more than a bothersome discomfort.

Today, his focus was split between his lessons and the timing of his act of *Intidhar*—the preparation for the coming of *Imam Mahdi*. He had been the most unlikely candidate for the honor. Only two years before, he had been *Kafir*, openly non-Muslim in both actions and faith. Now his knees and elbows were rough from the *Salat*. His heart was pure. He had been uniquely chosen as the direct instrument in the elimination of *at-Taaghoot*. His was the most sacred act in destroying all things worshipped other than the one true God, *Allah*.

"*Laa ilaha illa Allaah*," he muttered, his attention fixed on the crowded street before him.

Three police cars sat at the curb in front of the large courthouse. Their light bars whirled and flashed, strobing reds and blues. A huge mass of onlookers, packs of journalists, and suited federal officers jockeyed for position around the building's front doors.

Achmed sat in the little car, waiting across the street some fifty yards away, just outside the barriers blocking the downtown street. He watched for the signal to move. Though he did not know what the signal would be, he had been assured he would recognize it when it came.

A slight change in the movement of the milling crowd signaled the prisoner would soon emerge from the building. Achmed ignored the silent driver waiting with him. He opened the door and stood on the hot pavement of the street. Reaching into his coat pocket, he grasped the plunger trigger, gripping it tightly in his right hand as he nervously awaited the signal.

3

JOE MERCER BRACED HIMSELF AGAINST the pressing bodies of the mob. He pushed against the weight of the crowd with his hands against the glass as writhing onlookers pressed into him and his group. He gave an assuring glance to one of his protesters.

His participation in these demonstrations had led to his arrest on numerous occasions. His repeated liberation from jail with no subsequent legal backlash confirmed he was the embodiment of the American way. His First Amendment rights were sacrosanct even to those against whom he protested.

He was an activist leader. His job was to provide direction and purpose to mindless protestors. His demonstrations had always been aimed at helpless citizens or opposing activists. This day, however, was different. Where previously the police had disrupted his activities, this time he and his group were to disrupt the duties of law enforcement.

His experience with the police had taught him you always got a warning. He knew his initial act would draw that warning. The aftermath of the second act would warrant a far more committed reaction.

Mercer squinted to see through the thick tempered glass outside the modern courthouse building. Killing a man was never easy. The task was made much more difficult when the man was in police custody and wore a Kevlar vest.

His role as a leader placed him in proximity to the direst acts imaginable. He had seen much violence and death in his commitment to the cause. He believed his job was crucial, and the darkness he sometimes embraced was a means to a required end. At times, the cause demanded a high price. He believed in his work and was willing to do what it took to succeed.

He turned, locating the uniformed officers stationed strategically within the milling crowd. He had to be cautious in selecting a path free of impediments which could delay the group. Timing was everything.

He found a route clear of law enforcement. He mustered his courage as his time drew near. Today he wasn't concerned about the killing of the man. He only had to draw that first warning.

His gaze returned to search the inside of the courthouse. Through the tinted windows he saw a phalanx of uniformed officers making their way down a long hallway toward the lobby. He spied his quarry. He caught only brief glimpses of the prisoner among the tightly packed bodies of the officers. Building security moved bystanders aside, making room for the approaching group.

The police escort spread wider as it left the narrow confines of the hallway, entering the wide lobby which housed the double doors of the building's entrance.

Joe saw the prisoner clearly now. He wore a black Kevlar vest over an orange inmate jumpsuit. His feet and hands were shackled, causing him to shamble rather than walk. His balding head and wire-framed glasses shone vulnerably under the fluorescent lights of the lobby. Mercer was surprised how small he seemed. In power, the important man had seemed a giant among his peers.

Franklin Cole looked around helplessly and fearfully. Today, all the power and fame were gone, replaced by shame and ridicule. The mob outside represented a national abhorrence for him. No one is hated as one who was once trusted unquestioningly.

The double front doors flung open as the police entourage moved confidently into the hot glare of the Houston afternoon. Cole squinted in the bright sunlight. Head down, the angry din of the crowd dulled his perceptions. He felt the impassioned sound of the mob and the pounding heat of the blazing Texas afternoon as a united assault upon his narrow shoulders and balding head. He experienced strange gratitude for the strong grips and irresistible force of the officers as they carried him through the crowd. It seemed at times his feet left the ground as he was taken from the courthouse to the police convoy which would end with him in a secure private jail cell.

A quick movement to his right drew him from his reverie. A long-haired man, his face twisted in hatred, was thrown to the ground by one of the guards as he rushed the officers surrounding the prisoner.

Some distance from the police entourage, Joe watched the long-haired man struggle with the arresting officer. He gestured to his followers. He and the fourteen angry young men moved as one, shouldering through the pressing crowd, roughly shoving curious onlookers out of the way. Joe Mercer plowed through the mob on an intercepting course with the prisoner escort.

A tall man holding his two children fell back from the advancing protestors. Three men in expensive suits complained as they were jostled and moved aside. Joe was a large man with angry eyes.

With remarkable speed, they drew to only a few yards from the security detail. On cue, the protestors raised their signs and their voices in chants.

"NOTUS – We won't go! No right, no rich, no po po!"

Joe and the National Organization of Trotskyite United Socialists broke through the crowd at a perfect right angle, converging upon the slowly advancing police guard. Joe pressed headlong toward the detail. The officers were well-trained and acted immediately upon their training, turning to face the protestors, pressing forward against the impending attack.

Joe bent low and leapt headlong into the officers like a linebacker rushing an offensive line to sack the quarterback. The angry NOTUS protestors followed. The impetus of Joe and fourteen sprinting men overwhelmed the half-dozen guards.

Camera shutters clicked and video cameras whirred as the press struggled to gain a vantage point from which to record the melee unfolding before them.

The converging reporters' movements hindered the frightened bystanders' flight from the violence. The shifting mob tangled, and many fell to the hot concrete, trampled by others. The tone of the angry mob changed by degree as the wail of the frightened and the injured added their voices to the din.

Those few guards who were not struggling to regain their feet rallied after the surprise of the initial assault. They moved to reform the security cordon around the prisoner. The officers did not wait for their fallen comrades to join them. Rather, with desperate strength, they fairly carried the prisoner as they again made their way toward the awaiting police cars. The officers stationed amongst the police cavalcade at the curb moved toward them, trying to usher the panicked crowd out of the path of the diminished security detail.

The terrified Cole, and the few guards who escorted him, finally broke free of the packed throng and entered the open area near the line of police cars.

Cole felt vulnerable and exposed as the three remaining officers in his escort struggled through the diminished crowd near the awaiting police cars. Two of the fallen officers appeared from behind them, rejoining the prisoner escort as they neared the police cars.

Franklin Cole looked up from his intense focus on the ground and his efforts to remain above his shambling feet. As if through a narrow tunnel, he saw a dark-headed young man in a long black coat slide between two of the police cars. The young man's dark eyes locked with Cole's as he drew his right hand from his coat pocket.

Cole saw he held something metallic. He couldn't see clearly what the dark-headed man held, but it glinted in the summer sun. The dark man spread his arms wide as if to offer Franklin Cole a welcoming embrace. As his arms rose, the coat opened, and the congressman saw the rectangular packs and loose wiring of an explosive vest.

The police noticed the man in the coat too late. Their attention had been on the crowd and the protestors behind them. They drew their weapons to neutralize this new threat. Their weapons never came on line for a shot.

Joe Mercer grappled with two uniformed officers as the blast shook the crowd. He and the officers fell to the hot sidewalk, their ears ringing with the concussion of the blast.

4

CARSON BRAND ENTERED THE LITTERED alleyway with a measured step and a cautious eye. Although it was mid-afternoon, the tall buildings on either side cast cool dark shadows upon the stained pavement of the alley.

According to the man he had left bleeding and bound on a dirty floor, the tall building to his right was where he would find Christina. In addition to the reluctantly provided information Brand was able to draw from his tormented informant, "enter through the alley in back" had been uttered with an honesty wrought by the same pain.

Brand had passed by the front, noticing several seemingly unassociated men sitting loosely about. Their interest in Brand confirmed they protected the vulnerable front entrance. Brand had moved past them casually.

Set within the building's spray-painted bricks was a peeling metal door with a slide viewport set at eye level. There were no windows on that side of the structure. The steel door was the lowest of several built at the rusty landings of a zigzagging fire escape which served each of the ten floors of the old building.

Brand stopped before the steel door. He glanced around once more. Nothing stirred around him other than the rare breeze which lifted trash in lazy circles in the tight space between the buildings. There was no knob or handle on the door.

With one last look down the alleyway, Brand beat the door with three hard knocks. He listened for any indication of movement within. He detected none. Either no one was inside, or the steel door was thick enough to mask the sounds.

He waited a full minute with no answer to his knock. He was about to turn from the door when he heard a scraping sound as someone worked at the mechanism that secured the door. Brand watched as the viewport slid slowly with a reluctant squeak.

A stripe of a dark face and black narrowed eyes surveyed him blandly through the narrow viewport.

"What do you want?" a whiny voice asked through the port.

"I was told to meet Oscar here," Brand replied as innocuously as he could.

"There is no Oscar here, white man," was the quick answer.

"Bullshit," Brand argued without heat. "Open the door and stop wasting my time."

The doorkeeper's eyes shifted down and away as he considered the direct manner of the stranger.

"Who said Oscar is here?"

The voice held a new quality. Brand thought he detected doubt, maybe fear.

"Don Rojas sent me."

The eyes focused on him once more. They held him with a steady stare.

"Wait."

The slide again closed over the narrow port, and Brand waited for several minutes before it was opened once more.

This time the eyes in the viewport belonged to someone else. They were green with flecks of gold at the edges.

"Who are you?" a female voice asked suspiciously.

Brand looked at his feet as his impatience grew. He glared at the green eyes.

"I don't have time to stand out here in this alley while you decide whether or not Don Rojas will punish you for blocking me out. The answer is yes, he will. Open the door and stop wasting time."

The green eyes hesitated a moment more before the viewport slid shut. Metal scraped and clicked as she unlocked the door. It swung open reluctantly on groaning hinges. Inside the doorway stood an older woman wearing too much makeup and a small dark man holding a snub-nosed revolver.

"Enter," the woman commanded.

Brand considered the smaller man for a moment before he complied. The gunman's dark eyes held a menacing light. Brand recognized him as the first who had answered the door.

The woman looked him up and down.

Carson Brand was just over six feet tall, athletically built for a man who rarely worked out or ran. His arms and legs were sturdy from a life of labor. The old woman shifted her assessment to his blue eyes. They were dark as a stormy sea.

She glanced at the small man holding the gun.

The gunman gestured with his pistol.

"Against the wall," he commanded in a high, pinched voice.

Brand stepped inside and put his hands against the painted concrete wall just inside the doorway. The gunman frisked him rapidly with practiced efficiency.

"He is unarmed," he told the woman.

She watched Brand as he faced her once more.

"What do you want with Oscar?" she demanded.

"I am to speak only to him," Brand said in return.

The woman weighed this as she considered him gravely. After she studied him for a few long seconds, she seemed to come to a decision.

"Oscar has not been here for several days," she explained with unexpected candor. "We are concerned at his absence."

"I see," Brand said.

His thoughts returned to the memory of Oscar bound hand and foot with duct tape in a dark apartment in Houston's 3rd Ward.

"Can you help me then?" he asked.

"With what?" she asked suspiciously.

"I am looking for a friend. Her name is Christina. She came in on what you call the 'Vaca Train.' She is Latina, attractive, and speaks English."

The gunman growled as he brought the pistol up to fire at Brand.

Brand struck the gunman's hand as the pistol belched flame. The bullet cracked wickedly as it bounced off the concrete wall. He snatched the gun hand, pulling the smaller man toward him. He grabbed the man's head and slammed it against the wall where he had frisked him.

With a groan, the gunman folded, unconscious.

Brand collected the pistol from the limp hand, dropping him to the floor. He adjusted his grip on the pistol, training it on the woman. His ears rang from the loud report.

"No more tricks," he warned. "Oscar lied to me. I will punish you if you lie."

The woman said nothing. She merely stared at him. Brand noted she seemed to be without fear.

"Let's go," Brand said, gesturing with the pistol.

She obeyed without any resistance. Brand's caution grew at her ready compliance. He followed her along a dark hallway. At the center of the long narrow corridor, a single bare bulb provided a dim, raw light. They passed under the bulb, continuing toward the darkness at the other end.

Brand strained to hear anything which might give away a trap or an ambush. He heard only the faint sounds of distant machinery and the ringing in his ears.

The woman led silently with a slow gait. She turned to the right, and they climbed a dark staircase within a dingy stairwell. The first landing was visible in the dusky glow of another bare bulb in the ceiling. Brand glanced upward through the center space between the railings. The stairs disappeared into darkness above.

They mounted the stairs in darkness until they reached the landing for the third floor where she pushed the bar on a heavy door. Inside, the stench of filth, excrement, and something he could not place assailed his nose. He guessed it must be death.

A long wide corridor stretched toward the opposite side of the building. At the end of the long hallway stood another sturdy steel door. Judging by the direction they faced, Brand presumed it was one of the outside doors opening onto the fire escape he had seen from the alley. Several side doors led into adjoining rooms on both sides of the dark hallway. The building appeared to have been an office complex at one time.

The woman stopped. She turned slowly until she faced him.

"If she is here," the crone explained in a withered tone, "she is in one of these rooms on this floor. If she is not on this floor, you cannot help her."

She waited for his reaction. He sensed she expected him to visit violence upon her. With surprising insight, he realized she was not without fear. She was without hope.

"You lead," he ordered.

She shrugged, turning away from him as slowly as before. She shuffled to the first door. Inside, a man was atop a blonde woman who stared blankly at the ceiling. He writhed as she lay inert, unresponsive to the base act forced upon her body.

Brand felt disgust rising in him. He wanted to shoot the man. He clenched his teeth and pushed the woman roughly toward the next door, taking out some of his anger on her.

At the next entrance, two women sat against the far wall, clutching one another as they eyed Brand with dread. Neither was Christina.

In this way, they went from room to room, each view a new and more horrible sight to Brand. At the last doorway near the end of the long hallway, Brand paused, focusing upon the naked body of a woman with long black hair. She lay on the floor, her bruised back toward him.

Was she Christina? He pushed the woman into the room.

"Turn her over so I can see her face," he ordered the older woman.

She looked up at him impassively.

"This is not your Christina," she assured him.

"Do it," Brand repeated, his voice a growl with his anger and a growing sense of dread.

The woman shrugged, pulling the naked woman onto her bruised back. The face he saw was vacant of expression and unfamiliar.

Brand grabbed the older woman and shook her upright.

"How did you know she was not Christina?" he demanded of her.

The wretch smiled at him as though he were the pathetic one.

"Christina is dead."

Brand struggled to make sense of what he heard.

"Don Rojas gave instructions she was special and was to be treated as such."

She looked into Brand's eyes to make certain he understood.

"She is dead and gone. She is as dead as *Señor* Rojas."

Brand stared at her in disbelief. The woman knew more than she had given away. Brand felt a twinge of remorse as he struggled to believe Christina was dead. His journey to rescue her had been long and arduous. Rojas, the head of the Gulf Cartel, had died at his feet in Mexico less than a month before. At gunpoint, one of his henchmen had told him about the "Vaca Train" upon which Christina had been taken to Houston.

This woman knew everything, yet she had allowed him inside.

"Why did you lead me here?"

The woman's heavily made-up face screwed into an evil mask. Her expression froze like a building gargoyle as she listened to a nearly inaudible faraway noise. Brand canted his head to identify the sound. He soon recognized what he heard: it was the pounding of slamming doors and the heavy staccato of boots on smooth concrete.

He had walked into a trap.

From his place near the naked woman and the old crone, he heard the stairwell door bang open. Several pairs of feet scuffed along the long hallway.

Brand felt a familiar buzz of anger rising in him. The feeling was akin to a light-headed euphoria. A raging hunger consumed him as he anticipated the conflict to come.

The memory of Christina haunted him, torturing him with the realization he had failed her. He stared at the grinning wretch who allowed women to be treated this way. He listened as unseen assailants closed in on him. All of these caused his blood to run hot in his veins. He felt the familiar heat of an irresistible urge to act, and to act violently.

He struck the woman hard across the face with the pistol barrel. She fell soddenly—unconscious. Brand turned his attention to the approaching menace in the passageway. Checking the pistol for ammo, he counted five rounds.

Moving slowly along the hallway, three Latino males carried pistols as they searched the floor. They checked the first room cautiously. They snickered and spoke softly at the sight of the man atop the woman.

Brand heard them speaking in whispers and muted laughter. Although he didn't understand Spanish, he guessed they commented on the man and the woman he had seen earlier. He crept to the wall beside the open door, leaning against the wall out of view of anyone who would peer into the room.

The three Latinos crept cautiously from one door to the next. Inside each, they found only drugged and beaten women. With fading vigilance, they approached the last doorway. Their confidence in finding the intruder was waning. Had he gotten away in time?

Brand heard them outside the door. One of the men peeked around the doorjamb. He saw the two women lying on the floor. He turned to inform the others of his findings when Brand crushed his nose using the pistol grip of the black revolver.

The other two fell back from the attack as Brand turned tightly into the hallway. He lifted the stunned man with his left arm, covering the two men with the pistol in his right. His first shot sent shards of plaster into the nearest man's face. The other Latino shot the man Brand held upright. Brand felt the body jolt as the slug struck deeply. Brand shoved the wounded man at them and fired wildly as he turned toward the steel door leading to the fire escape.

Three rapid strides brought him to the door. He shoved the bar, pushing the rusty door ajar. He slid through the narrow opening, slamming the heavy door as a volley of slugs pinged off its solid surface.

The weathered steel stairs creaked a rusty warning as he descended, leaping from landing to landing. The platform ended some fifteen feet above the alley pavement. A ladder was hinged from the bottom landing in an upright position. It was secured with a quick-pull release pin. Brand tore at the mechanism. Frozen in place from years of rust and weather damage, the pin did not move.

He heard a scraping squeal as the door above swung slowly outward. He guessed the prospect of gunfire had slowed the pursuit for the moment.

Brand leaned out over the railing and fired a shot up the fire escape. The two Latinos retreated, jumping against the brick wall behind the cover of the steel landing.

Brand stuffed the pistol into his waistband and stepped over the railing. He grabbed the ladder and lowered himself hand over hand until he hung from the bottom rung. His feet were more than eight feet off the ground.

A shot exploded above him. The bullet nearly parted his hair. He let go, landing in a controlled roll—feet, calf, thigh, hip. He leapt to his feet and moved to cover against the building. Keeping near the brick wall, he ran along the alley toward the street.

Shots rang out above him. Bullets pinged off the pavement dangerously close, adding an additional urgency to his flight.

At the street he ducked right. He looked around the corner toward his backtrail. He saw the third-floor door slam closed as the Latinos re-entered the building. Brand felt certain they would contact the sentries occupying the front sidewalk, enlisting their aid in the pursuit.

Brand turned from the alleyway and cautiously headed away from the danger. With a conscious effort, he held his pace to a casual walk, wary of signs of pursuit. His body stiffened in alarm as he heard an approaching police siren. He hurried to the curb and dropped the gun into a nearby storm drain.

Just ahead, two Houston PD cruisers roared around the corner, grinding to a halt before him. Four uniformed officers stepped from the cars and trained their weapons on him. Blue and red lights whirled. Stoic voices from police radios filled the air as Brand raised his hands in surrender.

"On the ground!" one of the officers shouted, pressing his weapon forward to cover Brand.

With raised hands, Brand lowered himself to his knees. Two officers converged upon him, aggressively pushing him flat onto the sidewalk. They cuffed him, then frisked him. They lifted him to his feet, roughly shoving him against the brick wall where they frisked him once again. They emptied his pockets, opening his wallet.

"Carson Brand," one of the officers said, reading the name from his driver's license.

More police cars arrived on scene. An older officer approached the group.

"Is this him?" he asked.

"Yes, Lieutenant," was the reply.

"Take him."

"Lieutenant, we haven't investigated the gunshots yet."

"We'll take it from here. Get him in a cell ASAP."

"Yes, sir."

"What is the charge?" Brand asked.

"Shut up."

5

THEY CALLED IT GLADIATOR FLOOR. On the seventh floor of
the Harris County lockup, guards staged fights and bet on the outcome.
The 7th floor of the Harris County Lockup was one of Houston's best-
kept dirty secrets, and Brand was now a part of that secret hell.

Carson Brand was housed with the hardest gang bangers in the pod.
The guards staged fights and bet on the outcome. Every tattooed hard
case was trying to make his bones. Every other prisoner tried only to
survive.

Brand was new, making him a target. His introduction was short but
compelling. A fellow inmate broke down the details moments before he
was singled out to participate. You fought when the guards told you to.
There was no refusal. Those who refused to fight were raped.

Brand's bare feet felt raw on the concrete floor. The lean, sinewy
black man across from him glared fiercely. His tattooed skin shone with
sweat. Corded muscles moved beneath slick skin like angry pythons
within a shining sack. Tattoos covered him from the top of his bald head,
down his torso, and into the black and white striped jumpsuit, draped
low where it was tied off at his waist.

From their cells, inmates yelled, craning their necks for a view of the
combatants through rough gray bars.

Three guards grinned cruelly.

"The white boy was going down," one said to another.

Walker was their longest-reigning champion. Of all the inmates, he enjoyed the fights most. Others fought because combat was preferable to the alternative. Walker thrived on the conflict. He reveled in the notoriety and the stench of fear running down his opponents' legs.

"The new guy is no match for Walker," said the third.

"Put your money where your mouth is."

Brand saw the guards but could only guess at their conversation. His sole preoccupation was the fierce black man before him.

Brand quartered his body slightly. He flexed his knees in a ready position. He had no idea how the attack would come, but he knew it would happen soon. He felt himself growing angry. He disliked being pressed into a fight he hadn't started. He certainly resented the obvious opinion he was an easy victim for the tattooed inmate.

Walker approached Brand casually, his hands hanging low along his sides.

The guards chuckled. They had seen this technique before.

Walker continued his forward advance until he saw the smallest movement as Brand tried to create distance between them. With incredible speed, his right hand shot toward Brand's face. Brand turned his head but caught the blow on his jaw. He fell hard to the concrete, banging his head as he did.

Walker was on him. He kicked Brand. If Brand had not covered his ribs with his left arm, one would be broken.

Walker backed up. The crowd cheered him. He lifted his hands victoriously, spinning for his fans.

The guards laughed. The one who bet on Brand frowned.

The cell block went silent as Brand stood slowly.

Walker had his back to him when he rose. With a surprised look on his face, he turned, facing his vanquished foe.

"You dumb motherfucker. You coulda quit and walked away from this. Now they gonna carry you out."

Walker ran at Brand, slick muscles and hard fists. He brought a right from nearly the ground with enough power to punch through and grab his backbone.

Brand stepped to his left. He delivered a hard right.

Walker caught the blow fully in the center of his face. The impact was magnified by his forward momentum. He felt his nose break and his teeth rattle loose. Walker's momentum shifted, causing him to stand upright. Brand drove a sharp left into Walker's throat.

Walker fell, holding his throat, trying to open his airway.

Furiously, Brand stepped in. He bludgeoned Walker's face with several hard and unnecessary blows.

The guards emerged from their stupor, rushing to pull Brand from atop Walker.

Walker lay unconscious, his face a tattered, bloodied mess.

In his frenzy to get at Walker, Brand struggled to shake off the guards' restraining holds. A kick to his torso and a billy club to the head turned out the lights.

BRAND WAS IN SOLITARY CONFINEMENT when he was collected and led to the visitor's hold. He entered the room bound at wrists and ankles with heavy shackles.

Alone in the room stood a tall thin man in a suit holding a red folder. He nodded to the guards, and they sat Brand at the center table. They used a spare set of cuffs to shackle him to the table.

The guards hesitated over Brand.

The man in the suit waited for them to leave. Finally, he spoke with the authority of a federal officer.

"Give us the room, gentlemen."

Reluctantly, the guards retreated behind a heavy door with bulletproof glass.

Brand considered the man in the suit with a disinterested expression.

"So, you are a hard case now," the man in the suit observed dubiously.

Brand said nothing.

"I am Matthew Kilgore, DEA. You are in a lot of trouble, Mr. Brand."

Kilgore approached the round steel table, sitting across from Brand. He set the red folder on the table before him.

"What would you say if I offered to get you out of here today—right now?"

"You people put me in here," Brand replied immediately.

"Your recent activities have drawn a lot of attention from highly placed individuals on both sides of the law. I don't believe you will last long in here once it is known you single-handedly wiped out the Gulf Cartel."

Brand remembered Detective Hernandez's list of crimes he had committed. He had since added many more, but he had not wiped out the cartel. He had merely been on hand for a coup.

"What's in the folder?"

"We dug deep on you."

Kilgore opened the file at the center. Notes and official-looking forms were clasped to both flaps of the folder. Kilgore closed the file without reading it.

"Based on your impressively speedy creation of a very considerable rap sheet, the law will imprison you for the rest of your life. How do you feel about that, Mr. Brand?"

"It sounds like I am in a tight spot."

"I want you to go to work for me," Kilgore replied simply. "As a private citizen, everything you have done over the past months is a criminal offense. As a federal asset, all of those things were done in the line of duty and would likely warrant some type of award or citation."

Brand shook his head at the irony.

"Join me and walk away from this mess clean. Allow yourself to be appropriately rewarded for a job we have been trying to do for a long time now."

"It sounds like I have no other choice."

"You don't—at least not a choice that ends well for you."

Brand looked down at his chains.

"What exactly am I agreeing to?"

"Freedom. I'll assume your answer is yes. It will take some time to work out the details with local law enforcement. Unfortunately, you may have to spend a few days here before we straighten this out."

Kilgore rose, tucking the red folder under his arm.

"Once you're released, you will have to stay in Houston for a few weeks. You will attend training classes to learn the skills you will need for the job."

Before Brand could ask Kilgore to elaborate, the agent ended the conversation with a gesture.

He hesitated before leaving.

"How did you get out of Mexico without us catching you?"

"Seriously?" Brand asked incredulously. "I walked across a shallow part of the river and grabbed a ride. An army could have crossed without you knowing it."

Kilgore smiled at Brand's candor.

"We'll look into that."

Kilgore turned and moved to the door.

The door lock buzzed, and the awaiting guards moved aside as Kilgore left.

7

THE FOLLOWING MORNING, BRAND WAS placed in a line of inmates in prison garb. Chained together, they were instructed to follow a yellow line along a narrow hallway into a concrete room with a low ceiling and a judge's dais at one end.

The prisoners shuffled awkwardly down a narrow aisle between steel benches. A guard led them to the front row and sat them as one on the long bench.

Prosecutors sat at a table to the side. They looked at laptops and typed one-handed as they waited for the proceedings to begin.

The bailiff stood.

"All rise," he called loudly.

The shackled inmates stood as a clean-shaven, pockmarked-faced judge in black robes entered, taking a seat behind the heavy bench.

"Sit," the bailiff commanded.

Brand and the other inmates sat.

After several busy minutes of paperwork and hushed conversations between the judge and one prosecutor after another, the judge adjusted his microphone and leaned forward.

"Alvin Ames," he read from a page in a tan folder.

"Here, sir," a voice among the inmates answered.

"You are charged with aggravated assault. Bond is set at $25,000. Do you have an attorney?"

"Yes, sir."

"Robert Ames," the judge read.

"Here, Your Honor."

"You are charged with theft by check under $500. Bail is $1,000. Defendant is eligible to apply for PR Bond. Do you have an attorney?"

"No, sir."

"Can you afford one or do you need a public defender?"

"I need a public defender, sir."

The judge pointed at the back of the room.

"The court will appoint counsel."

"Carson Brand," the judge said as he continued reading from the list.

"Here," Brand replied.

"Criminal trespass. Bail is $10,000. Can you afford counsel?"

"No, sir."

"The court will appoint counsel."

Brand felt relief wash over him. The charge seemed serious, but he was not facing any of the grave charges the Fed had listed. That was good news.

"William Camey," the judge called.

"Here, sir."

"Possession of a controlled substance, misdemeanor. Bail is $5,000. Can you afford counsel?"

The court proceedings continued in this way for just over an hour, after which the inmates were returned to holding or to their cells if, like Brand, they were housed already.

8

AMY LANDRY WAS IN NO MOOD TO HANDLE a day filled with rude gang bangers and angry druggies. Her ex was up to his tricks, and the sting from their latest highly contentious phone call was fresh. She hated it when he upset her. She was certain he counted it a victory when she responded to his unreasonable demands with any level of emotion at all. Her patience was not a credit to her faith. She struggled with her anger toward the man's self-serving actions.

Since the divorce and throughout the continued custody hearings, he had presented to the courts a front of reasonable calm and decorum. A long enough phone call, or bitter enough face-to-face, would shatter the brittle façade, revealing his true nature. He handled the limited public exposure in their numerous legal proceedings with ease, never showing any sign of his temper.

The morning traffic was heavy as she drove toward the courthouse annex. As she left the crowded expressway, a black SUV cut her off, and she narrowly avoided colliding with the car behind her.

Her blurred vision hampered her driving, and she cursed her weakness under her breath. She dabbed at her wet eyes, looking in the rearview mirror to assess the damage to her appearance.

"Damn you, Justin," she muttered, blinking back angry tears of frustration.

She berated herself for giving him control. Her thoughts shifted to her son Peter. The tears flowed once more.

"Dammit," she repeated.

She parked her car in the reserved lot for the Public Defenders' Office. She locked up and entered the building. She smiled at the guards with a warmth she did not feel and passed through security with little delay.

Her heels clicked as she strode down a long, wide hallway and entered a large room housing nearly a dozen desks. Most of those were occupied by public defenders reviewing their caseloads for the day. She turned to the right where her desk stood.

The desk was empty save for a fresh stack of red folders in the metal inbox at the corner of the desk. Unlike most of the staff, she did the bulk of her work at her private office in South Houston. She found the dark, utilitarian nature of the Public Defenders' Office depressing.

She sat in the chair behind the desk and thumbed through the folders. Each represented a court-appointed client. Most of the cases were drug-related. She pursed her lips blandly as she found a DWI among the files. The last file contained a criminal trespass case—Carson Brand.

She guessed he was probably some gangbanger thug caught on a wealthy homeowner's lawn. She read the first few paragraphs of the police report.

Wow, she thought. The perpetrator had been arrested outside of a human trafficking operation. At least one person was found shot inside the building, and several female victims were rescued from the site. Her client was not armed, but witnesses reported hearing gunshots moments before he had been apprehended.

Amy closed the folder and stood the pile on end, tapping them into order. She glanced at her watch. The morning session would begin in less than a half hour. She stood, pushing the chair under the desk with her hip. She gathered her briefcase and left the office. She made her way along the long hallway to the courthouse.

It was early afternoon when Brand was escorted once more to the visitor's hold. He was directed to sit at one of the tables. He was surprised the guards did not shackle him to the table as before.

A few minutes passed before the heavy door was opened and a well-dressed woman entered. She carried a soft-sided briefcase. She sat across from Brand.

"I am Amy Landry from the Public Defender's Office. How are you, Mr. Brand?"

"I've been better," he replied.

She dropped her business card on the table.

"I have been appointed by the court as counsel for your defense. You are accused of criminal trespass, a Class B misdemeanor. I have reviewed the police report, and I think we can get a plea deal which will include a small fine and community service, or we can try the case. I recommend you take a deal."

"What are my chances of winning at trial?"

Amy extracted his folder from her briefcase. She thumbed through the pages within the file.

"Well, two witnesses place you in the building, one of whom claims you went upstairs with her. A man was found injured with a concussion, the result of his head making impact with a wall. Your fingerprints were found on the inside handle of a fire escape door. You seem to have been present when the place was broken into by gang members who fired shots, wounding one man. I am unsure why there are no associated charges filed in that incident.

"The good news is you have no prior arrests, and the building was being used in a human trafficking ring. Slavers and smugglers rarely press charges. But I think you would be wise to leave this thing behind you. I might be able to talk the prosecutor into a Deferred Adjudication deal which would remove the conviction after a couple of years' probation if you aren't charged with another offense during that time."

Brand considered the information. The old woman didn't mention to the police he had struck her. A misdemeanor seemed very lenient considering what he knew he could have been charged with.

"Alright," he said. "What do we do now?"

"You are scheduled for arraignment tomorrow morning at 9 a.m. We will talk with the prosecutor about a deal."

"Thank you, Ms. Landry."

She considered Brand for a moment.

"You seem like a decent type. What happened to you to land you in this mess?"

"Is that an official question?" Brand asked with a faint smile.

"Partially," she replied. "I have worked in the Public Defender's Office for just a few months. You are not our typical client. I work outreach in my spare time and thought I might offer some help or advice."

Brand agreed.

"I appreciate your interest. I was looking for someone—a girl—and I guess I was in the wrong place at the wrong time."

Brand felt a little guilty at the small exaggeration about his role in the case.

"A girl," Amy repeated. "Is she a victim of a human trafficking ring?"

"She was."

"Oh my God," Amy said with genuine alarm in her voice. "Did you find the girl?"

Brand looked down with real emotion dimming his vision.

"I found out she is dead."

Amy watched as Brand struggled to conceal his emotions.

"I am so sorry."

"Thanks," he said with a forced composure. "Hopefully, uncovering the operation will prevent any more of this type of thing from happening—there anyway."

"Hopefully," she agreed.

Brand watched her expression darken as she fought with her thoughts. At length, she collected herself. Once again, she was the dispassionate attorney. She stood, packing the file into her briefcase.

"Court tomorrow morning. I'll see you then."

Brand's thoughts went to Christina. With an effort, he focused on the present and his predicament.

"Do I get to post bail and get out of here?"

Amy hesitated before she spoke. She could see Brand was upset. She forced herself to soften her tone.

"You can contact a bail bondsman if you want. Your court date is tomorrow. I recommend you save your money and spend one more night here."

Brand realized it was a stupid question.

Amy stopped at the door, waiting for the guard to release the lock. She turned to Brand once more.

"Carson," she said warmly. "It's going to be okay."

Brand nodded his thanks for her concern.

Two guards entered the room as Amy left. They lifted Brand to his feet and escorted him back to his cell. That night, there were no staged fights. Brand managed to get some rest.

9

AT NINE, BRAND WAS SITTING IN A COURTROOM in the court annex building next door to the jail. Attorneys spoke to their clients and to awaiting prosecutors.

Amy entered the courtroom and gave him a smile of recognition as she passed. She stopped before a seated prosecutor. Brand watched her, as did most of those seated in the courtroom. The attorney was blonde and fit.

At the long prosecutors' table, Amy spoke quietly with a dark-haired, matronly woman in glasses.

Brand watched the exchange curiously, unable to hear the conversation. Amy spoke with animated emphasis.

The prosecutor listened with an air of disinterested patience, waiting for Amy to finish her statement. The prosecutor replied at length.

Amy looked at Brand for a moment as she considered what she had heard. She spoke once more to the prosecutor.

The prosecutor shrugged her shoulders. She spoke briefly to Amy in return.

Amy turned away and moved to the court clerk, seated on a lower seat next to the judge's dais. She spoke with the clerk. After a few minutes, the clerk handed her a stapled stack of paperwork.

Amy returned to where Brand waited on a long pew-like bench, crowded with prisoners awaiting their time in court. Amy had a curious smile on her face.

"The state has dropped all charges," she said in a muted tone. "Apparently, your role in exposing the slave ring weighed heavily in the decision."

"That is great news," Brand said with obvious relief.

"It is very good news," she agreed.

Amy considered Brand for a long moment.

"I need your signatures on this paperwork. After you are out-processed, you are free to go."

"Alright then," Brand said, leaning back against the hard back of the bench.

Brand signed the forms where Amy indicated. He handed the papers to her and sighed his relief.

She reviewed the documents before looking at him with genuine interest.

"Who are you?" she asked in a conspiratorial tone.

Brand looked at her blankly.

"You should have gotten at least six months' probation and a fine for this offense."

Brand drew a hesitant breath, about to protest what seemed to him a breach of trust.

Amy shook her head, closing her eyes as she more carefully crafted her thoughts.

"What I am saying is the prosecutor had an iron-clad case. All charges were dropped for non-judicial reasons. That never happens."

"I don't know what to say," he stammered, struggling to understand.

Amy watched him with a steady stare as her mind worked. Finally, she shook her head, dismissing her quandary for the moment.

"What are your plans?"

"I guess I will collect my belongings from the jail and find work. I need to stick around for a few weeks. I have some unfinished business here in Houston."

Amy nodded.

"Do you have some place to stay?"

Brand looked at her with a puzzled expression.

Amy looked uncomfortable. She struggled to shape the intimate tone of her question as casual concern.

"You are saying you will need to be local for a while. I might be able to help you find work temporarily."

Brand smiled.

"What did you have in mind?"

Amy pulled a business card from her briefcase.

"This is my office number and address. Come by or call when you are released. I can help you find temporary work until you get on your feet."

Brand was about to refuse the second card. Instead, he accepted it, not wanting to explain she had already given him one. He struggled with the confusion he felt at Amy's interest in his welfare beyond their attorney-client relationship.

"Thank you," he said. "I have a couple of things to take care of first, but I will contact you as soon as I am able."

Amy nodded to Brand, then to a waiting guard.

The guard approached and collected Brand. He led him out the double doors at the rear of the courtroom.

Amy watched him go.

She checked the time on her wristwatch and rose hurriedly. She had little time to get to her next consultation.

10

BRAND'S RELEASE WAS MORE INVOLVED than Amy's casual explanation had indicated. He signed numerous forms documenting his release. He was immediately led to the out-processing officer, who one-fingered a computer keyboard as she filled in the blanks with information he provided.

Guards returned him to his cell, where he gathered his few belongings, after which he was moved to a large holding cell.

The large steel room was filled with inmates awaiting release. A loud group occupied the center of the holding cell. Most of their rough talk was about how hard they were going to give it to their girlfriends when they got out. Some of the conversations included tales of past crimes and misdeeds. Brand determined that many of those being released had spent a lot of time in and out of jail.

Brand looked around the crowded holding cell. There was little available space on the painted steel benches attached to the walls or bolted to the floor. Brand saw an available space on a bench against the far wall. He moved through the crowd toward the bench. He watched the men on either side of the space for approval to join them as he approached.

One was a small Hispanic man who studied his feet. The other was a large man with long hair and stern eyes. He watched Brand intently as he drew nearer.

Brand's eyes went to the bigger man, then to the space between him and the Latino. The big man moved aside an inch or so. Brand squeezed into the gap, wedged between the two men.

He gave his attention once more to the loud group in the center of the cell. Of the half-dozen men, three were Latinos with gold-capped smiles; two were bearded white men, arms crossed as they shook their heads at what they heard.

The last was an impossibly thin kid with a mullet. His voice was pitched louder than needed to be heard within their tight group. His manner indicated he was aware of his place on center stage.

"You won't have your bitch for long calling her that," one of the Latinos said with a laugh and a shake of his closely shaved head.

The skinny youth, who appeared to be in his early twenties, stretched as he launched into a loud response.

"I call all women bitches," he said with a flourish of his hands. "It ain't insulting to them. Sometimes I gotta break them down if they get too lippy, but mostly they understand what I mean when I call them bitches."

"That's some bullshit," the Latino disagreed. "You spend a lot of time with your dick in your hand."

His observation was met with a cell-wide roar of laughter.

The skinny kid didn't seem to be embarrassed or angry at the ridicule.

"All bitches want a gangsta. Black chicks deny this because of racism. White chicks love a gangsta. They giving the middle finger to their daddies and brothers when they stroke it with a gangsta."

A cacophony of oohs grew in reaction to this aggressive observation.

"Settle the fuck down," Skinny said with a minimizing gesture of his waving hands. "This ain't about what's right or wrong. This is about human nature."

Skinny addressed the Latino.

"You a good-looking man to any bitch. They be all over you, am I right?"

The Latino looked down and shook his head with a wry smile.

"Don't be scared," Skinny said as his gaze took in the entire room. "I run off more bitches than any of you here has seen. The ones I keep around, I hit that shit like it owes me money. And every one, I call my bitches. True story."

Brand shook his head and avoided Skinny's searching gaze as the latter looked for anyone with whom he could debate further.

The room was awash in vigorous conversation, most of which decried Skinny's theory while others discussed how long he would be outside of jail before he was returned in cuffs or on a gurney.

"Interesting view on life," the big man beside Brand mumbled.

Brand looked at the man with a sidelong glance. The long-haired man was looking fully at him.

"Yeah," Brand agreed. "That approach never worked for me."

The big man chuckled.

"Joe Mercer," he said, extending his big hand to Brand.

Brand shifted as he was able to face Mercer more comfortably.

"Brand," he replied, taking the man's big hand.

"Getting out on bail?" Mercer asked.

"Charges dropped," Brand replied, hoping to end the conversation.

"Congratulations. A free man."

Brand looked around him.

"Almost, I guess. You are getting out on bail?"

"Yeah," Mercer replied with a shrug. "I figure the same outcome as you when it goes to trial."

"That's good. Hope it works out for you."

Mercer smiled, his good humor falling short of his dark eyes.

"I figured you were going to be here a while based on your performance in pop."

Brand looked at him curiously.

"Performance?"

"I saw you take that banger apart upstairs. Nice work."

Brand watched Mercer for a moment, trying to get a fix on where he fell on the subject of his fight.

"I was up there a few days before you hammered that guy. He was undefeated—not even close—until he ran into a buzz saw that looked like an all-American boy."

Brand looked around him at the awkward compliment. Skinny had moved to the far corner of the holding cell. He was engaged in an earnest conversation with two men. His words were buried within the steady din of the other inmates' voices.

"He had it coming, as far as I'm concerned," Mercer said affably. "Things will go easier now for the poor bastards stuck up there."

Brand made no rejoinder.

"You live in Houston, Brand?"

"I'm from San Antonio."

"Too bad. I work for a group that could use an all-American boy with an edge. And it pays well too."

Brand looked at Mercer. The big man smiled as he recognized he had Brand's interest.

"It's nothing illegal, but the work involves some late nights and eyes like a potato."

Brand smiled.

"You and me are a lot alike," Mercer continued. "We possess a broad skill set most only think they have. I can always spot a guy in a crowd who can take care of himself. You are not one of those guys. You are a sleeper. You don't set off alarm bells. That is a valuable trait in my line of work."

"What line of work is that?" Brand asked mildly.

Mercer's reply never came as the room quieted.

Two guards approached the steel gate of the holding cell. The first guard unlocked the gate and opened it.

"When I call your name," he instructed, "step forward and stand on the yellow line. Aguirre, Louis; Brand, Carson; Cameron, Victor; Flores, Raymond; Mercer, Joseph; Wolfe, Caleb."

As those called stopped at the gate, the guard asked each man his name and date of birth and again instructed the prisoner to follow the yellow line.

The yellow line brought the prisoners before a half-door where another officer handed them net bags containing their personal items. Brand signed for his property and changed into his clothes.

There was no place to dress privately, so the prisoners hid their nudity as best they could, quickly changing into their street clothes.

Paperwork in hand, Brand and the others followed the guard to a steel door. The lock buzzed, and the guard opened the door, nodding his permission for them to leave. Brand walked out of the dark hallway into a hot, bright afternoon. He paused as he relished the heat and his freedom.

He pocketed his wallet, which held a useless bank debit card, his driver's license, Amy Landry's cards, and a few singles. He dropped an orange locker key into his front pocket.

Mercer paused beside him, securing his belongings.

"You interested in my proposition?" he asked without looking at Brand.

Brand turned toward Mercer, sizing him up.

"What kind of money are we talking about?" he asked.

"The group I work for is funded by a rich and powerful businessman. He is very particular about who works for him. But when he picks you, he makes sure you want to stay. Money keeps me around. Like I said, it is legit. Call it security work if you want to name it."

"Like a security guard?" Brand asked reluctantly.

"More like corporate security."

Brand made no reply. The job was still unclear to him.

"I have a couple of things to take care of today. Give me your number and I will call you for a meeting tomorrow."

"This offer has a deadline," Mercer warned. "If this is a brush-off, just say so. I don't have time to waste on bullshit."

Brand considered Mercer seriously. His sudden display of temper was significant.

"I'm not sure of my plans yet. I'll call you one way or the other tomorrow. Text me your number. I don't have my phone with me, but I'll save your info when I get it back."

Mercer pulled his phone and texted his information to the number Brand provided him. He pocketed his phone and held Brand for a long moment with a gaze making the latter's senses draw tight within him.

"Tomorrow then," Mercer said and turned on his heel.

Brand watched the long-haired man walk through a parking lot filled with police cars, then onto a sidewalk along a busy street. He disappeared around the corner of a building.

Brand walked to the sidewalk and looked both ways as he tried to gain his bearings.

He wandered for several blocks until he saw a metro bus terminal at a distance. He made his way to the partially covered stop.

A homeless man lay sprawled on the only bench, forcing waiting passengers to stand around him.

Brand shouldered through the huddled throng and surveyed the route map on the back wall of the glass and aluminum shelter. He memorized the bus route numbers through downtown.

The schedule showed the bus arriving in fifteen minutes. Brand turned from the map. He looked down at the homeless man in a green military field jacket. The smell of whiskey, body odor, feces, and urine assailed his nose.

Brand kicked the bench upon which the vagrant lay.

"Get up," he said loudly. "You are taking up space and stinking the place up."

Several of the waiting passengers favored him with a grim look. Others veiled their approval for fear of reprisal from more compassionate members among the waiting passengers.

The homeless man grunted and rolled over on the bench, turning his back to Brand.

"There are ladies here who are standing," Brand pressed.

"Fuck off," was the muffled reply.

Brand grabbed the collar of his green field jacket and pulled the vagrant from the bench. He hauled him out of the bus stop structure and dragged him along the sidewalk some twenty yards from the bus stop.

The vagrant flailed his arms wildly, trying to strike Brand. His legs kicked uselessly as he was dragged unceremoniously, then dropped onto the hot sidewalk.

Brand turned casually and returned to the bus stop.

"You assaulted me, asshole," the homeless man spat through the gaps in his yellow teeth.

Brand turned his head, watching him with a measured stare.

"You all saw him," the filthy man told the crowd as he rose slowly from the sidewalk. "He attacked me. You are all witnesses."

Three women took seats on the bench, giving rebellious looks at the angry vagrant.

"Hey," he complained, "that is my spot."

"Move on, shit bird," one of the other men at the bus stop ordered.

The homeless man seemed surprised at the attitude of the crowd.

"I should sue all of you," he yelled.

"Move on, you bum," another man said, his voice gaining confidence as he felt the support of the others.

The homeless man spat on the sidewalk.

"Fuck all of you."

He stared at each member of the crowd. His gaze stopped on Brand.

"Another word," Brand warned, "and I will drag you around the corner and knock out the rest of your teeth."

The vagrant opened his stained mouth to retort. The look on Brand's face stopped him. He turned silently and trudged away.

Brand again faced the street to wait for the bus. Those around him raised their eyes and smiled at him.

Brand changed buses twice before arriving downtown near the Greyhound station. He crossed the busy street and entered the station lobby. He went to the wall of lockers and inserted the orange key into one of the locks. He turned the key and the door opened. From inside the locker, he withdrew a blue gym bag. He pulled his cell phone from among the clothing and personal items within. The battery was dead. At the bottom of the bag was about $1,300 in cash, the remnants of approximately $2,000 with which he had left San Antonio weeks before.

Brand pocketed the cash, zipped the bag, and left the station. Across the street, he spied a coffee shop. He crossed the street and entered.

He ordered a cup of coffee, black. The clerk favored him with a disapproving frown.

"No one drank coffee anymore," Brand noted. Everything had to be flavored or covered in whipped cream.

He had taken up the coffee habit in basic training. He had drunk two cups with ice at every meal to keep him awake through the long hours of training.

Brand sat on a stool against a long window wall. He plugged his phone into one of the many charging stations along the elevated bar top. He sipped his coffee as he waited for his phone to charge.

Outside the window, the sidewalks were packed with pedestrians on both sides of the street. Traffic moved by sluggishly. Honking horns voiced the drivers' frustration at the slow progress.

He glanced at his phone screen. It read five percent charge. He powered it on. The phone pinged and buzzed to life. One of the pings was the text from Mercer. He saved the number in his contacts and set the phone on the tabletop.

Brand watched the traffic as it thinned with the passing of rush hour. He waited for another half hour until his phone was at eighty percent charge. He rose, unplugging the phone, and gathered his bag.

He walked out onto the sidewalk and turned right. The auto and foot traffic had diminished to the point he was alone on the sidewalk when a black SUV pulled up beside him and the rear window slid down.

Kilgore waved him over from the back seat.

"Get in, Mr. Brand."

"Are you following me?" Brand asked.

"Get in," Kilgore repeated.

11

BRAND WALKED AROUND THE TRUCK and sat beside Kilgore in the back seat. Two agents sat in the front. The truck pulled away from the curb.

"For the next twelve weeks," Kilgore said without looking at Brand, "you will undergo a training regimen with one of our training pods."

Brand looked at the side of Kilgore's face as he delivered this information.

"What kind of training? Agent training?" Brand asked.

The man in the front passenger seat snorted and favored Brand with a disapproving look.

"It's okay, Spencer," Kilgore said with a dismissive wave. "Your position with us is not as an agent, Mr. Brand. You will be a contractor."

"A contractor? What does that mean?"

"You don't qualify for agent status," Agent Spencer said with a sneer. "You are not a college grad, and you are not agent material. Sorry, dipshit. You..."

"That's enough, Spencer."

Brand eyed Spencer with a dangerous look. "You got a mouth on you," Brand observed significantly.

Spencer turned in the front seat and gave Brand a level look. "You better keep yours closed, or you'll find out how lucky you have been lately."

"I said cut it out," Kilgore said loudly. He looked directly at Brand. "We are taking you to the pod now."

Brand favored Agent Spencer with a black look. He felt a familiar buzz building behind his eyes and in his gut.

Spencer held his gaze for as long as he was able. He was familiar with the stories of Brand's anger issues. As much as he wanted to discount the claims, there was something about the new guy that made him reluctant to press him further. Instead, Spencer shook his head authoritatively and turned his attention to the road ahead.

Brand watched the agent for a long moment as he fought the nearly irresistible urge to grab him by the throat and cave in his face.

Finally, he mastered himself and looked at Kilgore. The thin DEA agent watched him with an amused twist to his mouth.

"Are you finished?" he asked significantly.

Brand looked at his hands in his lap but did not reply.

"You will train under the supervision of a private contractor. You will do what is required of you without question. If you graduate the course, you will work in the field for us as a special operator."

"Graduate?" Brand repeated. "What then?"

"That depends on you," Kilgore replied, his expression as vague as his answer. "I can tell you this. If you fail, you will find yourself in a cell for the rest of your life."

Brand considered Kilgore's words soberly. He sat back and watched the passing cityscape. They drove another forty-five minutes, the urban sprawl giving way to tawny grasses and brackish marshes.

The driver turned the SUV off the paved road and followed a winding dirt road several miles until they halted before a wide ranch gate. Spencer stepped out and opened the gate, closing it after the SUV passed through.

The road twisted its way through a wetland region where the swampy marshes bordered both sides. Wind-twisted trees rose from the dark waters. Reeds and thick algae littered much of the surface of the swamp.

Another turn brought them out of the twisted groves and swampland and into a squat compound of large portable buildings. Within the complex were several off-road vehicles and a fenced area containing what appeared to be an intricate obstacle course.

The driver parked in front of a corrugated metal building with windows across the front. Kilgore looked at Brand. He seemed to be appraising his reaction to the place.

"This is your stop, Brand. I'll be in touch."

Brand sat there for a moment, unsure what to do next.

Spencer turned his head and favored Brand with a black look. "Get out, tough guy," he ordered.

Brand bit his tongue. He really wanted to whip this guy's ass. An uncharacteristic caution checked his violent desires. Kilgore's threat of a lifetime in prison held his attention and his temper.

Without a word, he stepped from the vehicle. He stood there holding his gym bag as the driver shifted into reverse and backed the SUV onto the roadway. In a moment, the SUV had disappeared among the twisted trees and foul water of the surrounding swampland.

Brand faced the dark-tinted windows of the building before him. He mounted the long porch and entered the single door at the center of the building. Inside, a lean, bearded man in a black T-shirt and tattooed arms sat at a desk, tapping on a computer keyboard.

"Carson Brand?" he asked with an official tone.

"Yes," he replied.

"I am Mr. Wilson, cadre member. Welcome to Specialized Training Operations Pod, Houston."

"Thanks."

"Thanks, Mr. Wilson," he corrected, tapping the Enter key on the keyboard.

A nearby printer buzzed as it warmed up to print. Several sheets printed, sliding into the catch tray. Wilson stood and gathered the printed materials. He was just under six feet tall and rawboned. Brand got a sense Wilson was someone who could handle himself. He moved with unmistakable confidence. Brand found himself remembering Mercer's observations about spotting people who were skilled if pressed.

Wilson returned to his desk with the paperwork. He tapped them together and stapled the corner. "Read and sign, Mr. Brand."

Brand moved forward and scanned the printing on the sheets. He didn't bother to read much of what he was signing. It occurred to him that his agreement or disagreement with what he signed was useless. He had to train here, or he was headed to prison.

Brand grabbed a pen from a nearby holder and scratched his initials on the indicated lines after certain paragraphs and signed the bottom of the last page. He handed the signed papers back to Wilson, who looked over the forms before placing them in a file folder on his desk. He looked at the clock, then stood.

"Follow me, Mr. Brand," he said as he walked to the front door.

Brand followed him outside. They crossed the wide dirt compound, passing the obstacle course. They entered a long barracks building directly across from the main office. Narrow beds and tall wall lockers lined both sides of the room. Two doors at the opposite end opened into a latrine with clinically white sinks and urinals.

Brand was reminded of the squad bay in which he had lived during basic training some ten years before. Wilson pointed at a metal cot on the right-hand wall. Like those around it, it was neatly made with white sheets and a green blanket.

"This is yours. You will find your uniform in the wall locker. Get dressed. You have less than an hour of personal time."

Wilson turned on his heel and left Brand alone in the barracks.

Brand opened the wall locker. The locker looked military. Everything was folded with machine precision. Two pairs of black Durashock boots sat ready beneath the hanging uniforms.

After changing clothes, he put on the boots and zipped them up. He tightened the laces and knotted them. He tucked the ends into the boot tops, hoping his basic training memories served him well in donning the uniform.

The uniform reminded him of the BDUs the military used to issue years before. The fabric was a rip-stop material, light but sturdy. A black ball cap embroidered with the text 'S.T.O.P.' hung from a side hook in the locker. Brand lifted the hat from the hook. Under the acronym was written, "Specialized Training Operations Pod, Camp Bravura – Coastal Training Facility."

He carefully folded his street clothes and stowed them in the empty bottom drawer. He closed the locker door and sat on the cot, laying the hat next to him.

His thoughts were filled with nervous speculation of what he would face in this new life, in what appeared to be a paramilitary training camp.

He thought about Natalie. The day she died, they had been arguing about breaking up when a gunman burst through the apartment door and opened fire. His back still ached where he'd been shot.

Christina came next. She had betrayed him, yet he'd never stopped believing she was better than her choices.

Both were beautiful. Both were dead.

He admitted to himself he felt nervousness and a slight fear of the unknown as he waited. He drew some comfort from his limited military experience. The barracks and the clothing were familiar. Wilson's—Mr. Wilson's—demeanor was familiar.

He listed the unknowns: what type of training he was to receive and the likely severe levels of discipline he presumed would accompany the training. The latter troubled him. He had never been good with overbearing authority.

CRAIG RAINEY

He heard vehicles approaching outside. He stood, waiting at the end of his bunk. He felt a grim appreciation for the quiet solitude of the barracks. He knew it was about to change.

12

HE HEARD FEET HIT THE DIRT LOT AS SEVERAL individuals dismounted unseen vehicles. A hoarse voice yelled unintelligible commands, followed by the sounds of a group sprinting. The footfalls grew louder as they approached the front door of the barracks.

The door burst open, and about a dozen men entered. Their uniforms matched his but were caked in mud and grime. They moved to their bunks and stripped off the filthy clothing, rushing toward the showers.

The newcomers ignored Brand as they conducted their ablutions. The few who waited at their bunks for an available shower covertly eyed him while busily rummaging through their lockers. Brand felt conspicuous in his clean, pressed uniform, standing uncomfortably by his bunk.

He sat and turned his attention to his hat, listening to snippets of conversations from the latrine. The men spoke about the day's training, the weather, and what was to be served at chow.

Brand got the impression the group was relatively new to one another. There was none of the casual humor or teasing typical of men sharing the collective tribulations of intense training. Hardship quickly created bonds of temporary friendship, but the sidelong glances of those waiting for shower space confirmed his suspicions. If they had shared a bond, he would have been questioned or messed with. Instead, they ignored him. He was the new guy—but not new enough to warrant curiosity.

Men returned from the showers one by one. Some wore briefs, while others returned naked. They moved to their bunks, glancing at Brand as they dressed. The last man to leave the showers, heavily muscled and naked, eyed Brand fiercely as he approached. Brand could tell the man was trying to intimidate him with his physique and nudity.

Brand, who had played sports and trained with men in the military, wasn't fazed.

The big man went to the locker beside Brand's bunk. Opening it, he turned to face Brand. "New meat, stop looking at my dick."

Brand was surprised at the aggression. The naked man held his gaze. "You like what you see? Are you a dick lover, boy?"

Brand turned his back to him. He wasn't sure of the code of conduct here, and he didn't want to start his time with a black mark on his record.

"Smart move, faggot. I'll let you suck it later."

Brand looked at the floor. His eyes blazed with rage and a growing desire to hurt the bigger man.

His father's advice came back to him.

Keep a low profile. Never volunteer for anything.

"What are you smiling at, bitch?" a threatening voice interrupted.

Brand turned to his tormentor.

The man was fully dressed now, his uniform fitting him well. He was a specimen.

Brand stood and faced him. The name tag on the uniform read "White."

"White," Brand said evenly. "I don't know you, but I know your type. I suggest you put your teeth together before I remove them."

White sneered at the smaller Brand.

"What we have here is a badass," he said to the group watching the drama unfold. "He's my bitch. I love a little fight in my bitches. It makes the prize sweeter."

Brand struck him in the face with a fast, hard punch. White was surprised, but the blow didn't stun him. Brand felt the impact of White's return punch. It knocked him over his bunk, and he felt like he'd been hit with a cinder block. White rounded the foot of the bunk and tackled Brand as he struggled to rise. Both men rolled across the vinyl-laminated floor from the force of the collision.

White grabbed Brand's uniform blouse with one hand, reaching for his neck with the other. Brand pushed away with both arms, creating a gap between them. He brought a knee up into White's groin.

White abandoned his grip on Brand, clutching at his aching testicles. Brand crushed White's nose with a headbutt, then grabbed White by his short hair and delivered three quick punches to his face. Blood flowed, and White grunted with each impact. Brand's hands went to White's throat, squeezing with all his strength.

The men in the room rushed to pull Brand off White. They grabbed his arms and wrists, struggling to release his grip on White's throat.

White clawed ineffectually at Brand's hands. Finally, the others succeeded in pulling Brand away.

Brand fought them as he tried to get at White again. His eyes blazed with hatred, and he muttered low growls, spitting as he writhed and flailed against his restrainers. He inadvertently struck one of the men holding him, who fell back. Brand made another move toward White, but three more men jumped on him, pinning him forcefully to the floor.

The door to the barracks opened, and a tall man in black fatigues stepped inside. He surveyed the scene, waiting until Brand seemed sufficiently subdued.

"Chow," he announced mildly.

He turned on his heel, closing the door behind him.

"Can we let you go?" one of the men restraining Brand asked.

Brand nodded.

"You need to say it," the same voice commanded.

"You can get off me," Brand said tightly. "I'm okay."

Cautiously, they released him. He looked around. To a man, they watched him with alarm, waiting to see if he'd go after White again. He thought he saw a glimmer of amusement in their eyes behind their grim expressions.

"Let's go to chow," said a red-haired man with a name tag reading "Moore." His was the same voice Brand had heard earlier.

Brand brushed off his clothing and stepped away from White, who lay groaning on the floor. The group moved toward the front door, leaving White struggling to rise. His face was a bloody mess.

Brand walked with them across the lot to the mess building, similar to the headquarters building but without large front windows.

Inside, the main hall was filled with the smell of cooking. Brand realized he was hungry. Slowly, he mastered his anger.

Moore gestured toward the chow line. Brand grabbed a plastic tray and selected a plate pre-filled with meatloaf, mashed potatoes, and green beans. He filled a white plastic cup with iced tea and took a seat at one of the long tables. Moore sat beside him.

Brand dug into the meal, clearing his plate in under five minutes. He wiped his mouth with a paper napkin and drained his iced tea.

"I like to see sparks fly off a plate," Moore observed appreciatively.

Brand chuckled at Moore's humor. His glance went to the front door. White hadn't entered the dining hall.

Moore noticed Brand's attention to the door. "White won't be joining us, if my diagnosis is correct. You broke a couple of bones in his face, I think. They'll transport him."

Brand nodded.

"White's been a pain in our ass since we got here three days ago. He's an ex-law enforcement goon, probably SWAT. No one had the guts to shut him up until you."

"I was lucky," Brand said dispassionately.

Moore considered Brand's calm demeanor. "If you say so."

Mr. Wilson approached the table and paused before Brand. "Report to the office, Mr. Brand."

"On my way," Brand replied. He turned to Moore. "Thanks."

"No problem," Moore said, though he didn't understand why Brand was thanking him.

Brand dropped his tray at the kitchen window and made his way to the office building.

Inside, Mr. Wilson was again seated at his desk. He looked up from his computer screen and jerked a thumb toward an open door behind his desk. "In there, Mr. Brand."

Brand entered the office, which contained filing cabinets and a large desk. The man behind the desk was the same one who had called them to chow after the fight with White.

"Take a seat, Mr. Brand," he said, indicating a single chair before his desk.

Brand obeyed.

"You broke Mr. White's nose. You may have broken other bones in his face. That is assault, Mr. Brand."

He opened a folder on his desk and read a few pages silently while Brand waited.

"We are not a typical military unit, Mr. Brand. We are a training facility for military, law enforcement, and private security firms. Our trainees are not protected by the color of the UCMJ. If Mr. White decides to press charges, you could go to jail. Your DEA affiliation will only get you so far here."

Brand shrugged.

"You are not concerned about the possibility of prison?"

"I doubt my concern will change his mind one way or the other. It's been a long day, sir."

The man nodded in understanding. "My name is Mr. Crabtree. I am the commandant of this facility. I expect you to conduct yourself as a professional, Mr. Brand. If you can't, we are highly creative in our dealings with malcontents and troublemakers. Am I understood, Mr. Brand?"

"Yes, sir."

"I have a call into the DEA. They may decide to deal with you internally. Report to formation tomorrow morning as usual until I figure out what the DEA wants to do about White. Dismissed."

Brand rose and returned to the barracks. Blood stained the pale vinyl flooring where White had lain. Brand went to the latrine, found a wall locker with cleaning supplies, and grabbed a spray bottle and rag. He cleaned the blood from the floor, disposed of the rag, and returned the spray bottle. Back at his bunk, he sat against the metal headboard.

His fellow trainees returned to the barracks one or two at a time. Moore arrived and stopped before Brand's bunk.

"Lights out at twenty-two hundred; reveille at oh-five hundred."

Moore came to the side of Brand's bunk and extended his hand. "I'm Dennis Moore, ex-Army infantry. Pleased to meet you."

Brand sat forward and accepted the handshake. "Carson Brand, ex-National Guard artillery."

"Weekend warrior, eh?" Moore said with a ridiculing expression.

"Yeah," Brand replied with a frown. He'd heard it all when it came to being a part-time soldier.

As Moore retreated to his bunk, Brand noticed the others grinning at him. National Guard service didn't impress active-duty troops. He might as well have claimed to be an Eagle Scout.

Brand removed his uniform, hung it in his wall locker, and slipped under the stiff sheets and rough green blanket of his bunk.

The lights clicked off automatically at ten o'clock. Brand guessed they were on a timer. He slept soundly, waking only when the lights turned on automatically at five a.m. the following morning.

In the first moments of the early morning, Brand relived his dim memories of basic training. Harsh fluorescent lights attacked his sleep-blurred eyes. Unlike his days as a seventeen-year-old basic trainee, he was now an early riser by nature.

He had been a carpenter and framer in his former life before the murder of his best friend and his girlfriend. In the construction business, the days were long and hard. He had developed the habits of a hard worker, rising early despite fatigue, excuses, or being hungover. Those habits served him well here.

The trainees dressed, saying nothing as they donned their uniforms. Most had military backgrounds and seemed to fall back on practiced habits as they prepared themselves for the day. Brand had been there for less than three days and had no idea what to expect outside the barracks. He grabbed his black leather dop kit and moved toward the latrine to shave and brush his teeth.

White's bed was as it had been the previous night. Brand guessed he was still in the hospital. He must have received more than a broken nose in the beating.

Brand finished his grooming and returned to his bunk, where he pulled on his boots and then made his bed. He regarded the tight covers over the thin mattress with pride. Part of his military training had included PLDC, Primary Leadership Development Course, at Camp Shelby, Mississippi. His bunkmate had been a former Marine. He had taught him to make a bed off which you could have bounced a feather.

He followed his fellow trainees out the door and into a military formation before the barracks. Moore took his place before the squad of twelve trainees. Brand presumed he was the squad leader or perhaps a platoon guide, informal ranks with which he had become familiar in basic training.

The office door opened, and a thick-limbed, muscular female instructor in black fatigues approached the group. Another instructor followed her and took a position behind and to the side of the female instructor.

Mr. Crabtree stepped onto the porch and closed the office door.

"For the newcomer, I am Ms. Newsome," the woman announced. "I am your primary instructor for this preliminary training block."

She jerked a thumb over her shoulder.

"This is Mr. Theil. He is my assistant instructor and your primary point of contact for this module."

Newsome turned away from the group and moved back to the office.

Theil stepped forward.

"Mount the transport, men. Move out!"

Brand moved with the group as they double-timed to a waiting black deuce-and-a-half. The others climbed the tailgate and took seats along the sides. The truck bed was open overhead. The sun was rising in a red pool on the horizon. Brand grabbed the handle on the tailgate and pulled himself into the vehicle. He took a seat next to Moore.

Moore nodded at Brand as the truck pulled away from the compound. The trainees rode for just under half an hour. They entered a fenced compound surrounding a large hangar-like building and an obstacle course within an oval dirt track.

Mr. Theil appeared at the rear of the truck.

"Dismount," he yelled.

They climbed out of the truck bed and formed a two-squad formation before Theil.

"Spread at five-yard intervals and ground your blouses!"

So began a rigorous period of physical training. Brand was not one to hit the gym or the running track, and the training was difficult for him. Many of the other trainees were physically fit but also struggled to keep up with the workout. Brand pressed himself to stay with the group. His focus was to finish ahead of the last man if it came to that.

The physical training continued for a full hour. The segment ended with a two-mile run on the oval dirt track. Brand staggered across the finish line among the main group.

A table was set up with a stainless-steel water can and plastic cups. They drank deeply and panted as they struggled to recover their wind.

"Break's over," Theil announced. "Move to the hangar."

He pointed with a flat hand to the large metal building at the end of the fenced compound. The group gathered themselves and double-timed it to the hangar.

Inside, Brand saw the burly female instructor, Ms. Newsome.

"Take a knee, men," she said.

The trainees obeyed gratefully.

"This segment will introduce you to basic hand-to-hand and close-combat techniques. How many of you have experience with close-combat training, martial arts, or hand-to-hand combat?"

Three hands went aloft. Several of the trainees glanced in Brand's direction. They seemed surprised that his hand did not rise. Brand ignored the expectant looks. His father's words sounded in his ears: Don't volunteer for anything. Keep a low profile.

"Good," Ms. Newsome said with a straight face. "You three are my demonstrators. Front and center, please."

The volunteers reluctantly joined Ms. Newsome, lining up behind her and to the side.

Newsome turned to the class.

"This segment will give you a basic skill set in a number of disciplines. We employ techniques from Judo, Taekwondo, and Sambo. To perfect any of these skills will involve an investment of time and resources we don't have here. Our time here will help you assess whether this type of work suits you."

She turned to the first volunteer. She pointed to a spot before her. The volunteer, a dark-haired man of medium build, moved to the indicated place.

"The first technique is called Block and Control."

She turned to the demonstrator.

"Attack me with a punch—full speed, please."

The demonstrator moved immediately with surprising speed. He executed a powerful right cross at the muscular woman. She lifted an elbow and parried the blow and, with impressive quickness, stepped toward him and used her elbows to block other punches. Grabbing his wrist and throwing him to the ground, she finished him off with a heel kick looking very real.

The demonstrator curled into a ball and groaned.

"Always finish any of these techniques with a kill blow. Finish your opponent!"

She helped the man to his feet. She motioned to the second man, who approached with an air of dread.

"The next technique is Evade and Dominate."

Brand watched as she instructed the second man to approach from behind and execute a chokehold. She dispatched him with the same adroit skill as the first.

"Next demonstrator," she commanded.

The third man shook his head doubtfully.

"The next technique is Defend and Counterattack."

The remainder of the morning was filled with drills where Brand learned those techniques and the many variations of them. They broke at midday to paper plates and food from thermite containers. After an hour's lunch, they filed into a warm classroom complete with desks and a large dry-erase board.

Written in big letters on the board were the words Situational Awareness.

Brand studied the subheadings beneath the big blue letters as he waited for the class to begin.

Profiling is the law of probability.

Reading threat indicators:

Profiling is the law of probability.

Reading threat indicators:

Scanning the area nervously, non-pro scan

Hide the face—attention to phone, book, etc.

Concealment—hoodie, sunglasses

Sweating or paleness.

Newsome took her place at the head of the class.

"This class is on Situational Awareness. There is no way you can stay at high alert in every situation. This block of instruction will provide you with the tools you need to recognize bad actors, even at less than full observation mode.

"Action always beats reaction. This means you will always be at a disadvantage. An attacker will always get the first move, meaning you will have to react quickly based upon your training. If you don't see the attack, your training will be useless, and you will die."

Brand settled back in his seat.

13

THAT EVENING, BRAND ENTERED THE BARRACKS. He moved to his bunk, noticing White's wall locker was open, clothing strewn across his bunk. Brand felt his pulse rise at the prospect of a repeat encounter with the bigger man.

Brand opened his wall locker and undressed. He stuffed his dirty uniform into the green laundry bag and withdrew his dop kit along with a change of underwear. He made himself busy as he waited for White to return to his bunk. Brand heard the shower running and presumed White was in the latrine. He resolved to choose the site for a fight if White renewed their conflict.

Three trainees returned from chow and took their places at their wall lockers, preparing to retire for the evening. Each of them noticed White's belongings on his bunk and silently anticipated the pending conflict.

The sound of the shower ended. White appeared, naked, his face bruised and bandaged.

Brand busied himself at his wall locker, watching White surreptitiously from his peripheral vision. He saw White glare at him through black bruises under each eye.

Brand disliked averting his gaze. It seemed like a submissive gesture. He remembered Crabtree's warning about further trouble. The idea of failing the course and subsequently going to prison for the rest of his life kept his pride in check.

White interpreted his averted gaze and passive front as fear.

"Hey, fag," White said loudly, facing Brand.

Brand turned to the naked man and held his gaze squarely.

"You are a dumbass, White," he said evenly. "Get dressed and mind your business. They will kick us both out of here."

White hesitated, considering Brand's warning. Finally, he dropped his gaze.

"This isn't over," he muttered, turning to his locker.

"Yes, it is," Brand corrected him with a warning tone.

Brand turned from White to see Moore standing near the front door, listening to the conversation. Moore watched silently, seeming to come to a decision about the new man.

Training continued with no further trouble. White made it clear he hated the smaller man, but he limited his displays of dislike to glowering stares and muttered comments unintelligible to those around him.

Aware of the conflict, the cadre never pitted the two trainees against one another during hand-to-hand drills.

As with the boxing program so many years before, Brand developed a considerable skill set as he absorbed the training. The other trainees avoided Brand as a sparring partner. Even Moore, who had grown friendly toward Brand, frowned reluctantly when paired with him in hand-to-hand drills.

Brand grew in skill and understanding. The hidden psychology behind many of the non-combat tools was fascinating. Ms. Newsome, the gruff female instructor, was knowledgeable and thorough, emphasizing the cerebral aspects of the discipline over the physical.

Newsome stood on a mat before the trainees wearing a gi with a black belt.

"We train for the reactions of our targets to fight-or-flight responses. The first rule is to avoid appearing as a threat or danger to the target. This is accomplished in several ways, but the easiest is to avoid verbal threats or threatening actions, which will reduce the likelihood of your adversaries entering fight-or-flight reactions."

Newsome paused and surveyed the men before her in the large training hall.

"Mr. Brand, front and center, please."

Brand obeyed, stopping a few feet before the muscular woman. Newsome extended a flat hand, palm up, toward Brand.

"Mr. Brand is aware he will be required to attack me to demonstrate a technique. Does he appear afraid?"

Laughter rose discreetly among the men.

"You are right, he is afraid to fight me," she announced.

Brand gave her a startled look.

"Mr. Brand just demonstrated a fight-or-flight response to my threat. Does that confirm he is frightened?"

The laughter ceased abruptly.

"Most of you agree fighting against Mr. Brand is an unpleasant prospect. Why would he be afraid or resort to the fight-or-flight response? Because, gentlemen, we all experience fear. Fear is not the enemy. Fear is as necessary as pain in identifying hazards to our survival or well-being. The enemy is our reaction to fear. Mr. Brand, are you reluctant to fight me?"

Brand made no reply.

"Is that a yes?"

Brand maintained his silence, crossing his arms over his chest.

"Notice how Mr. Brand processed his reaction to my line of questioning, settling on a passive wait-and-see posture. This is the least desirable outcome when dealing with the fight-or-flight response. At the beginning of our interaction, Mr. Brand was uncertain what to expect. The longer I delayed, the more time he had to acclimate to the threat I posed. That delay increased the hazard he posed to me. It is our goal to come to that decision before our adversary does."

Rigorous physical training continued daily, most of it taking place on the central PT grounds and obstacle course in the center of the compound. Early morning PT was followed by hours of hand-to-hand, close-combat training.

Over time, Brand found while he was tired at the end of the long days, he was no longer exhausted and sore as he had been at the beginning.

Brand kept to himself. During off hours, while the men talked, played cards, or participated in outdoor sports, Brand interacted with no one but Moore. He liked the man and felt comfortable around him. As for White, his bruises faded, but his hatred for Brand did not. Brand avoided the man when possible. Many nights, he awoke to find White lying on his side, eyes open, watching him.

On those occasions, Brand stared back until White rolled over, his back to him. Brand lay for a long time afterward, watching the rhythmic rise and fall of White's body under the sheets, wondering if he was asleep or faking it.

Two days before the end of training, Mr. Crabtree called Brand to his office.

Brand knocked on the commandant's door frame.

"Close the door, Mr. Brand," Crabtree said from his seat behind the desk.

Brand closed the door, taking the seat in front of Crabtree's desk.

The commandant leaned back in his chair, interlacing his fingers before him. Brand noticed a West Point Academy ring on his right hand.

"I have received glowing reports regarding your training success here. You have come a long way since your rough beginnings."

Crabtree paused to see how his words affected Brand.

"The DEA would like you to continue your training in our advanced weapons techniques POD. The training will take place over two weeks.

You have the middle weekend off. The next class begins two weeks from Monday—here."

Brand looked down, organizing the itinerary in his mind.

"Any questions?" Crabtree asked.

"No, sir," Brand replied. "I guess I'll see you two weeks from Monday."

Crabtree picked up a form from his desk. He read from the text on the page, looking up at Brand as if surprised he was still there.

"Dismissed."

14

TWO DAYS LATER, A CAB COLLECTED BRAND at the compound office. Brand produced Amy Landry's business card and gave the driver Amy's office address. He wasn't sure what made him decide to see her other than the fact he had no other prospects in Houston, he had two weeks to kill, and he knew no one else locally.

Amy's office was a suite in a three-story office building in South Houston. It was nearly five in the evening when he arrived at the front doors. Inside the lobby, he checked the directory, locating her name and suite number. He wasn't sure if she would be in her office, but he knew no one else in town and had few options.

He passed through the cool lobby to the small elevator bank. He pressed the button and took the elevator to the third floor. He followed the signs indicating suite numbers until he stood outside a dark wooden door with a black and white nameplate reading 'Amy Landry, Attorney at Law.'

Brand tried the handle. The door opened. Inside, there were two rooms: a reception area with a large desk and an office. The receptionist's desk was empty save for several table trays holding bland pamphlets for alcohol and drug addiction classes and several charitable outreach programs. Apparently, Amy ran her practice alone.

Brand spotted her through the open door to the adjoining office. Amy sat at her desk, working on paperwork.

She looked up, surprised to see him. She paused as she remembered his name. As her recognition returned, she smiled at him with professional courtesy.

"Hello, Mr. Brand. I didn't expect you."

"Call me Brand," he said, entering her office.

He stood behind a chair before her desk, pleased she had remembered his name.

"Sorry to drop by like this. I don't know anyone in town. You mentioned you might help me find temporary work."

Amy's brow furrowed, as if he were hinting at something with his explanation.

"Is this a bad time?" he asked, taking a step back. "I've made you uncomfortable. I'll come back when it's a better time."

"No," Amy said with a quick smile. "You just surprised me, is all."

Brand waited for Amy to continue.

"It's been a long time since I offered to help you. Did you get your personal business taken care of?"

Brand looked confused as he struggled to recall their last conversation. He smiled as the memory returned.

"Oh, yeah. I did. Thanks for asking."

"You took a chance, coming by here after so long. I am rarely in my office."

"I thought of that," Brand agreed. "If I missed you, I figured I would try you tomorrow."

"You have my phone number, don't you?"

Brand watched her face, gauging if she was annoyed at the intrusion.

"Your office is kind of on my way," he lied. "Anyway, I'm old-fashioned about the phone. Face to face is always best for me. The reason I am here is I am interested in the job you mentioned last time."

"That's right. I remember," she said with an understanding smile. "That was nearly three months ago."

Brand struggled with an explanation.

She watched him significantly. She relaxed after a moment.

"You look thinner than when I saw you last. Have you eaten?"

Brand put his hands in his pockets as he thought about her question. The training had obviously taken off some weight. He hadn't noticed the loss.

"Not what I would consider food," he said lightly. "Can I buy you dinner?"

Amy looked off-balance as the power dynamic shifted.

"It's just food, Amy."

Amy looked surprised at the familiar address.

"Brand...I am your attorney—a female attorney. It is inappropriate for me to go to dinner with a client. I asked if you had eaten to suggest a nice place nearby for you to go if you hadn't."

"Of course," Brand said. "I meant nothing by it. I am obliged to you for everything you have done for me." He paused before adding, "Technically, you are not my attorney anymore."

Amy frowned at the observation.

Brand cleared his throat. "Where is the eatery you were going to recommend?"

"Cali-Café, right around the corner."

"I'll try it. Thanks, Amy."

He turned to leave.

"Brand," Amy said.

He paused at the doorway.

Amy struggled with a thought. Finally, she sighed, letting her thoughts go unsaid.

"Come by in the morning. I'll help with the job."

"Thanks."

Brand took the elevator downstairs. Rush-hour traffic was building to a frenzied pace as he entered the nearby Cali-Café. He took a seat by the window, watching office workers moving along the sidewalk, heading home after a long workday.

Brand felt a profound sense of loneliness seep into his thoughts. He had no home, not after Natalie was killed. Since then, he had been on the run. The training had delayed the emptiness temporarily. He looked along the street, searching for a motel sign. He saw none.

"What will you have?" a voice asked.

Brand turned from the window. A waitress with blue hair and a nose ring eyed him suspiciously.

"I'll have a burger, fries, and a Coke."

The waitress stared at him with a combination of impatience and ridicule.

"We don't serve meat here, sir."

Brand chuckled affably.

"Oh, I see, Cali-Café. Can you bring me something hot with maybe a little tofu to give it some texture?"

The waitress raised her eyebrows as she wrote on her pad.

"Anything else?"

"Iced tea?"

"Green?"

"Do I have a choice?"

"Not if you want tea."

"That would be great."

She turned on her heel and went to turn in his order. Brand looked her over. She wore tight, torn jeans, black canvas high-tops, and a Cali-Café tee.

"Freakin' hipsters," he muttered.

He looked out the window in time to see the back of a shapely blonde as she walked by. She wore low pumps, and her legs looked great. She entered the café. He watched as she disappeared into the doorway. She reappeared inside the café. It was Amy. He stood as she approached his table.

"I decided I would join you," she explained.

Brand gestured to the empty chair across from him.

"Please. Have a seat."

She settled in the chair, placing her briefcase on the floor near the window.

The waitress returned with Brand's green tea. She smiled at Amy.

"Friend of yours, Amy?" she asked, as if Brand wasn't there.

"Could you bring me a red and a glass of water, Star?"

Star, the waitress, left to fill the request.

"A regular, I take it," Brand observed.

"It's close, and the food is good. Star is a bit possessive. What are you having?"

"I don't know. I'm leaving it to Star to decide."

Amy laughed quietly. She looked into his eyes as though she were working at a puzzle.

"What's your story, Brand?"

Brand shook his head.

"I'm from San Antonio. I own a little construction business—at least I used to—and I am stranded in Houston for the next few weeks."

"No family? No friends? No girl?"

Brand studied the tabletop. He finally looked at Amy.

"Nope. Just me."

"You don't strike me as a recluse, or a stalker, or a ne'er-do-well."

"Thanks. I'm not any of those things. I have learned to have a sense of humor about things I used to take seriously."

Amy said nothing in return. Brand got the impression she was sizing him up.

"I really appreciate your dropping in," he said. "I am enjoying your company."

Amy smiled.

Star returned, placing a half-filled wine glass and a glass of water before her.

"Anything else?"

"Not right now. Thank you."

Star eyed Brand with an evil look, then left.

"I don't think she likes you," Amy joked.

"You think?" Brand asked innocently. "I thought we were warming up to one another."

They laughed.

A silence filled the void for a moment.

Brand hadn't spoken to a woman in some time. Ms. Newsome didn't count by his standards. Amy was attractive, and she seemed genuine. Brand welcomed any semblance of normalcy or, more accurately, anything resembling his old life before tumult upended his average Joe world.

He sipped green tea as he considered Amy's blue eyes and ready smile.

"So, what about you?" he asked. "What's your story, Amy Landry?"

Amy smiled.

"I grew up in Connecticut but moved to Houston when my dad transferred with his company. I was a sophomore in high school then. I got an academic scholarship to Rice, got my law degree, and joined the bar.

"I worked for a number of charities as legal counsel for disadvantaged and exploited women's groups. I did a lot of good, but it didn't pay the bills. I started my own private practice and argued some smaller civil cases and some criminal defense. I got in with the court and was offered public defender work. The need for PDs is large, so I am almost completely booked with my court-appointed cases."

"You are obviously good at what you do, considering how my case ended up."

"That wasn't me. In fact, I had nothing to do with your lenient treatment. The prosecutor said she was following instructions directly from D.A. Perkins. She gave me no additional information."

Amy raised her glass and sipped the wine. She sighed with pleasure.

"I needed that," she said with closed eyes.

They were silent as Star brought a plate to Brand. She set it before him.

"Bon appétit," she said with little feeling behind her words.

Brand watched her go with a wry smile. His gaze returned to Amy.

She was studying him intently.

"Again," she said. "Who are you? How does a guy in the construction business in San Antonio end up in a human trafficking warehouse in Houston?"

Brand placed his napkin in his lap as he thought about her question. He rested his wrists on the table edge. He wasn't willing to open up to her about the last few months of his life. The events were hard even for him to believe. His new role with the DEA was unclear to him. He thought it best to tone down the details.

He took a breath, laying his hands flat on the table as he assembled the details of his story. He looked at her with a look confirming the gravity of what he was about to reveal.

"The girl I was searching for worked for a Mexican cartel. I met her after a friend of mine was murdered in Mexico. She helped me...we helped each other. We got separated. I escaped. She didn't. Now she is dead."

Amy's attention was fully on him and his words.

"I managed to track her to Houston. I learned she had been seen in that building. I was lucky to get out alive."

Amy watched him as she absorbed his story. She shook her head. She clearly saw he was holding back. She accepted he would remain a mystery for the present.

"Brand, I am so sorry for what you have been through. I know you don't want to tell me everything. I understand totally. Your friend murdered in Mexico and meeting a girl who worked for a drug cartel..."

Amy hoped he would give a bit more clarification. He made no additional comment. She hid her frustration.

"What are you going to do now?" she asked.

"I'm not sure yet. I've got a few things in mind but nothing in stone."

Brand picked up his fork and took a bite from the plate.

"This isn't a bad start."

He leaned the fork on the plate and sipped his green tea.

"Why don't we just sit here for a while?"

Amy tasted her wine.

"That sounds nice."

They shared small talk as Brand ate. Amy finished her wine, and Star brought her another.

Brand placed his napkin on the empty plate.

"I am full," he announced with a puffed-cheek exhale.

"Well," she asked with a smile. "How was it?"

"I have to admit it wasn't bad."

"You strike me as a steak-and-taters man," she joked, adjusting her position in her chair.

"It shows, huh?" he admitted. "I believe being a finicky eater is a character flaw."

"Is that right?" she asked with feigned displeasure. "I am a vegetarian."

"Your only flaw," Brand returned playfully.

Amy laughed lightly, pleased with his compliment.

"Oh, you are a clever boy. Quite the charmer."

Brand shrugged.

"Just being honest."

"Do you have somewhere to stay tonight?"

Brand met her gaze.

"I didn't mean to..."

"Relax," Brand said with a dismissive gesture. "You are not my attorney. I am not a client. We enjoy each other's company. There is no need to complicate it. Do you want to get out of here?"

Amy had given her attention to the nearly empty wine glass as Brand spoke. She waited until he finished before again meeting his gaze.

"Yes."

15

BRAND WOKE WITH THE SUNRISE. Amy lay beside him, sleeping soundly. The clock on her nightstand read 6:38 in red letters. Brand rose quietly and made his way to the bathroom. When he returned, Amy was up and wrapped in a flowery robe and furry slippers.

"You are an early riser," she observed. Her tone was open, but Brand sensed a hint of awkwardness behind her smile.

"You too," he returned with a wink. "Coffee?"

"You read my mind."

She turned toward the bedroom door.

Brand crossed the space between them and wrapped his arms around her waist. He turned her toward him and kissed her, pulling her against him. She returned the kiss and his embrace.

She felt him hardening against her stomach.

"Wow. You are insatiable," she said with admiration. "I have to work today, and you have an interview to make."

"You work fast," Brand said as he released her.

"I am going to arrange an interview with an organization I volunteer for on occasion. It is a campaign organization."

"Like an election campaign?" Brand asked.

"Exactly. Most of the campaign staff are volunteers, but they hire temporary staff to manage the volunteers. You will probably distribute door hangers, pass out handbills, and generally help out as they need you to. This is an easy gig, and the work you do is for a good cause."

Brand looked at her blankly.

Amy saw his resistance to the idea. She frowned and leaned back from him.

"I believe it will be a good environment for you considering what you have been through."

Brand shrugged his understanding.

"Sounds good. When do I start?"

Amy smiled.

"I will drive you over on my way to the courthouse."

Brand sat in the passenger seat as Amy drove through heavy traffic. They arrived at a downtown office building. The large windows along the crowded sidewalk were covered with red, white, and blue posters soliciting votes for the candidate for Congress, Randy Chappell.

Amy parked the car and led Brand through the double glass doors into the office. The ground floor was a glass-fronted open space. Inside, the office was a maelstrom of ringing phones, bustling volunteers, and harried management staff trying to direct the enthusiastic activities of the group.

Amy guided Brand through the roiling throng to a closed back door sporting a large colorful nameplate which read 'Candidate Chappell.' Amy knocked, then opened the door without waiting for an invitation.

Inside sat a man behind a desk. At a distance in the corner, a well-dressed woman sat on a leather sofa.

The man behind the desk was obviously Candidate Chappell. He was in his late thirties, tanned and handsome. He wore a white starched shirt and tie. His sleeves were rolled halfway up his forearms. He was frowning as he talked on the phone. His face changed drastically as he greeted

Amy silently with a broad gleaming smile. He lifted a finger indicating the phone call.

Amy looked at the woman in the leather chair. The woman smiled politely at Amy before she gave Brand her attention. She looked him over critically, as though she could see through him.

"That is exactly why you should support us," Chappell said into the phone. "You don't have to be a union shop to expect the help you need from your government resources."

Chappell listened to the other side of the call.

"Coffee?" he asked Amy in a whisper as he covered the mouthpiece of the phone.

Amy shook her head. She looked at Brand with a questioning expression.

Brand shook his head.

Chappell gave Brand a once-over as he continued to listen on the phone.

"Well, that sounds promising," he said expansively. "I think we can come to an arrangement. Speaker Cole was a polarizing personality, but his poor judgment landed him in cuffs, not any action on my part."

He waited for the response.

"I have no problem with that. In fact, I look forward to it. Talk soon."

Chappell hung up the phone. He glanced at the woman in the leather chair. She considered him mildly. Brand felt Chappell was looking for approval, and she wasn't giving it. Chappell returned his attention to Amy.

"Amy. So good to see you. Is this a business visit?"

"Not legal, per se. I have a capable candidate for your campaign staff. This is Carson Brand. He is a former client."

Brand saw a small dark cloud smudge Chappell's smiling exterior.

Amy spoke again with abruptness, giving Brand the impression she needed to talk the candidate into the idea.

"Is everything okay—since the incident?"

Chappell gave Brand a sidelong glance.

"We can talk about that later. Suffice it to say I don't need any additional complications."

Chappell pointed to the woman on the leather sofa.

"Brand, this is Camille, my fiancée."

Camille stood.

Brand was struck by her beauty. He struggled to hide his interest.

"Pleased to meet you, Camille," he said as casually as he could.

Camille smiled as she moved closer to shake his hand.

"My pleasure, Mr. Brand. So, what do we know about your new friend, Amy?"

Amy forced a smile, looking at Chappell as she answered.

"Brand is a good man," she replied. "He helped close down a human trafficking ring. I helped him iron out some details, but he has a clean record and seems to be a gentleman."

The last was said with a bit of an edge to her voice.

"Now that is remarkable," Chappell responded, giving Brand another long inspection. "A human trafficking hero may be too overqualified for our small operation."

"Randy," Amy urged. "He can hand out flyers and work with your street team. He is the right demographic, and he is well-spoken. I will personally vouch for him."

Camille remained silent throughout the conversation.

Brand glanced at her to gauge her level of involvement.

She watched dispassionately.

Brand looked at Amy. She hardly knew him, but she was vouching for him. He felt a bit uncomfortable that she put her name on the line with the important man.

Chappell pursed his lips as he considered her request. He looked at Brand with a blank expression as his mind worked. Finally, he focused, indicating he had come to a decision.

"Good enough for me, Amy. So, Mr. Brand, tell me about yourself."

"Please call me Brand. I came here looking for a friend. I didn't find her. Amy is overstating things. I didn't shut down a crime ring. My search for my friend led me to the human trafficking ring. The cops did the rest."

Brand gave Amy a sheepish smile.

"I will be in town for a few weeks. I am willing to help out where I can."

Camille inhaled softly as she covered her amusement.

Chappell gave Camille a quick glance then looked at his wristwatch.

"Amy, take him to Troy. He will put him to work."

He stood and offered his hand to Brand.

"Welcome to the team, Mr. Brand."

Brand took his hand and shook it gratefully.

"Thank you, Randy," Amy said with a big smile of gratitude.

"Thank you, Mr. Chappell. Good to meet you, Camille," Brand said as he followed Amy out of the office.

"Nice to meet you, Brand," Camille returned.

Troy's office was only two doors down from Chappell's, but it was a continuously active environment. Brand and Amy sidestepped two interns leaving the small office as they entered. Troy was a thin blond man with blue eyes and a large Adam's apple that bobbed as he talked.

Brand found it difficult to keep his gaze above the man's neck. The Adam's apple seemed to have a will of its own, sliding and leaping this way and that as it pleased.

"Troy Doell, this is Brand. He is the new guy. Randy asked you to put him to work." She pronounced his last name "Dell."

"Sounds good," Troy replied. "Good to meet you, Brand."

Brand dragged his attention from Doell's neck.

"You too, Troy."

"We are visiting a homeless shelter tomorrow morning," Doell said thoughtfully. "We could use all the help we can get."

"Does that work for you, Brand?" Amy asked him with a hint of leftover heat from their previous meeting.

Brand agreed.

"Sounds perfect."

"Meet us here at ten tomorrow morning," Doell said to Brand. "We have transportation arranged. Randy will be making a personal appearance there. We expect a large crowd."

"Thank you, Troy," Amy said warmly.

"Anything for you, Ames."

"So sweet," she said teasingly, caressing Doell's cheek fondly.

"Stop fooling around," Doell protested.

"Don't call me Ames," she countered with a stern smile.

"I'll try."

Doell turned to Brand.

"See you tomorrow, Brand."

"Tomorrow," Brand agreed.

Brand followed Amy to the front door. She didn't slow her pace for him. Outside she turned to him.

"Do you need a ride somewhere?"

She was all business.

"I'm fine for now. Thanks for everything."

"I'll check on you in a couple of days. Text me if you need anything."

Amy turned toward her car.

"Amy," he said as he stepped closer.

She turned, giving him a serious look.

"Brand, you don't have to..."

"I know I don't. I want to see you again. No strings attached. It is up to you, but I am for it."

Amy pulled one of her cards from her purse. She wrote on the back of the card.

"This is my cell. Text me your cell number. My office number is always forwarded, but I can't receive text messages there. If you still feel the same, call or text me."

Brand watched Amy get into her car. She was obviously angry with him, and he didn't know how to make things better. He remained there until she backed out of the parking spot without a glance at him. She shifted gears, and her car disappeared into traffic.

He turned on his heel to look for the nearest bus stop. He made a mental note of the street address for the campaign headquarters.

"Brand," a voice said from behind him.

Brand turned to see Troy Doell standing in the office doorway.

"Someone wants to talk to you," the blond man said.

"Who?"

"Come back inside. I want you to meet one of our team leaders."

Brand followed Doell back into the campaign office. They returned to Doell's office. Inside, a large man with dark, longish hair and dark sunglasses sat before Doell's desk. He didn't rise as Doell and Brand entered.

"Carson Brand, this is Joe Mercer. Joe, this is Carson...Brand, I mean."

"Hey," Mercer said. "I never got your call."

Brand nodded.

"Sorry about that."

He assessed Mercer. He slouched in the hard chair. His eyes were hidden by the dark, wire-framed sunglasses. He wore new jeans and heavy black tactical boots. His hands were broad, the fingers hairy on top and blunt at the tips. His tight tee shirt claimed global warming was time-released death for the planet.

Brand appreciated the irony of a man who appeared to be a hard ass wearing a politically sensitive message tee.

Mercer hopped out of the chair.

"Well, are you ready?" he asked Brand.

"Sure," Brand replied uncertainly. "For what?"

"Follow me."

Doell smiled at Brand as he followed Mercer out of the office.

Mercer led Brand out the back door of the campaign office. Several cars were parked in the small rear parking lot.

Brand followed him to a gray Honda Civic.

Mercer climbed in behind the wheel.

Brand settled into the passenger seat.

Mercer started the car, shifted the gear stick roughly, and the little sedan was underway.

"Funny how life works out, isn't it?" Mercer asked, looking around as he drove. "I guess you were destined to join the team. This campaign has several teams serving many tasks. The publicity group you were supposed to be assigned to is the street team. It hands out flyers and gins up support for the candidate. You are no longer on that team. The organization I work for contracts for a number of campaigns. We are called the Kinetic Team. Do you identify as a conservative or liberal?"

Brand shrugged.

"I have never thought about it."

"Do you vote?"

"No. It seems like a waste of time."

Mercer glanced at Brand.

"Votes are the product we produce, although sometimes our scope falls under the category of eliminating votes—like with opposing candidates.

"Today we are conducting competition impact. There is a rally about to begin near The Woodlands. We are going to drop by and see how things are going for the other team."

Mercer said nothing more during the hour-and-a-quarter ride to The Woodlands. The suburb of Houston was an upscale city whose residents lived among a heavily wooded city-wide shopping center. Hidden under the pine trees were every type of national and regional retail chain imaginable.

Mercer found a space for the sedan in a parking lot surrounded by tall trees. They left the car and followed red, white, and blue arrow signs labeled 'rally.' The signs guided them to a larger parking area where a small stage decorated with patriotic bunting lifted a group of well-dressed people above a gathering crowd.

Music boomed from large speakers positioned at each side of the stage. Vending trailers billowed the savory, smoky fragrances of barbecue on the grill, funnel cakes, and an impressive array of carnival-type fare.

Brand followed Mercer to the outside edge of the crowd. Most of the growing number of rally-goers were gathered near the stage, but many were spread out toward the outer edges of the parking area.

Mercer indicated a small group of nearly a dozen people hanging back at the edge of the parking lot, leading Brand toward them. Brand noticed they held signs on long sticks. The signs rested on the ground, unreadable. When they arrived, Mercer greeted them casually. Brand stood at a distance as he surveyed the group of youngish men and women. There was an overall sense of unrest among them.

"It looks like we are all here," Mercer announced to the group. "Hang back here until Candidate Sams takes the stage and is well into his speech. Disperse within the crowd. Don't congregate. I will give you the signal when it is time to rally in protest."

Near the stage, the crowd grew gradually until Mercer, Brand, and the group of protestors were no longer at the edge of the gathering. They were well within the throng when the buffer music stopped, and a blaring horn-led patriotic number heralded the commencement of the rally.

A portly man in an expensive suit took his place before the microphone in the center of the stage. His voice rose as the horn music faded to silence.

"Welcome, ladies and gentlemen. I am so pleased you have joined us on this glorious day to welcome our next congressman from the great state of Texas."

The crowd lifted their voices in cheers and eager applause.

"I am Mayor Bryan Tate. Welcome to our hometown barbecue picnic event for a great cause. Be sure to visit the caterers surrounding the event. You will find some of the finest regional tastes available in our fair city. Before we bring up Steve Sams, Republican candidate for U.S. Congress, let me tell you a little about him."

Brand tuned out the introduction disinterestedly as he looked around him at the crowd. Most of the rally-goers were older people. Many carried cardboard signs handed out at the entrances to the rally. Two police officers stood at the foot of the stage, surveying the crowd cautiously. Other uniformed officers prowled the outer edges of the rally.

The mayor droned on for some time as Brand busied himself with his observations and his thoughts.

The mayor's tone changed from a drone to an excited treble as he introduced the candidate.

"...the next congressman for the great state of Texas, Steve Sams."

A well-coiffed man stepped onto the stage, wearing an expensive navy-blue suit. To Brand, he looked like every other politician he had ever seen. The candidate began his speech as Mercer nudged Brand with an elbow.

"Stay close to me, brother."

Brand followed Mercer as he moved closer to the stage. The protestors separated and spread out among the crowd.

The candidate droned on as the protestors took their places throughout the crowd.

Mercer raised his voice as he yelled, "Fascist elitist pig!"

On cue, the protestors lifted their signs above the crowd and began a chant which quickly found a unified tempo.

"NOTUS, we won't go. No right, no rich, no po po."

Nearby rally-goers gave the protestors black looks. Some complained to the loud demonstrators directly. A sign dropped in the middle of the crowd as a protestor screamed at a rally-goer and shoved him. An older man in a red rally cap leveled the protestor with a strong blow to the face. Policemen waded through the crowd toward the scuffle.

Candidate Sams paused in his speech.

"Everyone please remain calm," he said. "Let the officers do their job."

"You are a liar and a cheat!" one of the protestors yelled from the crowd.

"There is no need for that, sir," Sams replied into the microphone. "We are in a free country allowing all of us our say, even if we disagree."

"Fuck you!" the protestor screamed back.

The protestor's sign dropped as a nearby man shoved him roughly. The crowd turned on the protestors, visiting upon them angry words and, in many cases, shoving and blows.

"Please remain calm, ladies and gentlemen," Sams begged as the crowd grew more active and the conflict escalated. "The police will handle these people."

Mercer sidled up to Brand.

"Time to go," he said in Brand's ear.

Brand looked at Mercer, who pointed toward a spot outside of the crowd. Brand looked in that direction. A camera crew stood before a large white van with a news channel logo on the side and a dish on top, capturing the melee on video.

"Come on," Mercer urged Brand.

They moved through the churning crowd, many of those attempting to flee the developing riot.

They arrived at the car. Mercer fired up the engine and made a beeline for the main road. They heard police sirens over the noise of the laboring engine.

Brand looked around for the police as Mercer weaved the car along side streets, making his way back to the freeway. Once on the highway headed to Houston, Mercer relaxed, regulating his speed to match the traffic around them.

"Pretty intense, huh?" he said proudly.

"This is the security work you do?" Brand asked.

"This is babysitting the mindless activists we ship in by the score for these events."

"What is NOTUS?" Brand asked.

"They are one of many special interest groups we work with for our counter-campaign efforts," Mercer answered as he changed lanes to pass a slow-moving truck.

"We work with a lot of groups: NOTUS, or National Organization of Trotskyite United Socialists; DASH, or Democrats Against Social Humiliation; CSJ, or Coalition for Social Justice. Most of them are splintered factions made up of angry kooks eager to gain media attention. That is the goal of every protest group."

"You sound like a promoter for crazy activists."

"We go deeper than that. We make a boatload off campaign promotion and countermeasures until after the elections. After that, the news cycle restarts on special interests or whatever issue catches fire."

"And this pays?" Brand asked incredulously.

"Handsomely. Insurrection is big business, my friend, and you are on the ground floor."

Brand indicated his understanding.

He watched the city pass by along the freeway.

"So, what did we accomplish back there today?" Brand asked.

Mercer smiled. He liked the 'we' in Brand's question.

"We contributed to a negative headline for Steve Sams and his campaign. The media will craft the story saying the rally-goers assailed protestors standing up for the rights of the working man. Negative press for Sams means an uptick in a poll number or two for our candidate. The media will spin the story. Our side will condemn the violence."

"The press is in on the game?" Brand asked in disbelief.

"Not directly," Mercer said thoughtfully. "Most journalists are leftists, and they use their access to the public to promote those issues they support."

"That doesn't seem very impartial."

Mercer shrugged.

"Walter Cronkite was wrong," Mercer observed. "He said once cable news meant the big three networks would no longer be able to craft the news. More access to news means we can change the news at the source, on the ground as it happens. Verification of a story is no longer a step in the news reporting process. The news cycle churns hourly instead of daily, which means it moves too fast to verify stories or confirm facts from multiple sources."

"That's why I don't vote. What's the point if the game is rigged with dirty tricks and subterfuge?"

Mercer shrugged.

"Perception is everyone's reality. Truth is subjective."

"This is a shitty business, as I see it," Brand observed.

"My friend," Mercer said with firm confidence in his voice, "the players who create and promote politicians are the feces of the species— the low of the low. Nothing has changed politically for more than fifty years. We make a nice living off a pointless process."

"You asked me before whether I was liberal or conservative. Why did you ask?"

"Conservatives don't do well in this business. They lack social passion when it comes to activism. Liberals are convicted in their beliefs, no matter how crazy or unreasonable. A liberal will sacrifice anything for the advancement of their cause, including their morals or core principles.

"Conservatives rail against a breach to their ideology. They may even get angry, but they never act. Protests are a liberal tool. Conservative messages don't play with the mob. It is too easy to label conservative values as racist or fascist."

"You have given this a lot of thought," Brand observed.

"I am a pro," Mercer said simply. "I have to be an expert at what I do just like you are good at whatever it is you do or did for a living."

Brand crossed his arms.

"So, what do we do next?"

Mercer smiled.

"That's what I wanted to hear. Let's grab a tasty beverage and I'll break it down for you."

16

RANDY CHAPPELL WAITED IN A LARGE LIVING ROOM with lofty ceilings and glass walls. An azure-blue pool sparkled outside. He poured himself a drink from an ornate decanter into a crystal highball glass as he watched the woman swim the length of the pool. He dropped an ice cube into the amber liquor and sipped the beverage as his eyes lingered on the swimmer.

Camille pulled water strongly with smooth, round strokes. At the end of the pool, she pivoted and pushed off the wall, moving underwater toward the opposite end. She swam below the surface the full length of the pool. She pulled her legs under her and stood, waist-deep in the water.

She moved slowly toward the submerged stairs, enjoying the cool water and the hot sun. Reaching above her head, she wrung water from her blonde hair as she pushed through the water. She stepped from the pool and moved to a nearby chaise lounge, where she grabbed a towel draped over one of the cushions. She dried herself thoroughly. Pulling a light pool blouse around her, she tied her hair in the towel.

Chappell appreciated her lean, shapely form. She faced Chappell's direction, but he was certain she could not see him through the reflective glass.

She walked to the large accordion doors and entered the room.

"Hello, Camille," Chappell greeted her.

Camille approached him with a smile.

"Hello, Randy," she purred and kissed him on the lips. "Have a drink."

The candidate looked at his glass with a tinge of doubt. Camille was touchy about decorum.

"Sams had a little problem at his rally today," he said seriously. "The video is all over the news. Some of the national cable outlets are running it."

Chappell sipped his cocktail.

"Really?" she said, with little surprise registering in her expression.

"I prefer not to be in town when this sort of thing happens."

"His problems have nothing to do with you, Randy. You were at a fundraiser in Dallas when the horrible attack on Speaker Cole occurred, but that didn't prevent the tough questions for you. Sams is running an unpopular campaign on antiquated issues. He will naturally blame you for what he can."

Camille watched Chappell as he took another long drink from his cocktail. She moved close to him and wrapped her arms around his neck. Her wet bikini top pressed against him. They kissed deeply.

"I'm glad you dropped by," she said, her breath caressing his cheek. "Why don't you help me out of these wet clothes? We have a big night ahead, and I don't want you to be late."

17

BRAND LOOKED AROUND HIM CAREFULLY. Mercer had picked a strange place to get a drink. The bar was crowded for a weekday. There were no women there, and the men gave Mercer and Brand plenty of attention as the two took seats at a small table near the front door.

The bar was called The Pink Poodle Lounge. Brand felt a bit uncomfortable at the overt attention paid to them by the patrons crowding the bar at that early hour.

Mercer looked at Brand.

"First time?"

"First time for what?" Brand asked.

"First time in a gay bar?"

"To avoid a long story, let's say yes."

"We can leave if it makes you uncomfortable."

"I'm fine."

"Welcome to Montrose, my friend."

"Thanks."

The bartender came around the bar and brought them two shot glasses filled with a purple liquid.

"Purple Geckos," the bartender announced as he placed the drinks on bar napkins before them. "Hello, Joe."

"Hello, Ross. This is Brand."

"Hello, Brand. Welcome to the Pink Poodle. Let me know if you need anything."

Ross favored Brand with a warm look before he returned to the bar.

Brand picked up the glass and drained the shot. He set the empty glass on the table.

Mercer held his glass aloft, waiting to drink until he caught Brand's eye.

"You like?" he asked Brand.

"Sure," Brand replied.

Mercer drained his glass and returned it to the table.

"Ah," he said dramatically, raising two fingers in the air at Ross. "I love 'em."

"Tell me about what we are doing next," Brand urged Mercer.

The latter was basking in the aftermath of the shot.

"Tomorrow, you meet the boss. Tonight, we drink."

Ross brought two more Purple Geckos, smiling mischievously at Brand.

"Ross," Brand asked the bartender, "would you mind bringing me a double bourbon on the rocks?"

"Coming up, handsome," he replied with a smile.

Mercer lifted his purple shot high.

"To new experiences," he toasted exultantly.

Brand lifted his glass and downed the shot.

Ross brought Brand his bourbon and Mercer a draft beer in a tall glass.

Brand sipped the bourbon with relish.

"A bourbon man," Mercer observed. "Always drink your bourbon with your gun hand to show your friendly intentions."

Brand sat back in his seat.

"As Mark Twain said," Brand quoted, "'Too much of anything is bad, but too much good whiskey is barely enough.'"

They lifted their glasses and drank.

Brand looked around the room over the rim of his highball glass. They were watched closely by a growing number of bar patrons.

"You mentioned this was not your first gay bar experience," Mercer said in a low voice. "Where was the first?"

"I said to avoid a long story, call this my first time."

"Pshaw," Mercer discarded the disclaimer with a wave of his hand. "Out with it, Brand."

Brand considered Mercer as he decided whether to tell the story or not. Finally, he leaned forward and spoke in a limited tone to avoid eavesdroppers.

"I had a friend named Bert. We had been friends since our teens."

"Where is he now?" Mercer asked curiously.

"Dead," Brand answered bluntly.

"Shit," Mercer snorted. "Sorry about that, brother."

"Forget it," Brand said with enough force to let Mercer know it still bothered him. "He was always cooking up a trip to Mexico or a vacation to Vegas or a weekend at the coast. He was a real rolling stone.

"One weekend he and I went to Shreveport under the guise of working there for a week. He really just wanted to hit the state-line casinos and sample some authentic Cajun food, so we went.

"We arrived after dark Sunday night. We crossed the border into Bossier City, Louisiana. The town had rolled up the sidewalks, and all the bars and nightclubs were dark. We decided to find a motel and settle down for the night.

"As we drove aimlessly around Bossier City, we ended up in an older residential neighborhood. We turned onto a street thinking we were traveling in the general direction toward the interstate. Directly ahead of us was an old house with big windows across the front. Inside, the place was lit up like a runway. We saw a bar and tables, packed to the walls with people.

"When we walked in, the place was full of beautiful women. There were only three men in the place: Bert, me, and the bartender.

"As the bartender fixed our drinks, we looked around. It was like we had entered the afterparty for the Miss America Pageant.

"When the bartender brought our drinks, Bert asked him, 'What is the story with a bar full of women in a dark town on a Sunday night?'

"The bartender told us Shreveport and Bossier were twin cities. Both had local colleges with a large female enrollment, the most refined and desirable Southern belles. Once the women graduated, they married the finest and most eligible Southern gentlemen.

"While they were in school, they dated their female classmates exclusively, the college thing."

"Bert asked the bartender if there was any chance of us getting one of those girls.

"The bartender assured him better men than Bert had tried and failed. He advised him to drink up and get used to disappointment.

"I looked up, and the bartender was standing there watching me. He asked me if I had ever considered a man for a lover.

"I told him there wasn't enough booze in his bar to make that happen.

"He said, 'Oh yeah? Let's find out.'"

Mercer laughed heartily.

"You don't remember the end of the night?"

"I know what you're thinking," Brand assured him. "I woke up the next morning in a motel room with Bert. My ass wasn't sore, and I didn't have a bad taste in my mouth."

Mercer laughed heartily at the story.

"That is a good one," he said appreciatively.

Brand drained his drink. The booze was taking hold. He was warming inside, and his mood was light.

"When we met," Brand asked carefully, "why were you locked up?"

Mercer gave him a startled look but quickly covered it.

Brand feared the question might have offended Mercer.

"Forget I asked. Just making conversation."

Mercer took a moment before he spoke.

"No," he said dismissively. "No problem. You will probably find out anyway. In our line of work, sometimes we get sideways with the cops. I'm sure you have heard about the celebrity activist who gets cuffed and stuffed for her role in a protest. They look at it like a badge of honor. The tabloids love it, and so does the cause. I'm no celebrity, but I still get locked up overnight occasionally. That time, I was taken in because there was an unusual amount of violence that broke out at a protest I was attending."

Mercer sipped his beer, eyeballing Brand over the rim.

"Was that the same day a congressman was assassinated by a terrorist with a bomb? Is that part of why you were in jail?"

"I was there with the protestors," Mercer said in a faint voice.

Brand thought he detected malice in the tone. He wrote it off to discretion.

"I was as surprised as anyone when the bomb blew up."

Mercer drank his beer. He watched Brand for a moment until finally he shrugged dismissively.

"Like I said when we met, the charges were dropped like they always are."

Mercer's expression changed after his explanation. Brand sensed he was happy with his answer, as though it might have gone another way.

"So how about you?" Mercer asked. "What brought you there?"

Brand shook his head. Mercer probably thought he was rejecting the offer to share. In fact, he was unhappy to relive any portion of the last few months in memory or words.

"I was in the wrong place at the wrong time," he replied simply but not completely honestly. "I was arrested for criminal trespass. The property turned out to be some kind of criminal enterprise, and the charges were dropped because I was helpful in exposing the illegal activities going on there."

Mercer watched Brand steadily. He felt there was more to the story but was unwilling to press Brand further for fear of upsetting their growing rapport.

"Well, that was a bit of luck," Mercer finally declared. "Like I said, tomorrow you will meet the boss. Drink up."

Brand raised his glass, relieved to shelve the subject.

They sat silently for a long moment. Finally, Mercer spoke once more.

"Where do you stay?" he asked.

"I haven't worked it out yet," Brand admitted, thinking of Amy's departure that morning. "I'm not sure how long I will be in town. Why do you ask?"

"I got the impression you and Amy Landry might be a thing."

"She was my attorney in the trespass thing. She isn't warming up to me these days."

Mercer sipped his beer and waved the subject of Amy Landry from the conversation.

"We need to get together tomorrow morning, and I was going to give you directions. Why don't you stay at my place tonight? Where did you leave your car—at the office?"

"My truck is back in San Antonio. I'm on foot right now."

"Then it is settled. No car and no home, we'll get you settled in short order."

Brand looked at Mercer with a doubtful expression.

"Not to worry," Mercer said abruptly. "Your ass won't be sore tomorrow."

Both laughed. Brand was somewhat relieved he didn't have to deal with the issue later.

18

THE NEXT MORNING, MERCER PARKED his car in a dirt parking lot before a frame house with large casement windows in the front. The building was unoccupied. The front door stood open, revealing an empty living room.

To the left of the house, a rectangular building was in the framing stages of construction. A single Latino, wearing heavy tool bags, worked on the building.

Mercer opened the car door and stood in the doorway. He leaned against the car as he produced a cigarette and lit it. He drew deeply and exhaled a large cloud of smoke.

"How do you feel?" he asked Brand as the latter stepped out of the car.

"I'm good," Brand replied.

Mercer squinted at him through a fresh cloud of smoke.

"You don't look good."

Brand smiled weakly. He felt seriously hungover.

Standing outside the car, Brand could see more of the property. Behind the house was a tall corrugated metal fence. It separated the front parcel from what appeared, from his vantage, to be an industrial complex. Over the fence, he saw the tops of Connex containers and metal sheds. A narrow pillar of black smoke billowed above the compound, rising on the still morning air. Brand smelled melting rubber mixed with burning garbage and the bitter odor of other nondescript flaming debris.

Movement drew Brand's attention as a shiny, dark, late-model Cadillac pulled smoothly off the narrow road and into the wafting dust of the parking lot.

Mercer leaned forward until he stood independent of the car.

The driver parked the shiny car and killed the engine. After a moment, he stepped out of the Cadillac.

He acknowledged Mercer with a quick look.

Mercer pulled on the cigarette.

Brand took stock of the newcomer. He was a thickly built Black man with neck tattoos and an exceptionally large gold wristwatch. He was dressed modestly in jeans, black boots, and a tight navy-blue T-shirt.

"You been back yet?" the driver of the Cadillac asked Mercer.

"We just got here," Mercer replied.

"Come on," the newcomer directed and walked toward the tall fenced-in area.

Mercer crushed the butt, and the three men moved to a narrow gate in the fence.

The newcomer gave Brand a sidelong glance.

"Who you?" he asked Brand.

"Brand."

The Black man grunted.

"Umar."

Brand made no response.

Umar looked at Mercer.

"I don't know if Sahib is here. We'll go back to the man cave and see."

Inside the fence, Brand discovered the source of the black smoke. A round Hispanic woman unloaded trash and junk from a stake-bed truck and threw it into a flaming fifty-five-gallon drum. She paid the three men no attention as they passed, feeding the multicolored flames inside the barrel.

The compound consisted of a wide dirt central area surrounded by welded steel sheds, shipping containers, and several buildings that were previously storage containers but had been converted to buildings with doors, windows, and welded porches at the entrances.

Umar led them to the largest of the structures and opened the left side of the glass double doors leading into the building. They entered a large room with tall ceilings. The opulence of the interior belied the drabness of the utilitarian exterior.

To the right of the doors was a large wooden bar complete with a stair-stepped back wall, neatly lined with liquor bottles. An impressive array of mounted game animal heads was hung high on the walls. A custom Harley chopper occupied a place among several vintage autos along the left wall. The main area was filled with overstuffed sofas and end tables positioned before a giant theater screen.

"I'll see if Sahib is in," Umar announced and disappeared through a doorway behind the bar.

Mercer turned to Brand.

"Some man cave, huh?"

"No kidding," Brand replied in awe.

"Sahib owns hundreds of properties."

"Where does he get his money?"

"We don't ask that question," Mercer replied with a little more aggression than Brand thought necessary.

Brand frowned but made no comment.

Umar entered the room ahead of a lean, dark-headed man in gray slacks and an expensive dress shirt. His face was covered with a closely trimmed beard and mustache. His dark eyes lighted upon Mercer, then more fully upon Brand.

"This is Brand," Umar explained with a meaningful look at the newcomer.

"He is with you, Joe?" Sahib asked mildly.

"New man," Mercer replied simply. To Brand, he said, "This is Sahib."

Sahib circled behind the bar. He took a seat and considered the two men.

"What has Joe told you about our operation?" Sahib asked Brand directly.

"He tells me he works security for protests and demonstrations."

Sahib laughed.

"Perhaps an oversimplification, but not inaccurate. So, you are interested in becoming a security guard?"

Brand didn't reply.

Sahib gave him a long moment to comment. Finally, Sahib looked at Umar.

"Mercer has brought us a shy guy, Umar."

Both men chuckled as they looked Brand over.

"Maybe he is Mercer's girlfriend," Umar said roughly.

Brand studied his shoes.

"Mercer," Sahib said lightly. "Does he speak or...?"

"Are we here to tell jokes and play grab ass?" Brand asked, looking Sahib in the eye.

Sahib's smile faded as he considered Brand seriously.

Umar turned toward Brand ominously, his formerly entertained expression replaced with a dark, dangerous look.

Mercer paled under his tan.

"You are one to speak your mind, I see," Sahib said soberly. "Is your lack of manners courage or stupidity?"

"It may be both," Brand admitted. "But I am not here to be the butt of anyone's joke. If you need help, I am here. If not, I can leave as easily as I got here."

"Is that what you think?" Sahib asked significantly.

Brand shrugged.

Umar's gaze never left him. His aggressive stance was obviously meant to intimidate him.

Brand had seen harder men than Umar. The threat irritated him more than it frightened him.

Brand glanced at Sahib. The man watched Brand with a mixture of surprise and amusement on his face.

Sahib smiled imperceptibly as he raised a hand toward Umar.

"Let us remain pleasant here," he said gently. "Mr. Brand is a serious man, I see. For him we will control our humor."

Brand watched Umar. The man descended from his state of high alert slowly and reluctantly.

Mercer cleared his throat uncomfortably.

"Brand is a good man," he assured the others. "He is intense, but he seems to be reliable and able."

Sahib listened doubtfully.

After a moment, he said to Brand, "I employ many men and women in many roles. I try to match their abilities to the task. You will work with Joe until we find a place perfectly suited for you. Is that agreeable to you, Mr. Brand?"

"Sure," Brand replied. "You can call me Brand."

Sahib shrugged nonchalantly.

"Joe," he said to Mercer. "On Saturday, take Brand with you to the event downtown. See that he gets a taste for the work."

"Yes, sir," Mercer replied.

Mercer turned to leave.

Brand followed him, casting a sidelong glance at Umar.

The latter watched him intently, exuding danger.

Mercer walked rapidly to the compound gate without a backward glance for Brand. He passed through the gate, Brand closing it behind them.

Brand managed to take his seat in the car before Mercer left. They drove in silence for several minutes. Brand looked out the window, ignoring Mercer, who was obviously annoyed with him.

Finally, Mercer broke his silence.

"What the fuck do you think you were doing back there?"

"Don't talk to me that way," Brand warned him. "I've had enough of the double-speak and talking down."

"Sorry if your feelings got hurt," Mercer retorted sarcastically. "You're gonna have to thicken up your skin if you want to cut it around here."

"My skin is plenty thick enough, Mercer. I'm not about to take shit from a guy who considers a junkyard full of shipping containers his palace, and a bunch of wannabe tough guys his protection from his mistaken belief he can say whatever he wants to me."

Mercer frowned and bit his lip. It was obvious he had misjudged Brand. It had been a mistake to bring him in. Sahib instructed him to take Brand along to the next job, so that was what he would do, but he would end the relationship as soon as he could.

"Where do you want me to drop you?" Mercer asked wearily. "The Grand Hotel fundraiser event is on Saturday night. You've got three days to get your shit together."

Brand frowned as he looked out the window.

"I saw you handle yourself in Harris County, but Sahib and his outfit are way out of your league. He is giving you another chance. If you don't have the common sense to think about yourself, at least think about the money."

"Drop me at a hotel near downtown," Brand finally replied.

Mercer drove toward downtown in silence. Brand was like no one he had ever met. What had he seen in his life that would cause him to react without fear?

On the Gladiator Floor, Brand faced off with a sadistic brute without showing any fear whatsoever. Prior to his fight with Brand, Mercer had watched Walker beat at least a half dozen men until they pissed and shit themselves. Many succumbed before the fight had even begun.

Brand stood in Sahib's private lair and insulted him. Brand had watched Umar fearlessly as the latter plainly displayed his deadly intentions. Umar had committed at least three killings he knew about. He was sure the man had killed many more prior to Mercer's joining the group.

He glanced at Brand. The latter continued to watch the world outside the car, ignoring Mercer. He couldn't help himself; he still liked Brand. The man was smart (other than his apparent death wish), had a ready sense of humor, and was capable in a pinch.

Sahib saw something in the man. It was not his concern to make those decisions for his boss. Mercer was surprised his anger toward Brand was diminished until he felt only annoyance.

Mercer took the next exit and drove toward his apartment. He would give Brand another chance, he thought. An involuntary smile tightened his lips. Besides, he mused, he liked having Brand around the house.

19

IMAM ABU MAZOORAH AL SHAHAN PATTED THE youth on the head. His smile beamed warmly upon the youngster. The Imam believed the strength of their cause lay with the young men and, at appropriate times, the young women within their sect.

"Blessed *Imam*," the boy asked, "how can so many be leaders?"

"Maabad, you and your brothers are the future of the world. You will learn to forget the laughter of your parents as they believe leadership to be hubris. When leading in the light of the Jamaat, leadership is a blessing from *Allah*."

The youth returned the old man's warmth in his upturned face.

"I understand, Blessed Imam. Thank you for your wisdom and guidance."

Shahan smiled. He lifted the boy's chin to look fully into his innocent eyes.

"Every Muslim, even a *Talib,* has a sacred duty to spread the faith of Islam," he told the youngster. "*Qur'an* 8:39 tells us to fight until there is no more tumult or oppression, and there prevail justice and faith in *Allah* altogether and everywhere."

"Yes, Blessed Imam."

"Be on your way."

The boy ran toward one of the framed buildings lined together in a neat row. He was soon lost within a large group of boys.

Shahan turned toward the large central building where a contingent of his adult followers waited at a respectful distance. Among them stood Sahib.

He watched the Imam approach with a welcoming smile.

"The guidance of a *Talib* from the master," he noted. "The Imam is truly the wise hand of *Allah*."

Shahan bowed to honor Sahib's words.

Sahib returned the courtesy.

The *Imam* moved through the group and led them into the large building at the far end of the fenced training compound.

Inside, Shahan led the way through a large doorway and into a narrow conference room. A long table filled the center. Soft chairs of Egyptian design lined both side walls. A head table stood at the far end of the rectangular room.

Shahan sat behind the head table. The others took seats in the comfortable chairs along the walls. Sahib sat to the side and closest to Shahan.

"Blessings upon you all. Many of you are new to our holy court."

Shahan turned to Sahib.

"Would you honor our guests with the miraculous story of our blessed purpose, Sahib?"

Sahib stood, greeting the newcomers as was customary for honored guests.

"Our *Jamaat* was founded some forty years ago to complete the act of *Taghoot*—to remove every false god, leaving only *Islam*. We have trained and mobilized hundreds of *Talib* in the service of *Islam*. It is certain one among our *Talib* is the 7th *Sultan al Fuqra*—he who will be present for Doomsday."

Sahib lifted a bent arm with an upturned palm, indicating Shahan.

"Our Blessed *Imam* is the 6th *Sultan al Fuqra*. He alone can remove a follower from a holy station. He alone may allow one into the Holy

Court of the Prophet Mohammed. Not all, but many of our *Talib* are reborn if deemed worthy with a pure heart and a spiritual connection to the *Imam*."

Sahib searched the faces of those seated around him.

"To succeed in the *Taghoot*, we must embrace the lessons of *Islam*. We are *Al Deen*—those submissive to the ways of *Islam*. We honor the *Salat*. We punish spiritual laziness—*Ahl Kusaal*. Ours is *Intidhar:* the total of actions made in preparation for the 7th *Imam—Imam Mahdi*—who will rule until the end of days.

"This training facility lies only a few miles from one of the largest cities in the country, in plain sight. Compassion, as they call it, holds them captive. They see our plight as that of any activist group. We shall be heard. We shall create change. We shall conquer the enemy from within without a shot fired. *Laa ilaha illa Allaah!*"

Those seated rose and repeated their praise of Allah in a unified voice of agreement.

"*Laa ilaha illa Allaah!*"

20

MERCER PARKED THE CAR IN A DARK ALLEYWAY near the Grand Hotel. Brand was reminded of the alley from which he had escaped under a rain of bullets some weeks before.

On foot, he followed Mercer to the mouth of the alley. The big man looked up and down the street before he turned to the right. Brand walked with him along the empty street until they arrived at the loading docks and service entrance behind the Grand Hotel. He and Mercer waited across the street behind the hotel, watching the service staff move in and out of the doorway and bay doors. After some minutes passed, the service door opened and a man in a red blazer gestured to them. Brand followed Mercer quickly across the street and through the open door.

"Hey, Joe," the man said. "Security is tighter than usual tonight. I can't help you beyond this."

Mercer pressed a roll of bills into his hand.

"Not to worry. We got it from here."

The man departed quickly as Joe moved along the utility corridor, his head on a swivel. Brand followed carefully. He had no idea what they were doing at the fancy hotel. He remembered Sahib referring to an event they were supposed to attend. Brand was certain they were not on the guest list.

The corridor ended at a pair of doors. Mercer opened one of the doors a crack. On the other side of the doors, they saw a wide carpeted vestibule crowded with waiters in red blazers and cooking staff in white clothing. They entered the crowded room and merged into the staff, heading toward stainless steel doors Brand guessed led to the kitchen. Mercer's hand was on one of the doors when a voice sounded behind them.

"Hey, you! What are you doing?"

Brand turned toward the voice. A large man with a crew cut and an earpiece glared at them. He approached in a businesslike manner. Brand turned toward the kitchen doors. Mercer was gone.

"Don't move, buddy," the man warned as he drew closer.

Brand pushed through the doors, drawing an angry cry from Crew Cut. Inside, two men held Mercer with his arms pinned behind his back. Brand backed out of the room. Crew Cut grabbed him from behind.

Brand reacted instinctively. He bent forward, pivoted on the balls of his feet, and tossed Crew Cut over his shoulder and onto the floor. He crushed his nose with a hard fist, slamming the back of his head hard against the floor.

Brand ran toward the double doors leading to the utility corridor by which he and Mercer had arrived. The hallway was clear of additional sentries. He arrived at the outside door and exited the service entrance. He ran along the shipping dock apron where he found cover behind a dumpster.

He watched the service door for pursuit. He expected men to boil out of the doorway, but none appeared. He thought about Mercer, captured by men with earpieces and law-enforcement-looking haircuts.

The door opened and three men, including the bloodied Crew Cut, hauled Mercer outside.

"It looks like your partner de-assed the A.O.," one of the men observed.

Mercer said nothing.

"You have been a pain in our ass for a while, Mercer," the same man admitted. "Your days of troubling anyone have come to an end."

"Cut the talk and arrest me already," Mercer said and spit on the concrete for emphasis.

"Arrest you?" Crew Cut scoffed as he rubbed the back of his head. "The cops won't hold you more than a day. This is a nice private place to show you the error of your ways. You can tell Chappell, or whoever it is you work for these days, this is a warning. Don't fuck with us."

Crew Cut stunned Mercer with a right to the face.

Mercer's long hair whipped forward as the impetus of the blow pushed him backward into the strong arms of the others.

To his credit, Mercer struck out, but his wild punch landed harmlessly against the muscle-padded shoulder of one of the other men.

His effort was rewarded with another hard punch to the face.

As one, the men were upon him, striking him whenever and wherever they could without hitting one of their own.

Brand waited, unsure whether he should help or not. The numbers were not in his favor. With a dogged determination, he stood from behind the trash bin.

None of the assailants noticed him as they gave Mercer their full attention.

Brand crept rapidly forward. He grabbed the nearest man by the collar and tripped him from behind. The man hit the concrete hard with a crunching sound.

Crew Cut and the other man turned toward Brand. They abandoned Mercer, focusing their rage on Brand.

Mercer shook his head, struggling to rise.

Crew Cut punched Brand in the face.

Brand absorbed the rush of the second man, who attempted to knock him to the ground. Brand spun with the man's impetus, rotating with his weight, throwing his attacker to the concrete of the loading dock. He kicked him in the ribs.

Crew Cut rushed to help his fallen comrade. Brand met him head-on. He pressed through his raised arms, landing two body blows in quick succession. The strikes only slowed the man.

He elbowed Brand in the face with a skillful forward attack. He moved to press his advantage as Brand fell to the concrete.

The man was on him, and they grappled for a dominant handhold.

Two blows from behind weakened the man with a shudder, his efforts noticeably diminished. As if he had sprouted wings, the attacker was lifted off the ground and fell back at a distance.

Mercer stood there a split second to check on Brand's condition before he followed Crew Cut and struck him several times in the face.

Brand regained his feet.

Brand tried to pull Mercer off Crew Cut, whom he continued to punch in the face.

"We need to go now," Brand warned him.

The other men struggled to rise. They would recover quickly enough to take up the fight if he and Mercer did not flee immediately.

Mercer stood and looked at Brand with a strange expression.

Brand turned, running toward their car.

Mercer followed on his heels. They arrived at the car in the alleyway. Mercer cranked the engine, and the little sedan lurched as he stomped on the gas.

Mercer narrowly missed running over the two sentries as they ran around the corner into the alley. They leaped clear as the little car barreled toward them before turning down the dark street.

Mercer drove in silence for some time before he glanced at Brand.

"Thanks for helping me out of that spot."

Brand watched as they passed dark buildings along the road. His head hurt from the blows he sustained in the fight.

"You have had some training in hand-to-hand. Military?"

"Something like that," Brand replied.

Mercer watched the road ahead, turning onto a busy downtown street. He ran a red light, and soon they were on a freeway moving well. He processed his thoughts silently for several minutes.

"I was wrong about you, partner," Mercer admitted through set teeth. "You could have left me, and I wouldn't have blamed you. Thanks again."

"Don't mention it," Brand deflected.

"How about a drink, partner?"

Brand considered Mercer.

"Seriously?"

"They knew me, they may know where I live. I know a place where they would never think to look for us."

"I think I know the place."

They parked across the street from the Poodle Lounge. The parking lot was jam-packed. Brand stepped onto the curb, examining his face in the mirror. He saw no blood, only discoloration around his left cheek.

Mercer was a bit more seriously injured.

"You better stop off at the men's room and clean yourself up," he advised Mercer.

Mercer limped slightly, indicating he was more injured than he appeared.

Inside, the doorman looked Mercer over curiously but gestured his permission to enter.

Brand went to the bar as Mercer moved toward the men's room.

Ross noticed him as he approached the bar.

"Geckos?" he asked Brand.

"Double bourbon on the rocks for me," Brand replied.

He took a deep breath as he reconsidered his answer.

"What the hell. Two Purple Geckos along with it."

"That's the spirit, Handsome," Ross encouraged him. To the barback he said, "Find a table for Brand and his friend."

The barback disappeared behind the busy bartenders as he moved to obey.

When Mercer arrived at the table, he looked better, but he carried bruises soap couldn't remove. He sat heavily in the available chair across from Brand. He lifted the purple cocktail and drained it.

"One more will take the edge off," Mercer predicted.

Brand looked toward the bar. Ross was already looking at them. Brand held up two fingers. He downed the Purple Gecko and sipped his bourbon.

"How are you feeling?" he asked Mercer.

"I'm going to feel it tomorrow. You?"

"I've been worse off many times."

"That karate stuff you were doing there. Where did you learn that?"

"It is called Sombo. I have had a little training."

"Well, you showed those guys a thing or two."

"We were lucky. They were most likely off-duty cops. Ex-military or corporate security guys would have had us."

Mercer pursed his lips, impressed with Brand's modesty.

"Let's drink to luck in the form of an All-American boy who carries a big stick."

They clinked glasses and drank.

Brand spun his glass in his hands, examining the tabletop and his thoughts.

"Those guys seemed to know you," Brand said. "Is that a problem?"

"I have been at this for a while," Mercer admitted. "It looks like they are keeping an eye out for me. It may be time for me to move on."

"That serious, huh?"

"This is a deadly business. Too much money is at stake. Those guys would have put me in the hospital for a while."

"I heard," Brand agreed. "So now what?"

"I will leave that up to Sahib. He has a lot of insight into this sort of thing. He works the campaigns and activists better than anyone."

Mercer watched Brand until the latter looked up from his drink.

"I need you to behave when we go back there. You don't want to make Sahib an enemy."

Brand considered Mercer.

"Please," Mercer implored him. "Give this thing a chance. It is a good thing for both of us."

Brand shrugged, then sipped his drink.

21

THE NEXT MORNING, MERCER AND BRAND were outside of Sahib's compound. Umar met them at the gate. He presented a stoic face, giving nothing away about where they stood with him or Sahib.

"Sahib is busy," Umar told Mercer, blocking his entry to the compound.

He looked at Brand with an expression impossible to read.

"Why is he here?" Umar asked, refusing to address Brand directly.

"We ran into some trouble last night," Mercer explained.

"We assumed you did. The event was not altered. You failed."

"Let me speak with Sahib," Mercer insisted. "He needs to know what happened last night."

Umar hesitated as he decided how to handle Mercer. Finally, he stepped aside.

"Only you. He stays outside," he warned, pointing a stiff finger at Brand.

Mercer glanced at Brand before he entered.

Umar closed and locked the gate.

Brand returned to the car in the front parking lot.

Mercer and Umar entered the man cave where Sahib sat on one of the loungers before the massive theater-screen TV. He watched the news with the sound off.

He glanced over his shoulder as the men entered.

They rounded the sofas where Mercer found a place before Sahib. He crossed his hands in front of him and waited for Sahib to speak.

"You failed to alter the event last night," Sahib said softly. "I do not tolerate failure. Please waste as little of my time as you can manage."

"We were jumped by a three-man team near the rear entrance," Mercer explained. "They knew me by name, and they were ready for us at our entry point. I believe my contact was compromised."

"You are here and not in jail. How does that happen?"

"They had no intention of turning me over to the police."

"How do you know that?"

"Because they told me as much."

Sahib's interest was obvious now.

"Tell me what happened."

"Brand and I entered through the service entrance. One of the waiters helped us in. We were about to enter through the kitchen when a guard yelled at us in the back corridor. I decided to make a break for it and enter the event immediately. I thought I could create enough of a distraction on the fly so that I could evade them long enough to button down the fundraiser. The rest of the team was inside the kitchen, and they captured me."

"What about the new man, Brand?"

"He opened the door, and when he saw I was nabbed, he turned to run. The guard on the outside grabbed him. He did some Kung Fu shit and slammed the guard on the floor. I didn't see him after that. The guards escorted me out the back entrance and began beating on me. They told me they would stop my activities permanently. They said it would be a warning for whoever I was working for not to fuck with them."

"Who are they?" Sahib asked.

"They didn't identify themselves, but they had cop haircuts, and they handled themselves like they were part of an organization."

"You don't look that banged up."

"They had just started on me when Brand appeared and took out two of them single-handedly. I took care of the last one myself."

Sahib showed his surprise openly. He looked at Umar as though he had won a bet.

"So, our new man is dangerous."

Umar shook his head and looked at his feet.

"Umar," Sahib said with authority. "Get the two envelopes behind the bar."

Umar hesitated.

"Do not make me repeat myself, Umar. This is a lesson you needed to learn!"

Umar strode to the bar and collected two white envelopes. He returned and handed them to Mercer.

"Give the new man the larger of the two for saving your life, Joe."

Mercer pocketed the envelopes.

"Thank you, Sahib."

"Tomorrow morning, have Mr. Brand go to the campaign office. You lay low for a few days until I can figure out who this new foe is."

"Yes, sir."

Mercer left and closed the door.

"Umar, do not question my judgment again when it comes to the capability of men. Go get my lunch."

Umar scowled as he moved to obey.

Once they were seated in the car, Mercer handed Brand the thicker of the two envelopes.

Brand opened the flap on the envelope. Inside was a sheaf of hundred-dollar bills. He estimated there was around $2,000 there.

"I told you," Mercer said. "I think you are in."

"It looks that way," Brand agreed. "What is this for? We failed, as your friend said."

"Umar isn't Sahib."

"What's next?"

"Tomorrow, I'm dropping you at the campaign office. I am going to stay out of sight for a few days."

"Have I been demoted to the street team?"

"I'm not sure. Stop sweating everything. You have money in your pocket, and there's more where that came from."

Mercer started the car and headed back to the freeway.

22

IT WAS LATE MORNING WHEN BRAND STEPPED onto the curb in front of the campaign office.

"Good luck," Mercer called to Brand before he merged the little car into Monday morning city traffic.

Brand looked at the posters on the windows of the campaign office. Chappell's face was displayed on each one with a different compelling message. He stepped to the front doors and entered the crowded office. As before, the place was as active as an anthill. He made his way to Troy's office.

Troy looked up from typing on his computer keyboard.

"Hello Mr...sorry...Brand. How do you like working with Joe? Quite a character, huh?"

"Yeah," Brand agreed half-heartedly. "I was told to report here. Any idea who I need to see?"

Troy thought about the question for a moment. He rose from his seat. "Wait here."

He left the office, returning in less than a minute.

"Go to Randy's office. Let yourself in. You are expected."

"Thanks," Brand said.

He left Troy's office, walking the short distance to the candidate's office door. He hesitated for a second, then opened the door and entered.

Camille was behind Chappell's desk. The candidate was not there.

"Hello, Brand," Camille welcomed him with a smile. "Please have a seat."

Brand sat in front of the desk.

"I hope you don't mind chatting with me for a moment," she said mildly. "Randy is running a few errands. I'm borrowing his office while he is away."

"No problem," Brand assured her.

"I wanted to thank you for saving Joe Saturday night. It could have been much worse if it hadn't been for you."

Brand accepted the gratitude silently.

"I appreciate the work you have put in with our Kinetic Team. We think your specific talents would be better served in a more intimate capacity with candidate Chappell. We would like you to join his security detail. The work isn't as exciting as what you are used to, but it is an upward move. Are you interested, Brand?"

"Sure."

"I hear you have had some training in hand-to-hand fighting. Can you tell me about your training?"

"I picked up some techniques here and there."

"Were you in the military or law enforcement?"

Brand gave his surroundings attention, reluctant to admit he had been a weekend warrior.

"I was in the Army National Guard for six years. Most of my training was the same as what regular Army troops go through. No law enforcement experience."

Camille was silent for a moment while she absorbed the information. She placed her hands on the desk and sat up straighter.

"Do you own a suit?"

"No, I don't. Do I need one?"

"You absolutely do! Come on. Let's get you sorted out."

She rose, turning off the desk lamp.

Brand followed her out the door, then to the rear parking lot where they entered a black sports car.

Camille started the car. Soon they were careening along a crowded street, zig-zagging through traffic, running red lights. She pulled the car off the road, halting before a valet station. She got out of the car and tossed the keys to the waiting valet.

"Keep it close," she instructed the young Latino.

They entered a small shop called Walter's Haberdashery.

Inside, Brand followed Camille to the back of the shop, where she spoke with a balding older man, a long measuring tape around his neck.

"Walter," she said. "I need this man in a tux and a couple of suits before Friday."

"Not a problem, Ms. Long," he replied without hesitation. He looked Brand up and down. "44 regular, I think."

"Black tux with all the accoutrement," she instructed, pronouncing the last word with a French accent. "For the suits, I have a few ideas."

Brand shrugged. He hadn't worn a suit since Easter Sunday church services with his parents.

Camille made her way to the 44 rack and looked through the suit coats until she found one she liked. She selected a charcoal coat with a muted pinstripe.

"Come here, Brand," she ordered. "Let's see how this looks with those blue eyes."

Brand obeyed.

Camille held the suit against his chest, appraising him critically.

"I think navy blue may be your color."

She draped the charcoal coat over a nearby rack and searched until she found a navy-blue pinstripe she liked. She pulled a coat from the rack.

Walter was nearby, and he beamed his agreement as she pressed the coat against Brand's chest once more.

"That's the one, Walter," she announced. "We'll take both, please; a black tux too."

Brand looked at the tag hanging from the sleeve. One suit cost everything he had in his pocket, including the cash he recovered from the bus stop.

Camille noticed him inspecting the price tag. She reached out her hand and touched his arm.

"I'm covering it. Consider it a work uniform."

Camille lifted a warning finger when Brand attempted to protest.

Brand pursed his lips.

Walter led him to a fitting area in the back and quickly marked up the suits for tailoring.

"They will be ready by Friday, end of business," he promised Brand.

Brand joined Camille at the front of the store where she had selected shoes, socks, three shirts and ties, and a belt.

Walter met them at the cash register.

"On Sahib's account," she said casually.

"Of course, Ms. Long. As I told the gentleman, the suits will be ready Friday before closing."

"That sounds great, Walter. We'll collect everything then," she replied.

Brand followed her out of the store. He walked beside her as they strolled along the sidewalk.

"It's after lunch," she announced. "Will you join me for a drink?"

"Sure," he replied because he doubted it was a request.

They walked another half block, entering a small but tasteful bar. They sat at a table in the back where they were the only patrons. A waiter took their order, then left quietly.

"Thanks for the clothes," Brand said. "Why would Sahib pay for my clothes?"

"Sahib is a major contributor to Randy's campaign, and he runs a PAC for him as well. You need to dress the part for your new role in the campaign."

Brand nodded.

The waiter returned with a double bourbon on the rocks for Brand and a martini for Camille.

"Cheers," Camille toasted, raising her glass.

They clinked glasses and tasted their cocktails.

"Tell me about you and Amy," Camille said with a casualness Brand felt was affected rather than sincere.

Brand swirled the ice ball in his glass as he thought about his response. He didn't want to make Amy out to be a one-night stand. He also didn't want to place too much emphasis on their relationship. It occurred to him it was none of Camille's business. He felt Camille was testing him, and how he responded would likely tell her more than what he said.

"I'm not sure what you are asking me."

"When we met, I got the impression Amy was a little possessive of you. I just want to assure you we love Amy and would never do anything to upset her."

"I don't know Amy well, but I like her," he explained.

"She is a good person. She has helped out with the campaign since Randy first decided to run for Congress."

Brand sipped his drink.

Camille smiled. She brought the martini to her lips and watched Brand over the edge. She sipped her drink, then set it on the table.

"Saturday night we are hosting a fundraiser dinner. You will provide personal security for Randy. Stay close, but not too close. Participate, but don't indulge. Blend in, yet be alert for any trouble."

"Are you expecting trouble?"

"The security detail that ambushed you and Joe is a concern. They used Randy's name when they threatened Joe. We are acting appropriately to prevent anything unpleasant."

"Who do I report to in my new role? Am I part of a security team?"

"For now, communicate through me. The assigned security detail for the fundraiser is provided by a government-run contractor. They handle most prominent candidates, and they are specific in their job description. We need you to fill the voids their contract leaves vulnerable."

"What makes you think I am qualified to handle the job?"

"Call it a combination of what I know about your abilities and an instinct I feel about you."

Camille lifted her glass and emptied it. Her eyes held a sparkle of...Brand couldn't place it.

He drained his drink and called the waiter.

Their visit stretched into the late afternoon. Brand learned a lot about Camille. She was, to all intents and purposes, Chappell's campaign manager. Although Troy Doell held the title, she seemed to make most of the decisions. She did not reveal how she ascended to her impromptu station within the campaign organization, but Brand suspected it had something to do with her beauty and underlying dominant will.

Brand learned she was from New England. She was a graduate of Harvard and grew up with money.

They talked about Brand's upbringing in San Antonio. She seemed surprised he had never gone to college.

Brand accepted his fourth cocktail from the waiter. He sipped it, then leaned back in his chair.

Camille eyed him with an unspoken interest.

"Tell me about you and Randy," Brand said. "How did he catch your eye?"

Camille smiled at his attempt to put her off balance.

"I would risk the truth that it was I who caught his eye. Randy is charming, smart, and ambitious. You only have to be in his presence for a moment to see that. He and I met at a golf outing at the club. My group was a hole ahead of his. He approached me in the club lounge. We hit it off. The rest is a combination of chemistry and mutual attraction."

"Do you love him?"

"Well, Mr. Brand, you are direct. Of course, I love him."

Brand looked at his drink. His eyes rose to meet hers.

"I think you two are good together—a perfect couple."

"Don't brood," she chided him with uncanny intuition. "I enjoy your company too."

Brand felt his face redden.

He looked into Camille's eyes. She was obviously enjoying the torture she was inflicting.

"I should get back before I am missed," Camille announced, opening her clutch.

"I'll get the drinks," Brand insisted. He pulled a folded sheaf of cash from his pocket.

"Thank you for the drinks, Brand," she said, her voice hinting at her remaining enjoyment of his pain. "Where can I drop you?"

"I can get home from here," he said, unwilling to admit he was homeless.

"Oh really?" she responded with genuine surprise. "Where are you staying?"

"I'm staying in a hotel for the time being," he replied. He would check into a room soon enough, ensuring the claim would not be a lie for long.

"I can drop you by, so you don't have to walk or catch a cab."

"I would rather you didn't," he insisted.

"Suit yourself," she said in a tone confirming her disappointment.

"Don't brood," Brand said playfully. "I still love you."

Camille gave him a look, causing Brand to pause. Her eyes blazed at him. She seemed genuinely angry with him.

"You should have Walter deliver your new clothes to your hotel," she said coldly. "I will text you the address for the event Saturday. Be on time."

She stood without another word and left him alone in the bar.

23

BRAND MET CANDIDATE CHAPPELL AND CAMILLE at the door to the expansive stone mansion in River Oaks, an upscale community of expensive houses and high-end stores and restaurants. The circular drive was filled with expensive automobiles.

To Brand, the event seemed more like a gala than a fundraiser dinner. Tuxedos and lovely evening gowns were the dress for the occasion. He overheard one of the staff mention the price was $30,000.00 per plate.

Although this was his first fundraising event, and his first time in a tuxedo, Brand enjoyed the people-watching and the elegance of the event.

Sometime after most of the guests had arrived, Chappell and Camille emerged from a long black limousine. The candidate looked sharp in his tuxedo, but Camille garnered the attention of all who watched them emerge. She was stunning in a red gown, plunging scandalously and hugging her curves as closely as Brand's gaze.

The contractor security detail took their place, establishing a cordon around them. Brand stayed outside of the secure perimeter.

He had been briefed by David Brymer, the Detail Chief. Brand liked the man. Unlike Agent Spencer with the DEA, Brymer had been friendly and helpful. He had assured Brand they worked with personally assigned security personnel regularly, and he would keep Brand advised when and where he might be needed. Brand was to stay in the immediate vicinity, but he would best serve Chappell by mingling and keeping an eye out for anything irregular.

Brand felt like the security commander was assigning him homework for the Situational Awareness classes at Camp Bravura. He planned to practice what he had learned, but with the screened guest list and the professional security team, he felt a bit superfluous.

Candidate Chappell and Camille were shepherded into the main hall of the mansion.

Brand followed closely behind.

A cheer, then enthusiastic applause, rose as the candidate made his entrance. He waved and smiled.

Camille beamed, leaning into Chappell as cameras flashed and raised glasses shimmered.

Brand left the entourage and circled around the perimeter of the room. He didn't have much experience, and his training was limited, so he decided to rely on his instincts. He remembered his time with Camille in the bar. She had never answered to his satisfaction why she thought his abilities were adequate for the task.

He was nearly a third of the way around the room when he spotted a familiar face in the crowd. Amy Landry sipped champagne and chatted with another woman near the massive fireplace on the back wall.

Brand altered his path, heading toward the two women.

Amy's companion, a busty brunette, noticed Brand's approach and whispered to Amy.

Amy turned with a mischievous smile that faded when she recognized Brand.

"Hello, Amy," he greeted her. "You look stunning. It is good to see you here."

"Hello, Brand," Amy replied with a less-than-welcoming tone. "Tamara Billings, this is Carson Brand."

"Hello, Carson," the brunette purred, giving Brand a detailed once-over.

"Call me Brand," he added with a smile.

"Call me anytime," Tamara countered.

Amy kept her eyes on Brand through the introductions. She had to admit he looked striking in his well-tailored tux. She promised herself that day at the campaign office she would never get involved with a client—or former client—again.

Brand smiled at the brunette.

Tamara was lovely in her blue gown. Amy, however, held his attention. He felt badly about the last time they had seen one another. He was not a womanizer like his late best friend, Bert, who had seemed to have grown a callus on his love-'em-and-leave-'em muscle.

"How have you been, Amy?"

Tamara ratcheted down her flirting at the sincere tone in Brand's voice. She didn't know the story of Amy and Brand, but she seemed to realize they shared a history and moderated her role to that of a supportive friend.

Amy considered Brand for a moment before she spoke.

"I have been fine. Has the campaign kept you busy?"

"You could say that," he replied. "I'm working tonight."

Amy seemed genuinely curious.

"Handing out fliers here?"

Brand scoffed at her sarcasm.

"Street team duties are 24 hours a day," he replied, playing along.

Amy laughed, her brittle exterior fading as the genuine, beautiful Amy appeared once more.

"After you left the other day, I was promoted to the Kinetic Team. It has been interesting, to say the least."

Amy's expression sobered.

"The Kinetic Team? I don't know much more than hearsay, but I would be careful if I were you, Brand."

"I don't know what you have heard, but it is a side of politics I have never imagined."

"I know enough about it to advise you to get out of it," Amy urged him with a cautious look around. "The campaign doesn't run that team, and I doubt Randy would condone it if he truly knew what they did on his behalf."

Brand was surprised at the gravity of her tone and the importance of her concerns. Her foreboding knocked him off balance.

"It is a non-issue now," he assured her uncertainly. "I'm working personal security for the candidate."

Amy considered him doubtfully.

"I see you two are getting along again," Camille said from behind them.

They turned toward Camille, where she stood holding a champagne glass. She smiled graciously as she took them in.

"Hello, Camille," Amy said with a brittle quality to her voice.

"Camille," Amy said, turning to Tamara, "allow me to introduce a friend of mine, Tamara Billings."

"Of the Billings oil family," Camille said as she raised her glass. "So good of you to contribute to our campaign."

Camille drank to the toast. She lowered her glass.

"I must admit I am surprised the Billings family would donate to the run of a Democrat for Congress."

"I don't represent the family in this," Tamara said demurely. "I am contributing on my own behalf."

She raised her glass in turn, giving Brand a sidelong glance to see if he was impressed with her reputation.

"In that case," Camille smiled, "we thank you even more. May I introduce you to candidate Chappell?"

"That would be lovely," Tamara replied.

Camille smiled at Amy and ignored Brand as she led Tamara through the crowd toward Chappell, who entertained his guests.

Brand faced Amy.

"What did you mean by Chappell not condoning the Kinetic Team?"

"Brand," Amy said in a lower voice, "there are things going on here you don't know about. There is a lot of money and power at stake. Those two things always draw a certain element. I should say they attract those who seek to benefit from both."

"Isn't that what politicians do when they seek office?"

"I am not talking about politicians," Amy retorted. "You asked my referral for a job. I intended you should hand out fliers and knock doors, not commit clandestine acts against opposing campaigns."

Amy knew more about the Kinetic Team than she was willing to admit. Brand understood she was not comfortable talking about the details.

She glanced around the room nervously.

"Amy," Brand said soothingly, "let's drop the subject for now. Let's talk about you. What brings you here tonight?"

Amy took a moment to calm her nerves.

"Randy invited me," she explained. "We are friends from school. We had a couple of the same classes at Rice. We dated briefly, which made us realize we are better friends than anything deeper. We maintain our friendship despite his growing fame and success. I guess our history together and my past work on the campaign keeps me on the VIP list for these things."

"I suspect you have a gift for understatement. There is more to you than just a public defender," he said, responding to her modesty. "You have an ambitious side anyone can see. You're smart and honest. I believe he probably sees those same qualities."

Amy looked at him closely. She had never been told those things. She was surprised Brand could see her for anything other than a pretty face.

"Thank you, Brand. It is very nice of you to say."

Brand smiled.

"I'd better move on," he said reluctantly. "I'm on the clock."

"I'll see you around," Amy said.

Brand continued his circuit, reaching the far wall, then drawing closer to the group surrounding Chappell.

A tall Black man appeared from one of the arched doorways. He stood stiffly as he rang a silver bell.

"Dinner is served," he announced in formal, clipped tones.

The crowd moved to the long tables in the center of the large hall. Folded placards identified seating positions.

Brand noticed Amy was seated farthest from Candidate Chappell. Friendship only got you so far in this setting, he thought.

Unsure what to do, Brand looked across the room where Brymer stood in a corner near the candidate, somewhat obscured by the tall, heavy drapes covering the end wall of the hall.

Brymer indicated a place near him.

Brand moved among the last of the donors taking their seats until he reached the indicated position.

The tall security man gave Brand a nearly imperceptible smile as he scanned the room. Every few minutes, his scan paused as he listened to updates in his earpiece.

The din of conversation quieted as dinner plates appeared before the diners and the dining commenced. Brand watched the guests, dismayed that roasted chicken, braised lamb, and a vegetarian plate could cost thousands. He was aware the meal was a token for a generous donation to a national campaign, but that level of wealth astounded him.

At a point when most of the guests were nearing the end of the meal, Chappell rose, tapping his champagne flute. All heads turned toward him expectantly.

"Ladies and gentlemen, a toast to you and your generosity. It is your support that breathes life into my campaign. Without you, I would not be the next Congressman for the great state of Texas."

Polite applause rose and glasses were lifted for the toast. Chappell raised his champagne glass and drank from it. The diners followed suit, their voices lifted with cheers and cries of "hear, hear."

"I learned earlier today we are leading in the polls by double digits."

Chappell smiled, pausing as the applause rose, then fell.

"Admittedly, we are early in a long race. November is still six months away, but if tonight is any indication of our future momentum, the future looks bright indeed."

The applause grew louder as the excitement rose.

"I would like to thank Kelly and Suzy Keller for their beautiful home so kindly opened to us for this event."

Chappell raised his glass, nodding to an older couple seated nearby.

"You have a magnificent home. We are privileged to share it with you this evening."

The couple raised their glasses and smiled, their gaze moving down the table in acknowledgment of their guests.

"I would like to share a bit more good news with you all tonight. We have gained the endorsement of the Teachers' Union, and the support of the I.O.A. For those of you who don't know about the I.O.A., they are the largest Muslim organization in America. With more than a quarter million members, they join us in making America a more inclusive and compassionate place for us all."

Cheers rose as Chappell's smile beamed proudly upon the crowd.

"When I was a boy, my father, rest his soul, taught me one of the greatest lessons in my life. He was a true son of Texas. His roots were firmly planted in the heritage of this great state. He valued more than anything else honesty, integrity, and commitment to the values that made Texas the republic it is. It is my goal—no, my pledge to you—to bring the strength of Texas.

"Thank you for coming tonight. There is plenty to eat and the bar is open. Enjoy the rest of your evening. I look forward to chatting with each of you."

The room filled with shouts and applause as Chappell received a standing ovation. As the applause faded, music sounded from speakers on stands around the room.

Brand moved closer to Brymer.

"Some party," he remarked to the tall man.

"Yes, it is," the security chief agreed with a nod.

"I'm not sure what to do here," Brand confided.

"We've got this, Brand. Why don't you enjoy the party? That attractive blonde you were talking to earlier has watched you the entire time she has been seated at the table."

Brand looked where Brymer indicated.

Amy raised her glass to Brand.

He smiled in return.

"Well spotted, David," he said, moving toward Amy.

Brymer watched Brand's back, pressing a hand to his earpiece to hear over the noise of the crowd and the music.

Amy rose as Brand reached her place at the table.

"Can I buy you a drink?" he asked her.

"I would like that," she replied.

They weaved through the crowd, arriving at the bar.

"Red wine?" Brand asked her.

"That would be great," she agreed.

To the bartender, Brand said, "A glass of red. Do you have any bourbon back there?"

"Of course, sir," the bartender replied cordially. "Do you have a preference?"

"A decent well bourbon works for me. The good stuff tends to have too much rye for my taste."

"I think I have just the thing for you, sir."

"Make it a double on the rocks."

"Very good, sir."

Brand handed Amy her wine, dropped a ten in the tip jar, and led her through the French doors where they stepped outside.

Illuminated by lovely hanging lights in the trees, they moved around a large swimming pool surrounded by tables and chairs. Many of the guests were already enjoying the cool night air.

Brand led Amy past the seats where they found a winding path through perfectly manicured landscaping. Fragrant flora perfumed the evening air as they walked together through the gardens. A gentle breeze freshened as their shoes crunched upon the crushed granite walk.

"I didn't say so earlier," Amy admitted, sliding her arm into his. "You really look great in that tux."

"Thank you," Brand said, looking down into her face. "It was a pleasant surprise seeing you here."

"It is nice. Sorry for my mood at first."

"Don't give it a second thought," Brand assured her. "I'm happy to be here with you on a perfect evening."

"It is a beautiful night," she agreed, looking around.

They walked for some time.

The silence seemed to weigh on Amy. As they walked along, she glanced up at his face, trying to understand what he was thinking. His expression gave nothing away other than he was occupied with his own thoughts.

He noticed her look and smiled at her.

Amy smiled in return.

"What are your plans once this thing you are doing ends, or you grow tired of it?" Amy asked.

Brand seemed surprised at the direct nature of the question.

"I have a busy couple of weeks starting next week—a personal errand I need to take care of."

"I get the impression you have a dual life, like a superhero. What do you do when you disappear for weeks at a time?"

Brand laughed. His life was extraordinary by any standard, but he was no hero.

"I am no Clark Kent," Brand assured her with a quiet laugh. "But you could very well be my Lois Lane."

Amy considered him seriously for a moment.

"The mystery continues with you, Brand. I am willing to listen if you need me to. I have a lot on my plate outside of work. Maybe this is all there is for us. At this point, I am okay with it."

"Me too," Brand agreed and wrapped an arm around Amy. "I'd better get back. I'm not sure what I'm expected to do here with all of the professional security, but it seems I am required to be seen."

Amy didn't understand what he meant but decided to let the subject drop.

They turned around and headed back toward the big house. As they neared the gala, the sounds of music and merry voices grew.

Tamara stood at the edge of the pool looking around her as they mounted the smooth stone surround bordering the pool. She saw them and stepped forward.

"Amy, there you are. I was wondering where you had gone. I see you have been occupied."

Amy blushed.

"Brand was showing me the gardens. They are quite lovely."

Tamara's eyes narrowed.

"I'll bet they are."

"Behave yourself."

Brand cleared his throat.

"I'd better get back. Thanks for the stroll, Amy. Good to see you, Tamara."

With that, he returned to the great hall. Many of the donors had left, leaving some half of the original number. Most of those remaining sat near Chappell, listening to him speak. Brand could not hear him over the music, but the politician had the rapt attention of the group.

Camille sat beside Chappell, her head cocked to the side as she waited dutifully while he worked the crowd.

She saw Brand enter through the poolside door. She watched him as he drew closer. She stood, excusing herself from the group. She moved away from them and toward Brand, who stopped at a distance from the table. She halted before him and turned so they stood side by side.

He smelled her perfume. He reflected on Amy, who was again talking to him after their first brush with the beautiful Camille.

"Have you been out prowling the grounds?" she asked in a businesslike tone.

"I ran into Amy. We took a walk. She and Tamara are at the pool."

Camille regarded Brand soberly.

"You are still on duty, you know?"

"That's why I am still here," Brand said without heat.

Brand looked around the room as he guessed at Camille's meaning.

"Sorry," he added.

Camille seemed suspicious of his easy acceptance of her reprimand. She looked at him carefully for any indication he was being sarcastic. Finally, she averted her gaze to scan the room casually.

"Can you do me a favor?" she asked after a moment.

"Sure. What do you need?"

"I left my phone in the limo. I don't want to leave to get it. The guests might see it as a signal to break up the party. Would you mind grabbing it for me? I need to check in with the office, let them know everything is going famously here."

"Okay," Brand agreed. "I'll be right back."

He took the long way around the room, exiting through the doors through which they had entered at the beginning of the evening. He checked with the valet, who directed him to the limousine parking area. Brand located the car and had the driver collect Camille's phone. He thanked him and returned to the hall. Inside, he did not see Camille where he had left her. He looked around. The bartender beckoned him to the bar.

"Ms. Long asked me to tell you to bring the phone to her in the study."

The bartender pointed toward an arched doorway leading to a dark-paneled hallway.

Brand followed the directions. He moved down the hallway, turning right and ending at a pair of heavy double doors. He tried the door handle, opening the door a crack. He saw Camille sitting on a leather sofa inside.

"Come in and close the door," she instructed.

Brand obeyed.

Camille stood, smoothing her gown. She went to a small bar where she had prepared two cocktails. She handed a crystal highball glass to Brand.

"Bourbon on the rocks."

Brand accepted the drink.

"Martini for me. A toast to bigger and better things."

They clinked glasses.

Brand finished most of the cocktail on the first drink.

Camille watched him over the rim of her martini glass as she sipped a small amount.

"What do you want from this relationship, Brand?" she asked without emotion, looking into his eyes.

"Relationship?" he asked with confusion.

"Between you and the campaign; you no doubt see that we value you as a team member."

Her tone and manner were formal, speaking to him as a subordinate.

He felt awkward, alone with her.

"I haven't given it much thought. This started out as a part-time gig until I got back to San Antonio."

"Is San Antonio still home?"

Brand emptied his glass.

Camille reached out a hand and took the glass from him. She returned to the bar and refilled it.

"I was born there," he said to her back. "Up until a couple of months ago, I had a small business, a home, and a girlfriend there. I have no one here, and I don't know Houston very well. I guess that leaves my future a little uncertain."

Camille returned with the glass, handing it to Brand. Her grip lingered on the glass, releasing it only after Brand shared the weight with her briefly.

"Are you reconsidering your role with the campaign?" she asked, sipping her martini.

"It's a long story," Brand deflected.

He sipped the bourbon. The alcohol warmed his belly and lightened his mood.

She paused a moment as she processed his reluctance to open up to her.

"As I said before," she continued, "there are unlimited long-term benefits to joining us permanently. A smart and talented man like you is in high demand. That demand creates a lucrative market value for the man who qualifies."

"What are my qualifications, as you say?"

"Let me ask you a few questions that will clarify that for both of us. Why did you come back to help Mercer after you and he had a falling out? He is nothing to you, but you risked your own safety and maybe your life by engaging a larger, well-trained group."

Brand shrugged.

"That was a snap decision," he explained. "Mercer and I get along fine. He didn't like how I handled my first meeting with Sahib. I presume you know what I am talking about."

Camille nodded.

"Still," she pressed, "not many, including Mercer, would have done the same for you, considering the odds."

"Maybe," he agreed. "I didn't give it much thought."

"Let's talk about your meeting with Sahib," she continued with a sip from her martini. "What upset you to the point things became unpleasant during the meeting?"

"I wasn't upset," he explained. "I don't enjoy deprecating humor. I particularly don't appreciate being talked down to by people I just met. Call it a respect thing."

Camille smiled with a genuine appreciation for his explanation.

"That makes sense to me," she said solicitously. "But you took a big risk, considering you didn't know the men you confronted, nor did you know what they might be capable of."

Brand shrugged once more. She was right about that.

"Finally," she said, "I am told you came to Houston to rescue a girl. There aren't many details, other than what you have told a small number of people here. Is she a girlfriend or a relative? Have you found her?"

Brand frowned. Camille was crossing a line with him.

"I don't want to talk about it," he replied firmly.

Camille leaned against the large desk.

"Your qualifications, Mr. Brand, are the sum total of what you are and how you react in demanding situations. You also seem to be able to keep things to yourself. All of these are necessary qualifications. Add to that the basic requirements of being skilled with your hands, and I think you are equal to the task."

Brand swirled the drink in his glass. Camille knew a lot about what he had done in the past two weeks. Many people reported to her. Much of her attention had been given to his activities.

"So, are you interested in moving forward, Mr. Brand?"

"Call me Brand," he replied absently.

His life was in a state of upheaval. He had no car, no home, no friends, and extraordinarily little money. If he accepted a full-time position, he would have to establish a life here. He didn't have the wherewithal to do so. What about Kilgore? He had given Brand scant information about his role as a contractor with the DEA. He knew only he was committed to two weeks of training starting Monday.

"Can you give me a couple of weeks to handle a few things before I commit to your offer?"

"I'll need a little more clarification if you are serious," she said in a serious tone.

Brand looked at her curiously. This was the second time she had reacted unfavorably to his rejection of an offer from her.

Her offer intrigued him, he had to admit, but he was reluctant to give her much information about his personal life.

"I don't like to talk about myself much," he said with genuine embarrassment. "I am homeless with no vehicle and only the money I have collected from the campaign. I need to work these things out if I am going to settle in Houston or take any position. I need a couple of weeks to make some tough decisions before I can give you an answer."

Camille gave him a concerned look and grasped his free hand.

"I suspected you might have been having problems. Don't let your current issues contribute to a poor decision."

Brand shook his head. Her tone indicated Camille cared little about his situation. His attitude hardened at her insincerity.

"The subject is not up for debate," he said flatly. "If you need me in two weeks, I will be available. If not, I am headed back to South Texas."

24

IT WAS LATE WHEN BRAND MADE HIS WAY between cargo trucks and the laboring service personnel filling the curved driveway before the mansion. He reached the street beyond the steel-trellised security gate. He felt pity for the catering staff. They would be at it until early morning, clearing the house of their wares.

A silver car was parked at the curb. Joe Mercer leaned against the rear fender, holding a paper cup with a lid.

"Hey," Mercer said with a grin.

"Who told you to pick me up?" Brand asked.

Mercer handed him the cup.

"Coffee?"

Brand accepted the Styrofoam cup.

"Thanks."

They entered the car. Mercer started the engine.

"Camille," he replied simply. "She said you were on foot and asked me to swing by."

"Thanks," Brand said mildly.

"She seems unhappy with you," Mercer observed pointedly. "She said I should talk some sense into you. I gather you two had a meeting, and it didn't go well?"

Brand said nothing. He watched the road and the early-morning traffic.

"Where is your place?" Mercer asked as they approached signs indicating a freeway ahead.

"I've got a room in a motel near downtown," Brand replied. "I'll give you directions."

During the remainder of the drive, Mercer tried to get the story of his meeting with Camille out of Brand, to no avail. Finally, they arrived at the long building lined with doors and wall-mounted air conditioners that made up the '50s-era motel where Brand had rented a room.

Mercer parked before a room with a black-stenciled "36" on the door.

"Home sweet home," Mercer teased. "Can I get you anything?"

"No," Brand replied. "Thanks for the coffee and the ride."

He stepped from the car, slinging his tuxedo coat over his shoulder.

"Are you still in hiding?" Brand asked Mercer.

"Yeah," Mercer admitted with some heat. "Sahib has me working on that new office he is building out front."

Brand smiled at the thought of Mercer working construction.

"Don't laugh," Mercer warned. "I'm not cut out for menial labor."

"I get that," Brand agreed. "By the way, I am going to be out of town for the next couple of weeks."

"I'll check with Sahib."

"I'm not looking for his approval. Let him know, if I am still working for him, that I'll be back in two weeks if he still wants me around."

Mercer frowned at Brand's rebellious manner.

"Brand," Mercer warned in a serious tone, "everyone in the campaign works for Sahib. He's not going to like you taking it on yourself to come and go as you please."

"Everyone works for Sahib?" Brand repeated incredulously.

"Everyone," Mercer said. "Don't do this."

"I'll see you later, Joe."

Brand leaned away from the car and fished his room key out of his pocket.

Mercer remained in the idling car, not backing out of the parking space as Brand opened the door, entered, and slammed it behind him.

The urge to follow Brand and reiterate the importance of his warning kept Joe outside the motel room for several minutes. Finally, he backed the car away, squealing the tires as he displayed his frustration.

PART FIVE

25

A YELLOW TAXICAB DROPPED BRAND off before the barracks at Camp Bravura. The compound was coming to life in the darkness of early morning. He paid the cabbie and carried his gym bag, along with a hanging bag containing his new suits, into the squad bay. Inside, most of the bunks were unmade as the trainees moved sleepily, readying themselves for a long day of training.

Brand's bunk was neatly made, and the wall locker was closed. He opened the tall doors and looked over the contents inside. His Durashock boots, T-shirts, and uniforms bearing his nametags were stowed as he had left them two weeks before. He deposited his personal gear in the bottom drawer and hung the garment bag. He dressed in his uniform.

Looking around, he saw no familiar faces. It seemed those who had gone through the hand-to-hand, close-combat training were not attending the weapons proficiency class. Brand smiled as a redheaded man emerged from the latrine wearing a towel and carrying a shaving kit. He was glad to see Dennis Moore. The latter approached his bunk.

"I was wondering if you would come back for Wep's," Moore said warmly, grasping Brand's hand in a friendly grip.

"Anyone else here we know?" Brand asked with a glance at the bunk next to him.

Moore shook his head, understanding Brand's question.

"White isn't here," he assured Brand. "I got here late last night, but I saw no one from the last class. You are the first familiar face I have seen."

Brand nodded.

"We'd better get ready," he urged Moore. "We'll talk soon."

"Glad you are here," Moore said affably. "See you at chow."

Moore moved to his bunk. Brand stowed his gear and changed into his uniform. He had checked out of his motel room in the early morning hours, not long after Mercer had left in a huff. The prospect of a 2 a.m. start to his day and an expensive cab ride was not his preference, but he saw no other way to get there.

Camille's interest in his personal life, and the certainty that his destination and purpose for the two-week hiatus would be passed along to her, prevented him from asking Mercer to drive him. He gladly paid the fare rather than reveal any more to her than he had already. He felt fatigue behind his irritated eyes. He was sorely in need of sleep.

Brand waited until Moore was dressed, then walked with him to the mess hall. They loaded their plates with eggs, hash browns, and S.O.S. Brand poured hot coffee into a large mug and joined Moore at one of the long tables.

"How goes the DEA gig?" Moore asked him.

"I haven't officially started with them yet," Brand replied.

"Contractor?" Moore asked with surprising insight.

"How did you know?"

"When you are an agent, you work through training cycles. Contractors are idle during the breaks."

"I take it you are full-time," Brand guessed.

"I'm ATF with the drug interdiction task force. We are working the border, looking for tunnels and mules."

Brand gave the plate his full attention. He had learned a lot about how the cartels moved product and people across the border over the last couple of months. Kilgore's warning, containing the list of potential crimes for which he could be charged, kept him silent about his past experiences.

"How did you spend your summer vacation?" Moore asked with playful affection in his voice.

"I did a little part-time work with a campaign for a future Congressman."

"Which one?" Moore asked with genuine interest.

"Randy Chappell," Brand replied without hesitation.

"Democrat, huh?" Moore observed with distaste. "I guess you've got to find work where you can."

"Are you one of those fascist Republicans?" Brand asked with a fake frown.

Moore considered him with a grave look.

"I'm kidding," Brand assured him. "You must be one of those right-wingers with an axe to grind. I don't see what all the fuss is about. Nothing we do makes a difference in Washington."

"Do you vote?" Moore asked him accusingly.

"Simmer down, John Birch. I'm apolitical by nature. No point in getting the red ass first thing in the morning."

Moore focused on his breakfast as he struggled to let it go.

"Sorry," Moore muttered. "I'm the farthest thing from apolitical. Sometimes I forget my manners."

Brand ate a bite of the S.O.S.

Moore looked Brand in the eye.

"I would be careful with the Chappell campaign. There are rumors they are involved with some pretty radical fringe organizations—donors, I mean."

Brand looked at Moore with interest. Amy had warned him with a similar expression on her face. He thought about Mercer, Sahib, Umar, and the Kinetic Team as a whole. Their brand of political activism concerned him from the start.

Although Mercer assured him what he did with the organization was normal in the business, Brand felt a growing doubt after separate warnings from two people unrelated to one another and who were from opposite camps and political viewpoints.

"Is that a personal or professional observation?" Brand asked Moore.

"Call it a bit of personal advice based on professional knowledge."

"Can you be a little more specific?"

"At least one of Chappell's donors has known ties to a suspected terrorist cell near Sweeney, Texas. I worked with the weapons task force for a couple of years. The camp appeared on our radar about three years ago when a large purchase of weapons was traced to them. There are many such cells throughout the United States."

"There are terrorist cells in America?" Brand asked incredulously.

"Absolutely!"

"What's stopping you guys from raiding them and shutting them down?"

Moore placed his fork on his half-empty plate as if he wanted to launch into the explanation unarmed.

"Profiling is the new defense against all law enforcement agencies, and these terrorists know it. Former terrorist training camps are now Islamic social education programs. They have exchanged their homemade bombs and AKs for textbooks and protest signs."

"That is some real conspiracy-theory stuff, Moore. You are an ATF agent. It seems you would risk ending your career if you were talking to anyone but me about this."

Moore leveled a stern look at Brand.

"Your response is exactly what they have created among the people of America. To most people, the idea that anyone would suggest any group would so cleverly work within the system to destroy it is unbelievable. It is not only unbelievable but offensive. So, the camps stay, and they grow."

"Based upon your definition, Chappell and his campaign are doing nothing illegal in their dealings with these people?"

"Technically, no," Moore admitted.

Brand shook his head.

Moore stood with his plate, his breakfast half-eaten.

"You have a phone," he said tersely. "Look it up online. The information is there."

Moore left Brand alone at the table.

After breakfast, Brand joined the trainees before the headquarters building. They stood in military formation as they waited for the day's training to begin. Although it was early, the sun was bright and well above the horizon, heating the morning air uncomfortably. When the door to the headquarters building opened and Mr. Theil strode onto the porch, Commandant Crabtree followed, closing the door.

Brand remembered Theil from the previous training module.

The thin instructor descended the steps and took his position at the front of the small formation.

"Trainees," he said in a stentorian voice, "mount the bus behind you for transport."

He extended a stiff arm, flat-handed, indicating a small black bus parked among the camouflaged vehicles along the fence that surrounded the obstacle course in the center of the compound. Brand moved with the group as they approached and then entered the bus. Theil counted the passengers before taking his place behind the wheel. He drove the bus to the front entrance gate of the compound, turning left onto the main road.

26

JOE MERCER FOLLOWED THE BLACK BUS as it headed north. The vehicle was two cars ahead of his. He wasn't certain Brand was on the transport, but it seemed reasonable that he was. He had followed Brand's cab from the motel to the entrance of Camp Bravura, as the sign read near the gate.

He had entered the fenced property only far enough to see a small compound. At a distance, he watched Brand leave the taxi and enter one of the buildings. Joe had turned his car around and driven back to the road.

He had to wait no more than an hour and a half before he saw the black bus exit the compound. Brand's mysterious behavior was becoming more bizarre with time. The compound looked like some type of paramilitary training facility. Why was he training as though he were either military or a cop?

A feeling of dread filled Joe with unaccustomed anxiety. He would find out what he could. For now, he followed the bus through the billowing dust it raised off the dirt road. He lagged behind as the bus turned onto the paved roadway. The bus traveled for nearly half an hour before it slowed near a guarded entrance on the left.

The bus turned, entering the gate monitored by a guard in a small glass building. Joe could not follow the transport inside the fence, and the dense tree line obscured any view of what lay beyond. He would wait until the bus reappeared. He decided to find a hiding place nearby, but not so close as to alert the guard in the guard shack.

Joe risked going to a convenience store to buy a drink and something to eat. He reasoned the passengers on the bus likely didn't travel half an hour and enter a guarded facility to stay a couple of minutes, then leave. He returned fifteen minutes later and found a shady place to park the gray sedan and wait for the bus.

The tree beneath which he parked the car was at the street side of the parking lot serving an abandoned building a few hundred feet from the guardhouse. Provided no one showed up at the abandoned building, he should be able to wait out the day there.

Cool in the tree's shade, Joe tore the cellophane wrapping off his king-sized burrito. He took a large bite as he mused. Was Brand law enforcement? Was he a plant within the campaign? If so, who sent him? Joe toyed with the idea of calling Sahib, or possibly Camille. He rejected the impulse when he inventoried what he knew thus far.

He drank from the straw sticking from the top of his tall plastic cup, then retrieved his phone. He pulled up his web browser app and searched for Camp Bravura. He found a website associated with the facility. It was advertised as a training facility and corporate retreat featuring group activities for team building.

Additionally, the training camp advertised specialized training programs for law enforcement, overseas contractors, and soldier-of-fortune-type civilians. The photos on the site depicted cops on shooting ranges, teens on obstacle courses, overweight corporate types involved in a mock combat game, and civilians training in hand-to-hand combat. Brand had proven himself skilled in a scrape. His training at a facility like Camp Bravura would explain his abilities.

Joe bit another large hunk from the burrito, washing it down with the cold drink. He remembered Brand's claim that he was a construction worker from San Antonio. Their conversations had supported his story of being a regular guy. Even drunk, he seemed genuine.

Joe recalled his angry departure after dropping Brand at his motel. Frustrated, he had called Camille to report that Brand was not going to be available for the next two weeks. She seemed annoyed also but said only, "Okay," before hanging up.

The only reason Joe had followed Brand to the gates of Camp Bravura was the frustration he felt at Brand's resistance to obey orders.

Brand was independent, and he tended to go his own way. Despite his doubts, Joe couldn't deny his fondness for the man. He had handled the Pink Poodle better than Joe had expected. Others he had taken there had not lasted an hour. Brand appeared to like the place. He also seemed nonplussed that Joe was gay. Significantly, Brand hadn't deserted him at the Grand Hotel.

Maybe there was a simple explanation. Joe would do a little more research on his own. If Brand tried to lie his way out of their impending confrontation, he would know Brand was not who he seemed.

27

THEIL DROVE THE BUS ALONG the private driveway. Brand saw no sign or any other indication of what type of facility they had entered. The narrow pavement wound through a neatly manicured wooded area, which opened into a broad grassy meadow. In the center of the green clearing sat a glass-fronted stone building. The roof was flat except in the front, where tall gables of glass and steel added the lone architectural accent to the large square building.

Theil stopped the bus in a small parking lot and opened the doors. He waited until the last trainee had exited the bus before he dismounted, pushing the doors closed behind him.

"Follow me, please," Theil said, leading the group toward the broad front doors of the glass-fronted building.

They entered a broad vestibule with high vaulted ceilings and marble tile on the floor. At the back of the entry room, a wide set of stairs climbed halfway up the height of the interior wall, at the top of which a pair of tall, ornate wooden double doors led to rooms beyond the bright lobby.

Theil halted them at the foot of the stairs, where they waited in a loose formation. Within a few minutes, one of the doors opened and an average-sized man in black BDUs appeared. He descended the stairs, looking the trainee group over man by man.

He was dark-haired. His face was carpeted with a thick beard. He surveyed the formation with piercing blue eyes. The thick black beard split near his jaw, and a smile of dazzling white teeth appeared in the gap.

"Good morning," he said in a pleasing voice. "Welcome to the Hascomb Weapons Training Facility. I am Mr. Lyndsey, armament expert and weapons master. I will guide you through the next two weeks of training. In this module, we will focus on small arms and light automatic weapons.

"Part of your training will include marksmanship skills and inert-to-armed transitional training. In other words, you will not only learn to be accurate with the weapons upon which you will train, but you will also be capable of carrying them securely, producing them quickly, and hitting your target from multiple positions and postures."

Brand received only a limited amount of weapons training at Camp Bravura and with his former National Guard unit. He was unsure what "inert-to-armed transitional training" was, but he was interested.

He looked around him, spotting Moore. The man had ignored him since their conversation at breakfast. Moore gave his attention to Lyndsey, showing some understanding of the techniques to which the bearded instructor referred.

"A few ground rules," Lyndsey warned. "From the moment you are fitted with a firearm, you will carry it with you at all times. It will be loaded for weight and carry familiarization. There is no downrange here. We are in a 360-degree environment. Conduct yourselves as such. Safety is always our primary goal. Follow me."

Lyndsey led the group up the stairs and through the large double doors. Inside was a vast open room with tall ceilings. There were task stations set up throughout the room.

Brand saw an enclosed shooting range behind a wall of fixed glass windows at the rear of the space. The instructor stopped before a table where a dozen pistols were displayed. Each sat before a stack of black plastic boxes containing new models of each display weapon. He turned to the group.

"Weapon selection is critical. Here we will choose the weapon that fits your body and shooting style. Please take a position along the line on the floor, toes on the line," he instructed.

The students obeyed.

Lyndsey pointed to a red dot on the far wall.

"Stand with your hands to your sides. Look at the red dot. Close your eyes. Keeping them closed, point your shooting trigger finger at the dot. When I instruct you to do so, open your eyes, keeping your hand on line with the dot."

Lyndsey waited until the trainees were in position.

"Ready," he called. "Locate your target. Eyes closed. Acquire."

Brand followed the instructions, pointing his finger where he had seen the dot.

"Open your eyes."

He opened his eyes. His finger was pointed at the dot nearly dead center.

"Notice you were able to acquire the dot without looking, merely from memory. You should be able to do the same with an appropriately selected weapon."

Brand saw the reasoning behind the drill.

"Now select a weapon that looks comfortable for you. This first pistol will not be your final weapon, so pick any one of them."

Each member of the group selected a weapon from the table. Brand was near the end of the line, and only three pistols remained on the table. He selected a Smith & Wesson 9mm. He returned to his place on the toe line.

"Again, look at the dot," Lyndsey directed them. "Once again, close your eyes and aim the weapon at the dot. Open your eyes on my command."

Lyndsey repeated the commands.

Brand opened his eyes. The pistol was pointed well below the dot.

"Notice none of you were able to acquire the target with your selected weapon. If your aim point is below the target, exchange your weapon for a model with a less right-angle design from grip to barrel. If your aim point was above, select the opposite."

The fitting continued for more than two hours. Brand sampled each of the dozen pistols. Lyndsey had the class experiment with sight orientation, concealed-carry size, style, and overall weight.

Brand's limited military career gave him training and practical experience with the M1911 pistol and the M-16. Recently, he owned a .45-caliber Glock 21. The gun was seized by the police when he and his girlfriend were shot in his apartment.

Because of his familiarity with the larger Glock, Brand presumed he would prefer a heavier-caliber load for his pistol selection. Instead, he found he preferred the lighter weight and thinner size of the 9mm Sig Sauer he settled upon.

During his turn at one-on-one training with the instructor, Lyndsey helped him with the fitting. He recommended a 9mm because of the size and the popularity of the caliber. Ammo would be easier to find even in areas where gun stores were not plentiful. The Sig passed the dot test, and Brand was able to hide the weapon where it was invisible under his clothing.

After each of the students had selected a weapon, they moved to the glassed shooting range, where Brand took a position at one of the shooting tables. A square frame held a paper silhouette target a short distance downrange. Lyndsey gave them a quick safety briefing, after which he instructed them to practice with their new weapons.

Brand expended a full box of cartridges in just under an hour. He was happy with the shot group. All were center mass, other than the dozen or so rounds he placed in the head of the silhouette. He was pleased with the pistol. It felt like an extension of his arm.

"Cease fire," Lyndsey commanded from behind the shooters.

They cleared their weapons and placed them on the shooting tables.

"It seems everyone has been fitted successfully. If your shot groups are loose, don't worry. Practice will remedy that. Let's talk about marksmanship for a moment."

Lyndsey approached one of the students, a muscular Black man. The instructor read his nametag.

"Cummings here shot an excellent group. He is, so far, the best with the new weapons. Mr. Cummings, do you have formal handgun training?"

Cummings maintained a modest front.

"Quite a bit," he admitted modestly. "I'm prior service and was an instructor for a while."

"I can tell," Lyndsey agreed. "Holster your weapon."

Cummings obeyed. He slipped the pistol into his concealed holster inside the front of his cargo pants. He faced Lyndsey, his hands clasped high on his chest.

"Stand at ease, Mr. Cummings. Relax for a moment while I break down our first training subject."

"I am relaxed," Cummings assured him.

"Very good," Lyndsey said.

He looked around at the group.

"Anyone can learn to shoot with skill and accuracy while relaxed on the range. In the field, you will not have the luxury of planning your shots or selecting where you will engage an attacker. Your enemy will choose for you. You might not be sitting in a chair or relaxing by the pool when the attack occurs. In fact, the conflict will develop while you are either emotionally or physically taxed. Under stress, your skill will degrade. Our goal is to ensure your degraded skill level is of a high enough proficiency so you can react and effectively defeat an enemy. The remainder of your live-fire training will occur while you are under duress."

Lyndsey returned his attention to Cummings.

"Mr. Cummings, stay with me as we make our way to our close-quarters mockup area. The rest of you follow and spread out around the training gallery."

The students moved to follow. Brand stayed behind for a moment. He went to his table and holstered his weapon before he followed. Moore stood at the door watching him. He quickly grabbed his weapon before catching up with Brand.

The remainder of the group encircled a mockup of a retail store, complete with stocked shelves, a front counter, and a cash register.

Lyndsey stood in front of the cash register with Cummings. He surveyed the group at the perimeter of the training area.

"I need four volunteers," Lyndsey announced.

He pointed to Brand and Moore.

"You two."

He indicated two other students.

"And you two."

Lyndsey positioned the four volunteers in the aisles of the fake store. He took a position behind the cash register.

"Mr. Cummings, you are about to buy something at the register. Using casual situational awareness, who other than you is armed in the store?"

Cummings looked around him.

"Moore," he said, pointing him out.

"Anyone else?" Lyndsey asked.

"Only Moore."

Moore looked surprised and uncomfortable.

"You are only half right," Lyndsey corrected him. "Mr. Brand is carrying also."

Lyndsey looked around the room critically.

"Everyone who left their weapons in the range," he commanded. "Give me 50 push-ups."

Brand, Moore, Cummings, and Lyndsey waited while the grunts and heavy breathing of the students conveyed their discomfort.

After the last student rose, Lyndsey said, "You will keep your weapons with you at all times. Please retrieve your weapons and return here."

The class moved to obey.

"Move it!" Lyndsey yelled. "We move at double time here!"

After the final student returned, Lyndsey held up a hand for attention. He looked at Cummings.

"How did you know Moore was armed?"

"He stands like a cop. His right hand was on his hip below where his gun is concealed, and he had his hips slightly forward, keeping the weapon clear for a draw."

"Very good. Why didn't you notice Mr. Brand in your survey?"

"I didn't see any indication he was carrying a gun. I'm still not convinced he is, other than he didn't drop for push-ups."

"Mr. Brand," Lyndsey asked. "Are you armed?"

"I am," Brand replied. He lifted his BDU blouse and revealed the pistol in his pants.

"How did you know?" Cummings asked.

"I saw him lag behind and secure his weapon," Lyndsey explained. "He apparently has no law-enforcement or advanced weapons training other than his time in the military. He favors his right side, with more weight distributed to his right foot, but that is not a clear indicator. Mr. Brand is comfortable with the weapon on him: unusual but not unheard of."

Lyndsey returned his attention to Cummings.

"Relax, Mr. Cummings. Be at ease."

Cummings smiled at Lyndsey.

"As I said before, I am relaxed."

Lyndsey turned to the group.

"Mr. Cummings is an instructor. In classroom environments, safety is the main concern. Part of the instructor training focuses on overt safety demonstrations, the appearance of safety leadership.

"In a traditional classroom environment, downrange weapons orientation is witnessed and acknowledged. In that environment, you announce when you clear a weapon, and you stand with your hands joined at your chest to demonstrate you are unaggressive."

Lyndsey faced Cummings.

"Mr. Cummings, your stance broadcasts to even the most casual observer that you are armed and dangerous. Mr. Moore stands like a cop."

Lyndsey pivoted, addressing the students.

"We must all learn to appear as Mr. Brand does: unthreatening and unremarkable. Your enemy practices situational awareness too. Don't display your carry. That is rule one. The second is to keep the weapon with you. You can't use it if you don't have it. Rule three is to make sure it is accessible."

Lyndsey glanced at his watch.

"You all have ten minutes to sprint to the front gate and back, execute 100 good push-ups, and 100 good sit-ups. After that, return to the gun range. Ready—Begin!"

Brand moved with the group in a mad dash for the big doors leading to the lobby. He was slowed at the doorways but soon gained on the group until he led the way to the front gate. He was first among the class to return to his shooting table at the firing range. Other than him and Moore, most of the trainees were not in shape. His and Moore's training over the previous three months, including daily PT and hand-to-hand training, had prepared them for the physical exertion.

Lyndsey had the students again expend a box of ammo, periodically dropping them for push-ups or sit-ups during the range work. Brand found accuracy difficult while breathing heavily and fatigued after the calisthenics.

"Shooting is a perishable skill, people," Lyndsey called out over the gunfire. "It is not like riding a bike. You do not get back on and achieve any level of success. Practice, practice, practice!"

This continued until the evening, when they mounted the bus and collapsed into their seats. Moore sat with Brand on the return trip.

Brand exited the bus before the headquarters building at Camp Bravura. He felt a weariness weighing on his muscles. His mind was fatigued from the long hours of concentration required to compensate for the extreme rigors his body had endured.

Moore followed him into the squad bay.

"I'm almost too tired to eat," he admitted wearily.

"I'm never that tired," Brand assured him, returning the look. He liked the man and was uncomfortable in the shadow of his disfavor.

"Shower and chow?" Moore asked.

"And bed immediately after I clean this pistol."

Moore laughed with little humor.

"Almost forgot."

28

AMY LANDRY WAS CONFUSED BY THE Carson Brand question. Randy and Camille sat together on the sofa in Chappell's office. Their expressions gave away nothing. She had not been given a clear reason why Randy had asked her to drop by the campaign office. Now she stood like a child before her parents after being caught breaking a rule.

"I know very little about Carson Brand," she explained. "I represented him on a misdemeanor trespassing charge. He was acquitted, and I helped him get a job with your campaign."

As Camille listened, she shifted in her seat, glancing at Chappell.

"It seems like you two have a personal relationship outside of the attorney-client privilege," she noted with a smile meant to soften the observation.

"That is none of your business," Amy snapped at her, her brow clouding at the intrusion. "If you asked me here to question my ethics, I would be very careful."

Randy cleared his throat uncomfortably.

"We don't mean any offense, Amy. We are curious about Mr. Brand's extracurricular activities. We hoped you could shed some light on his background—for the good of the campaign."

Amy studied Chappell blankly. To her, Brand seemed fairly straightforward, although he did pose a mystery as to how he ended up looking for a trafficked girl he claimed was killed before he could locate her.

"Amy," Chappell said gently. "You introduced him to our organization. You vouched for him. All we want is for you to help us understand more clearly who he is and what his intentions are."

Amy felt the blood drain from her face. If Brand was not working out for them, she was responsible for bringing him in. Her face softened as the gravity of her position became clearer to her.

"Has he done something illegal, or has he caused trouble in the campaign?"

Camille smiled brightly.

"Amy, have you noticed he disappears for days on end? Has he told you where he goes or who he may work for?"

Amy shook her head. She remembered his reappearance at her office after some three months away. He seemed leaner, harder somehow. To her, he had revealed little about his background.

"He told me he used to own a construction company, and his best friend had been killed."

Amy paused, watching the two for a reaction. Why was she feeling reluctance to share everything they had talked about at the Cali Café? She decided to add to her answer so she didn't appear to be hiding anything.

"He told me he has no friends, family, wife, or girlfriend."

The last caused her to blush slightly.

Camille smiled, seeing her embarrassment. She touched Chappell's arm reassuringly before she spoke.

"He also mentioned to me he was homeless and alone. He said he was broke. He told me this over cocktails prior to the fundraiser dinner."

Amy shifted her weight uncomfortably as she experienced a twinge of jealousy and tried to hide it from Camille.

Camille's expression conveyed that she noticed.

Amy looked at Chappell. He seemed nonplussed that his fiancée was having cocktails with strange men.

"I spoke with Brand at the benefit," Amy said with mild heat. "He told me he was not a part of the street team. He said he was assigned to the Kinetic Team and was now part of Randy's personal security detail. You obviously felt comfortable with what you know about him if you placed him in such a high-risk position within the campaign organization. My dealings with him have been less detailed and certainly not as trusting. Maybe you should have vetted him more carefully before you placed him so deeply inside."

Camille's eyes hardened at the implication that she had been careless.

"My referral," Amy said, "was for you to place him on the street team to hand out flyers and knock on doors to gin up support."

Chappell held up a hand to avert the growing conflict between the women.

"You are absolutely right, Amy," he said hurriedly. "We aren't saying there are troubles with Brand. He has been extremely helpful when he is needed. I think you are getting the wrong idea."

"He is a mystery to us. You said yourself he doesn't volunteer much personal information. We hoped you might know more about him than we do. Additionally, he seems to like you. I can't help but have some interest in a potential suitor. Call it a big-brother instinct."

Amy wasn't sure she was buying his explanation, but she admitted his concern pleased her. She and Randy had grown apart since Camille had entered the campaign. She liked the fact that he was voicing his feelings for her in front of Camille.

"I'm sorry for my temper," Amy apologized. "I may have overreacted."

Camille kept her gaze on Amy. Her face was stone as she fought to conceal her displeasure that Chappell was conveying even the most casual favor upon the lawyer. Amy's accusations rankled her deeply.

Amy endeavored to control her temper. She spoke exclusively to Chappell, shifting her stance away from the angry Camille.

"I do remember him saying his friend was killed in Mexico and the girl he was looking for had worked for a cartel at one time. That's all I have been able to learn from the limited conversations we have had about it."

Chappell processed these new facts for a moment before responding.

"A cartel?" he mused.

Amy could tell he was more interested in this last piece of news than he was letting on.

"We're sorry we upset you," Chappell said with a sudden brightening of his tone.

He rose quickly with an air of satisfaction at their conversation.

"Amy, it is good to see you despite the confusion. We'd better get back to it."

He crossed the distance and stood directly before her.

"I'll call you if you aren't too cross with my overprotective actions. I know we shouldn't have gotten involved in your personal life. Call it a force of habit carried over from our college days."

Amy smiled her forgiveness. It was pleasant to hear Randy refer to their younger days.

"I'm a little tired," she admitted, hoping to mitigate any hard feelings. "I, of course, am always worried when I refer someone, that it doesn't work out. I'm glad Brand is working out for you. I'd better go."

"Totally understandable," Chappell assured her. "Let me walk you out."

Amy and Chappell left the room, leaving Camille alone on the sofa. She stood, moving to the desk where she picked up the phone and dialed a number.

"We may have a problem," she said into the phone.

She listened to the voice on the other side.

"He was somehow associated with a drug cartel in Mexico."

She paused again.

"His girlfriend just told me."

Camille looked at her watch as she listened.

"Amy," she replied impatiently. "She is the girlfriend."

Camille listened to the reaction to the revelation.

"I have to go," she said impatiently. "I'll call you later."

She hung up the phone and left the room.

Chappell returned a few minutes later. He frowned at the empty office. He knew Camille would not go easy on him later.

29

OVER THE NEXT FEW DAYS OF TRAINING, Brand learned much about draw techniques. By his estimation, the Compressed Ready technique was the most reasonable and useful of the skills he acquired. He liked the economy of motion and the way it made the weapon a part of his body.

Lyndsey had warned against two sloppy habits common with the technique. He referred to them as bowling or fishing. The movement from clearing the holster to fully compressed was a smooth linear gesture. The two terms referred to rounding the motion from above the draw line or below.

He learned the way he had carried a weapon in the past was called the "Mexican Carry." The pistol was kept in the waistband without a holster. He wasn't sure if the name was a technical term or a jab at cartel members who seemed to use the method a lot.

The phenomenon of Auditory Exclusion interested Brand. He learned during times of high stress or duress, the mind allocates more energy to visual abilities, lowering the keenness of other senses, particularly hearing.

Friday afternoon of the first week left Moore and Brand off for the weekend. They stood at their bunks, packing their personal gear.

"Any weekend plans?" Moore asked as he zipped his tote.

"None," Brand admitted. "You?"

"I plan to eat a good meal or two and sit at the pool."

"Good plan," Brand agreed. "Mind if I join you?"

"Suit yourself," Moore said with a smile. "I could use a wingman poolside."

"Aren't you married, Moore?"

"Ever heard of the Man Code? Besides, I'm kidding."

"I know you are," Brand said. "All you do is talk about your wife and kids."

They lifted their gear and made their way to the door.

Outside the barracks, Agent Kilgore sat inside a large SUV parked in the middle of the wide parking lot.

Brand saw him and nudged Moore with his elbow.

"It looks like I have a ride. See you Monday."

Moore looked at the DEA SUV.

"Monday."

Brand moved around the truck and entered the back seat.

The driver put the vehicle in gear and headed toward the front gate. Agent Spencer sat in the front passenger seat. He eyed Brand evilly out of the corner of his eye. Brand guessed Kilgore had warned the agent not to stir up trouble.

Kilgore appraised Brand with a sparkle in his eyes.

"You are looking fit, Mr. Brand. How have you been doing?"

"As well as I need to, I guess," Brand replied curiously. "What brings you to Camp Bravura?"

"I haven't had a chance to catch up for a while. I thought we might get together and make sure you are still aware of the particulars of our agreement."

"I passed the hand-to-hand class, and the weapons training is halfway done without my killing anyone."

Spencer shot Brand a black look at the sarcasm.

"Are you armed?" Kilgore asked Brand but looked at the back of Spencer's head.

"Of course not," Brand replied. "I'm not technically law enforcement."

Kilgore looked at Spencer significantly.

"Good answer," he said. "We wouldn't want Agent Spencer to arrest you."

Spencer grunted his displeasure but continued looking forward.

"Brand, my visit with you is also partially business-related. I need you to do a little fieldwork for me tonight."

Brand looked at him.

"What kind of fieldwork?"

"We have been working a drug dealer with ties to Mexican drug suppliers. He is clever and has eluded arrest through very advanced means. He background-checks everyone who attends his drug distribution parties. He is holding one tonight at a country bar in Montrose. I need you to get into the party and get him on video and audio during the event."

"It sounds dangerous. What's the plan?"

"It could be if you don't play this right. So, we will make sure you know what to do. Do you still have your driver's license on you?"

"I do."

"Good. Many nightclubs swipe licenses and IDs upon entry. Most store the information for later in case the alcohol board or an investigation into overserving requires it.

"This bar, The Golden Stallion, runs the ID on the wire. They get their information within minutes. If you are not escorted out in the first ten minutes, you are good to go. We believe they are on the alert for a standard profile that fits most cops. Local law enforcement recruits only squeaky-clean individuals, usually with a college degree. You fit a profile they're less likely to flag. You should pass their initial check. You will wear a micro-camera and microphone. Do you own a suit?"

"It is back at the barracks."

The driver glanced in the rearview mirror. Kilgore spun his index finger. The driver U-turned.

"We'll go back for it."

"Speaking of driver's licenses," Brand said, "I am having trouble getting around with no vehicle and no address."

"What happened to your truck? I saw in the SAPD report you bought a new one after the other was torched."

"It was impounded and auctioned. At least that is what I was told by DPS. My apartment was locked, and I was evicted. My furniture and personal belongings were also sold at auction."

Spencer chuckled from the front seat.

"Are you enjoying this, dickhead?" Brand snarled at the agent.

Spencer flared and spun in the seat.

"I am enjoying this. You are a piece of cartel shit as far as I am concerned. If you weren't under Kilgore's protection, I'd..."

"You'd what?" Brand asked in a dangerous tone.

Kilgore raised his hand and began to intervene.

"Hold on, Agent Kilgore," Brand interrupted him. "This smart-ass in the front seat has run his mouth ever since I first saw him. He is one of those faggots who used to get his ass kicked in school. He got a badge and strapped on a gun so he wouldn't get his ass whipped anymore. It is his revenge on all the cool kids who used to make fun of him at school."

Spencer reddened from his hairline into his white shirt.

"Agent Spencer is highly decorated for his service with the agency," Kilgore assured Brand. "He has served for more than ten years. I recommend we all calm down and focus on the task at hand."

"I'm fine with that," Brand said in a low voice. "If you can't leash this loudmouth, I will."

"Why don't you give that a try," Spencer roared, spit flying out of his mouth with his rage.

"That's enough, both of you," Kilgore commanded in a stern voice. "I will write you up, Spencer, and I will toss you in jail to cool off, Mr. Brand. I don't give a shit whether you like each other or not. The job is the focus. Understood?"

Spencer struggled visibly to control his anger.

"Not a problem," Brand agreed coolly. He knew he had Spencer's number.

Spencer nodded reluctantly.

"I need to hear the words, Agent Spencer."

"I understand, sir," Spencer muttered through set teeth.

"I can't help you with the address right now, but we have a private impound lot with a few clean titles in it. We'll drop you there. You will requisition a vehicle for temporary use."

30

THE THREE AGENTS SAT IN THE DEA OFFICE situation room. Spencer glanced at the large monitor screen on the wall as he adjusted the controls on the receiver. The image showed the top of a steering wheel and glimpses of the road. Brand's micro-cam was functioning perfectly.

Kilgore sipped coffee while the third agent, the SUV driver, Bratton, read a spy novel.

Kilgore checked his watch.

"Tom," he said to Bratton. "Check in for us, please."

Bratton flopped his book onto the conference table and grabbed the SAT phone. He dialed a short log-in number. At the tone, he punched in the numerical check-in code and pressed pound. He returned the phone to the table and resumed reading.

"Our man should be there inside of ten minutes," Kilgore announced.

Spencer sighed and gave his attention to adjusting the video feed.

Kilgore sipped his coffee.

"What is the deal between you and Brand?" he asked Spencer.

Spencer fiddled with the dials on the large black video receiver.

"You said you didn't want to hear about it," he replied testily. "It's not important."

"If you can maintain your calm, I wouldn't mind discussing it."

Spencer tapped the video equipment absently as he attempted to formulate a response that would cast him in a justified light which Kilgore would understand and to which he would agree.

"Why did you recruit a guy who clearly is a criminal—a felon? He is guilty of at least a dozen violent crimes. He is unremarkable as a human and in his qualifications. He is a construction worker, for God's sake. At best, you should have made him a C.I., not a contractor."

Kilgore sipped his coffee as he thought about Spencer's complaint.

Bratton glanced over the top of his novel, watching Kilgore before again giving his full attention to the read. He smiled sardonically. The Spencer/Brand feud had provided him welcome entertainment of late. This conversation was bound to be interesting by his estimation.

"If I understand your objection," Kilgore began carefully, "your chief issue with him is he doesn't measure up to your qualifying standards for a contractor or even a casual member of our team. Additionally, you seem to have a hard-on for blue-collar stiffs. Finally, you consider him a criminal no matter the circumstances. How am I doing?"

"I think you put a dumbed-down face on it, but yeah, I think that will do it."

"I agree with much of what you say, Spence. He is not our typical demographic. He has broken laws, though most of those were in a foreign country. He has no CJ education or experience. If unchecked, I believe he would eventually end up on a post office Most Wanted board."

"Let's talk about what he brings to the table. He is a crusader. He took a cartel lieutenant under his protection and risked his life to save hers."

"She is reportedly dead," Spencer corrected.

"His actions were before that. He has survived a contract order by the cartel and avoided an APB by multiple levels of LEA. He survived capture by the cartel and managed to kill two leaders, including the head of the organization. We have tried to get to both for almost two years with no measurable results."

Spencer stared at the video display. Brand was pulling into a parking lot.

Kilgore finished his coffee in a gulp.

"He accomplished all of this with no training other than weekend warrior training during his six years in the National Guard. He is tough and resourceful. With a little specialized education, I think this boy could be Carson Bond instead of Brand."

Spencer snorted at the observation.

"Bullshit, Kilgore. This kid is no super spy."

"So, you just hate him," Kilgore observed dismissively.

"I think he is a piece of shit. I don't hate him. I just know the type. You will be left holding the bag when this thing goes sideways."

The Golden Stallion was an old warehouse converted into an urban western bar. The parking lot out front was packed with cars and pickups. Brand found a spot for his requisitioned Ford pickup near the street at the far edge of the lot. He stepped out and locked the door.

He saw his reflection dimly in the driver's-side window. In his new suit, he felt he was overdressed for a country bar and the old pickup. He pocketed the keys and walked toward the front entrance.

Four large men in cowboy hats eyed the mass of patrons as they entered the club. Many were dressed as Brand was. Most, however, appeared to be lean cowboys and sexy country girls out for a night of two-stepping. As Brand neared the entrance, one of the giants extended a hand.

"ID, sir," he said in a deep voice.

Brand pulled his wallet from the suit coat and placed his driver's license in the giant's huge mitt.

"San Antonio, huh?" the bouncer commented, reading the address on the license.

"Yeah," Brand replied simply.

"Go on in, sir."

He handed Brand his ID and stopped the next person.

Brand entered the vestibule where he swiped his ID through a card reader supervised by a steely-eyed man with a dark mustache.

The reader beeped.

"Have a pleasant evening, sir," the mustached man said with a smile that failed to reach his eyes.

Brand pocketed his ID and entered the club. He found a place at the bar. A large-breasted bartender approached.

"What'll you have, Handsome?"

"Bourbon rocks."

She favored Brand with a look-over and a smile.

"Coming up," she said, turning to fill his order.

Brand looked around the expansive club.

Music filled the high-ceilinged room. The place was packed to capacity, as far as Brand could tell. In the center of the room, dancers crowded an oval dance floor, resembling a NASCAR track.

Inside the center ring of the dance track, patrons filled seats at round tables and stools at an ornate bar. Throughout the club, tables and rail tops were surrounded by customers. Waitresses in short skirts hurried to serve drinks to their demanding clientele.

At the rear of the club, Brand spotted a double-door entrance with leaded glass bearing the logo of the bar, a rearing gold horse in a desert landscape. Kilgore had informed him he was to gain entry to the Stallion Club through those doors.

The bartender set his cocktail before him.

"First time here?" she asked, leaning forward, allowing him a better view of her low-cut neckline.

Brand smiled his appreciation.

"It is," he replied. "Big place. What's your name?"

"Star," she replied.

"Of course you are," he said, passing her a twenty. "I'm Brand."

"Pleased to meet you, Brand. I'll get your change."

"It's yours," he said with a nod. "I enjoyed the welcome."

Star smiled.

"Come by when you are ready for a refill."

Brand sipped his drink. He waited at the bar for ten minutes per his instructions. When he was confident a giant bouncer was not coming to toss him out, he moved further into the club.

He saw nothing out of the ordinary with the Golden Stallion. Growing up in Texas, he was familiar with the culture, nightlife, and people. Closely spaced tall tables looked like cowboy-hat displays. Pretty country girls in jeans and tucked boots, and lean-waisted men with large rodeo belt buckles were everywhere. All of these were standard fare in any country nightclub in the state. Nothing about the bar struck him as a place where high-dollar drug deals were being conducted.

He saw fewer men in suits inside than he had seen when he entered the club. A closer look around him revealed a man in a suit entering the double doors to the Stallion Club.

Kilgore had briefed him carefully as Agents Spencer and Bratton fitted him with the micro-camera and wires for his body surveillance equipment.

"You are to get close to the main guy, Moises Montez. He is our target," Kilgore had instructed as he geared up.

Kilgore had pronounced the name Moses. He had shown him several surveillance photos of a dark-eyed man with closely groomed facial hair.

"Your mission is simple: to get us video and as much audio as you can. You don't make personal contact with anyone. Go in, circulate, get close enough to some of the conversations where we can electronically eavesdrop. You are generating leads to further the agency's investigation, that is all."

"Understood," Brand had agreed, watching Spencer position a video camera on his suit coat.

"You may feel overdressed, but the party in the Stallion Club is private and there is a dress code. When you get to the door of the private club in the back, tell them you were invited to the 'Cattle Baron's Ball.'"

Brand had frowned.

"They don't hold Cattle Barons' Balls in nightclubs."

"So, you are an expert on that too," Spencer had scoffed as he taped a wire to Brand's chest.

"It's common knowledge, Yankee," Brand returned. "It's a part of Texas culture."

"It isn't important," Kilgore interrupted, tired of the continual conflict brewing between the two men. "That is the phrase that gets you in the door."

Brand indicated his understanding. He didn't want to get on Kilgore's bad side. The threat to his freedom was always front and center in his mind.

He approached the glass double doors and pulled the handle for the right door. Inside, he saw a completely different kind of party. The air was full of cigar smoke, a violation of the city's no-smoking ordinance being followed in the front of the club. The patronage was entirely male. The hosts and wait staff were exclusively scantily clad attractive young women.

Brand paused as another large bouncer blocked his path.

"I'm here for the Cattle Baron's Ball," Brand explained confidently.

"Name?" the giant asked.

"Carson Brand," he replied, looking around the room.

"I don't know you, sir," the bouncer said firmly.

"I don't know you either," Brand agreed. "This is my first time at the Golden Stallion."

The bouncer's face underwent an impressive transformation. His professionally courteous expression hardened to the grim countenance of an Easter Island obelisk.

"Are you trying to be funny?" he asked as the last of his courtesy evaporated in the growing heat of his deadly transformation.

Brand felt a rare impulse for caution take its place. He recognized this as a moment where he should employ charm rather than might.

"Not at all, big boy," he replied with a friendly smile. "You're too big and capable to be funny with."

The bouncer considered Brand's reply for a long moment. Brand hoped he detected a hint of softening in the man's countenance.

"I need to check before I grant you access to the Ball," he said finally.

As he placed his hand to his ear to actuate his in-ear radio, a voice called out brightly.

"Brand. Fancy seeing you again."

Brand looked toward the voice. He recognized Ross, the bartender from the Pink Poodle.

"Hello, Ross," Brand greeted the bartender. "Fancy seeing you here too."

Ross came closer and gave Brand a hug.

"Don't you look hotter than a bandit's pistol."

Ross looked at the bouncer.

"Beach, this is Brand. He is a friend. You remember Joe, Joe Mercer? They work together. Stop hassling Brand. Come along, handsome, let me get you a bourbon."

Beach opened his mouth to protest.

"Beach is very cautious," Ross explained with a wanton smile at the bouncer. "He got his name from Muscle Beach in L.A. He takes himself very seriously."

He patted Beach on the arm.

"Stop worrying. I'll vouch for him."

"He works with Mercer?" Beach asked in a cautious tone. He considered the information for a moment before his expression returned to its former thinly worn courtesy.

To Brand, he said, "Enjoy yourself at the Ball, sir."

Brand walked with Ross to a bar at the back of the room.

"I'm surprised to see you here, Ross."

"I work the Stallion on the weekends. I bartend at the Poodle during the week. The tips are way better here. Bourbon rocks?"

"As usual," Brand replied with a grateful smile.

"Is Joe with you tonight?" Ross asked, dropping a bourbon ball in a highball glass. He poured the bourbon over the ice ball and set the glass before Brand on a bar napkin.

"I'm not sure if he is attending or not," Brand replied uncertainly.

He was on unfamiliar ground. He appreciated Ross vouching for him. However, he was unsure whether the gesture was based on their brief personal relationship or on a recognition he was associated with Mercer as claimed. Why would Mercer's name get him into a drug distribution party?

"Interesting," Ross mused thoughtfully. Finally, he shook his head, dismissing his doubts. "You guys have more secrets than I can keep up with."

Brand sipped his cocktail as Ross moved to serve another customer. He looked around casually. A large table caught his attention. Those seated at the table were Latinos in expensive shining suits and cowboy boots. Three topless women sat with them, enduring frequent groping touches and lewd remarks. They spoke primarily Spanish. Most had neck tattoos and wore heavy jewelry. Brand recognized the men as cartel members.

He hid a frown. His experience with the cartel was unpleasant, mildly put. His thoughts dissipated as he noticed a table at the edge of the room where only two men and a well-dressed woman sat. Brand recognized the man with a well-manicured Van Dyke as Montez, his target.

The other man seated there was a smallish man with an acne-scarred face. He scanned the room with an evil gleam in his eyes, like a jackal on the Serengeti. The woman was dark and beautiful. She seemed to be more important than one of the female consorts and bouncing waitresses. Brand guessed she had a personal relationship with Montez.

Brand watched as a short man with a cigar approached the Montez table. Montez said something to him. He took a seat beside Montez. They spoke for a moment before the man again stood. Montez shook his hand. Brand noticed the gleam of a white business-card-sized paper in their palms. The newcomer pocketed the card and moved away. Moments later, another man sat with Montez. The card-passing handshake was repeated once more. As one man left the table, another man took his place beside Montez.

Brand realized the micro-cam was not oriented in a direction where video could be made of Montez's actions.

A waitress passed close to Brand. He stopped her, turning his body on the bar chair toward her.

"Excuse me," he said to her.

She paused with a smile.

"Hi," she greeted him. "Can I help you, sir?"

Brand pulled her to the side, clearing the camera's view of Montez.

"What is your name?" he asked with a smile.

"Cheyenne," she replied, returning his smile.

"I saw you earlier and couldn't resist talking to you," he said, half watching Montez. "What's the chance of you and me seeing each other later?"

Cheyenne smiled politely.

"Are you one of Mr. Montez's friends?"

"Of course," he replied.

Cheyenne's smile faded slightly. She replied with a darker tone to her voice. She raised her hand and adjusted her hair in a manner conveying her disdain.

"I'm sorry, sir. I am not a prostitute."

"That's not what I meant," he stammered.

Cheyenne turned her head curtly as she left him, continuing on her way.

Brand was confused and a little annoyed as he watched her disappear through a doorway around the bar. If Spencer were listening, he would give Brand a hard time about the rejection.

His gaze returned to Montez. Another man was seated beside him. However, this time the well-dressed woman was looking directly at Brand.

Brand scanned the room, trying to appear as if he were only looking around, like a guy on his own in a bar full of interesting people. He turned in his seat, facing the bar once more. He drained his drink and raised a finger to Ross for a refill.

Ross brought the bottle and poured him another drink at the bar. Brand was surprised at the Old West pour, especially in a nice bar. He looked up at Ross.

The bartender's face was solemn.

"You need to get out of here as fast as you can," Ross warned Brand. He ended the pour and returned to the other end of the bar.

Brand looked down each end of the bar. To the left, he saw Beach and another man of equal girth approaching him in a businesslike manner.

Brand stood, dropping a twenty on the bar. He turned toward the doors and the bouncers.

Spencer cursed loudly.

"He failed the backside security measure. He is fucked, Kilgore. We may be too if they find the wire."

Kilgore watched the images on the video screen. They clearly saw the two large men approaching Brand. Why was Brand moving directly toward them? Was he doggedly headed for the entrance, oblivious of the security bearing down upon him?

"Shit," he said, agreeing with Spencer's observation.

The video camera went black as the two bouncers filled the screen with their dark clothing. The camera tilted violently to the side. Grunts and the sound of straining men suddenly went silent as the audio device malfunctioned, likely from the impact of a blow during the struggle.

The image lurched in the opposite direction before the view cleared, and they saw Brand had somehow escaped the two bouncers and was moving toward the doors. He didn't seem to be sprinting.

Kilgore was impressed with Brand's self-control.

The silent images appeared surreal to the watching agents. In the main hall, a squat muscular man in a western shirt and cowboy hat appeared in the viewport. They saw, at the edge of the screen, Brand heft a metal barstool, clubbing the man violently with it.

In the silent movie, Brand moved toward the side of the club.

Bratton thought the video images looked like a first-person shooter with the sound off. He watched with silent delight.

The video image jerked upward sharply, after which another man, dressed similarly to the squat muscular man, fell into the frame as he struck the concrete floor. The image showed Brand moving past the man toward a set of security double doors at the side of the club. The doors burst open, and they saw a paved drive illuminated by tall streetlights. Brand sprinted along the side of the club, headed toward the front parking lot.

As Brand arrived at the front corner of the building, he turned his body, and the video screen was filled with at least a half dozen bouncers bearing down on him.

Brand turned and sprinted to his truck.

The agents saw his truck in the monitor. He was parked at the outside edge of the lot. The door opened, but the muted signal prevented them from knowing if he had time to start the truck. Between the steering wheel and the dashboard, they saw movement as Brand drove the truck over the parking stop and the curb. He turned onto the busy street and accelerated into traffic.

Kilgore slumped into his chair.

"Thank God," he gasped as though he had been beside Brand through the whole ordeal.

Kilgore's phone rang. He answered. Brand was on the other end.

"Hey, Brand."

"That didn't go as well as I thought it might."

"We didn't get much," Kilgore agreed. "Are you being followed?"

Brand checked his mirrors, then turned onto a side street. He pulled into a parking lot and turned off his lights.

"I don't think so," he said after a moment. "I'll be sure in a couple of minutes."

"When you are sure," Kilgore instructed, "come back here for debriefing."

The phone went dead. Kilgore set the cell on the conference table.

Spencer pulled the surveillance gear from Brand's clothes. Brand pulled the body tape off himself, knowing Spencer would take immense pleasure in ripping it off.

Kilgore reviewed the video and audio capture once more.

"Why did you call the waitress over?" he asked, pausing the feed.

"I needed to orient the camera toward Montez. I could see everything clearly, but I was turned away from him."

Spencer straightened, looping the wires.

"You're smooth with the ladies, buddy," he mocked Brand.

Brand considered him silently.

Kilgore cleared his throat, sensing the building conflict.

"That was a smart move," he said. "We didn't know they had implemented any additional internal passcodes. That is on us."

Brand was unhappy with the failure of the operation.

Kilgore sat back in his seat.

"Don't beat yourself up, Brand," he consoled him. "We got a lot of solid intel. We have every face in the local drug ring on camera. We know they pass drop locations and times through those cards Montez passes out. We placed members of the drug cartel at the scene, meaning they are Montez's source. Not bad for a couple of hours' work."

Brand buttoned his shirt and took a seat across from Kilgore.

Spencer stowed the gear.

Bratton read his spy novel, watching them with occasional glances over the top of the book.

"How do you know this Ross character?" Kilgore asked.

"He is the bartender at a gay bar in Montrose, the Pink Poodle. I met him when one of the guys I work with took me there after hours."

Brand looked at Spencer threateningly.

"If I hear another smart-ass comment from you, we are going to go right here and right now. You'll get a chance to see how tough you are."

Spencer's mouth was frozen in the open position, his next insult abruptly stemmed by Brand's threat. Kilgore watched until Spencer finally closed his mouth and returned his attention to the equipment.

"The guy who brought me there is Joe Mercer. He works for the Kinetic Team on the Randy Chappell election campaign."

Kilgore pointed at Bratton, who flopped his book down and retrieved a laptop from a bag below the desk. He opened the laptop and fired it up.

"That sounds a little clandestine," Kilgore continued. "What does this Kinetic Team do?"

"My experience has been that they disrupt opposing candidates' rallies and fundraisers."

Kilgore shook his head.

"Some job you found. Anyway, we will check out the bartender and this Mercer individual. Let me know about any blowback in your future dealings with them. They may know something that can help."

Brand shrugged his shoulders uncertainly. He rubbed his head with a scowl.

"Do you need to see a doctor?" Kilgore asked.

"It's just a bump," Brand assured him.

"Get out of here. We'll be in touch."

31

SUNDAY EVENING, BRAND PARKED HIS TRUCK in the designated POV parking at Camp Bravura. Once again, he wore jeans and a T-shirt. His suit was bagged over his shoulder as he made his way to the barracks. When he entered, many of the trainees were in their bunks, some alone, others chatting.

Moore was in his, looking at his tablet. Brand opened his locker and stowed his clothing.

Moore watched him over the top of the tablet.

"Long weekend?" he asked.

"Nothing special," Brand replied.

"That's a nice shiner you have next to your eye."

"That was an accident," Brand said cautiously. "How was yours?"

"I checked into a hotel and caught a movie and dinner. Stayed in."

Brand knew from a previous conversation Moore was from Indiana, where his group was based. He was married with a three-year-old girl and a newborn boy.

"Did you talk to your fam?"

"Yeah," Moore answered. "They're great; happy I'll be home next week."

"Are they serving chow this evening?" Brand asked.

"They are," Moore replied, laying his tablet on the bunk. "I could eat."

Brand secured his locker and followed Moore to the chow hall, where they selected pork chops and mashed potatoes. Brand swallowed a bite and drank from the red plastic cup. He watched Moore silently from across the table as the other man ate. Brand wiped his mouth, dropping the napkin on the plate.

"You mentioned the Chappell campaign was known to have ties to a terrorist camp in Sweeney. Do you have any specifics about how they are associated or who is involved within the campaign?"

Moore chewed. An amused look twisted his closed mouth and lit his eyes. He swallowed and sipped from his plastic cup.

"Interested in conspiracy theories, are you?"

"Usually UFOs," Brand joked. "For now, terrorist camps disguised as youth camps will do."

Moore twisted his mouth as he let go of his unhappiness that the barb hadn't struck home with Brand.

"As I said before," he began, "it is mainly rumor. We get a lot of uncorroborated leads and spotty information. What I have heard is there is a major donor who is associated with both the campaign and the camp."

"You don't know the name—even in passing?"

"It wasn't a case I was on, so my information is not very specific. What's your angle with these questions?"

Brand sat back in his chair. He looked around him as he considered his reply.

"I worked a short operation with the DEA this weekend. It was a drug thing, not terror-related. I got in a pinch, and mentioning the name of one of my campaign colleagues got me out of it."

"So, you didn't run into a door," Moore teased, touching his cheek and indicating Brand's bruise. "It sounds like you need to share this information with your handler."

"I did," Brand assured him. "I figured you might know what kind of people I'm dealing with."

Moore wiped his mouth as he moved on from the subject.

"No more shop talk. Do you play chess?"

Brand's brow furrowed at the dismissal and the offer to play a board game.

"Sure," he replied. "You have a board?"

"You don't?" Moore asked mockingly. "Come on. Let's see if you have any skill."

They returned their trays and trash to the kitchen window.

The day broke under dark cloud cover and an unseasonably cool breeze, promising rain. Brand and Moore stood together in formation. Theil conducted his daily headcount.

"Mount the black bus," Theil announced when he was satisfied all the trainees were present.

Brand and Moore sat together on the bus. The morning grew darker to the point that they arrived at the shooting facility to see lights shining through the tall front window glass.

Inside, Mr. Lyndsey met them in the front lobby.

"Follow me to the classroom."

He led the group down an adjacent corridor, and they took their places at tall desks with no chairs.

Lyndsey took his position behind the lectern at the front of the room.

"Weapons out and atop the desks, please," he instructed.

Brand produced his pistol from his clothing, locking the slide open and withdrawing the magazine. He placed the weapon on the desktop.

"After our classroom session this morning," Lyndsey began, "we are going to break down into smaller groups where we will practice the lessons we will cover here."

He moved to the long dry-erase board on the wall. He uncapped a marker and wrote in broad block text.

"Our goal today is to develop your reaction conditioning while under attack. These are the terms you will need to know."

He read the terms as he wrote them out.

"Force Multiplier: Any weapon you can use to increase your deadly effect on an assailant.

"Emotional Fitness: The level of your ability to perceive a threat and react within the confines of your training and without panic affecting your reactions.

"Waiting Your Turn: When confronted by an armed assailant while unarmed, survive the initial encounter long enough to create an opportunity to arm yourself, escape, or counterattack."

Lyndsey turned from the blue writing on the board.

"Alright, let's get started."

32

IT WAS DARK WHEN MERCER ENTERED the Pink Poodle Lounge. He took a seat at the bar. Ross dropped a bar napkin in front of him.

"Gecko, handsome?" he asked.

"Just a beer, Ross," Mercer replied vacantly.

Ross considered Mercer for a moment before he moved to fill his order. He returned with a cold bottle and a glass. He poured the beer, watching Mercer curiously.

"Where's your partner in crime?" Ross teased.

Mercer looked up abruptly, as if he were surprised at the reference. He stared at Ross vacantly, not understanding the question.

"Brand," Ross reminded him gently.

"That motherfucker is more trouble than he is worth," Mercer spat with uncharacteristic ire.

Ross stood straighter, grasping the empty bottle.

"So, you do know," the bartender said with a shake of his head.

"Know what?" Mercer asked suspiciously.

"Brand, at the Stallion Friday night."

Mercer struggled to catch up with the conversation. His mind whirled as new troubles with Brand dawned within his imaginings.

"What are you talking about?" he finally managed.

Ross's expression became grave as he gathered from Mercer's reaction that Brand had acted alone and without his knowledge.

"He showed up at the Cattle Baron's Ball Friday. He set off one of the girls, and security came for him. There was quite a tussle, but Brand managed to drop Beach and Cortez before he got away."

Ross watched Mercer keenly for his reaction to the news.

"He was there long enough to get a good idea of what was going on," Ross added.

Mercer paled under his tan and long hair.

"What did he say to you?" Mercer asked in a dangerous tone.

"Nothing," Ross replied innocently. "I asked him if you were alone, and he said he didn't know if you were coming or not. I made him a drink, and that was the last we spoke. It was busy, and I was in a hurry to keep up."

"How did he get in?"

Ross reddened noticeably.

"I vouched for him," he admitted quietly. "But I thought you two were an item. I didn't know..."

Mercer relaxed a bit as he drank beer from the full glass.

Ross waited, unsure if their conversation was finished.

"Thanks, Ross," Mercer said finally, dismissing the bartender.

Ross moved away reluctantly. He couldn't help feeling as if he had somehow betrayed Joe.

Sahib listened carefully. The news did not frighten him, but it demanded attention. In the past, his work had been harried by protestors, special-interest groups, and Christian activists. Previously, he had been protected by the color of the law. On rare occasions, he had taken advantage of existing hate-law statutes to dispatch protestors or aggressive trespassers. This new threat represented a danger he had never dealt with.

Joe Mercer waited for Sahib to react to the news of Brand's strange activities. He looked around, uncertain whether he should sit or remain standing out of respect.

"Have you told anyone else of this?" Sahib asked quietly.

"I haven't had time," Mercer answered. "It was late when I learned about this. I came directly to you first thing this morning."

"He is not law enforcement," Sahib mused. "Even a cursory search online reveals a minor criminal background. He may be a plant or a criminal informant."

"Unless they are training C.I.s in South Houston," Mercer disagreed, "he is affiliated with the police in some way."

Sahib considered Mercer with a more serious look.

"How much does this man know about what we do?"

"Not much more than what the news is reporting about their suspicions that we are organizing protests, and a small part of what we do in the Kinetic Team."

"He knows about this place and about me," Sahib observed with growing annoyance. "And it now seems he is involved in an investigation into whatever is going on at this country bar."

Mercer looked at his feet. His associations prior to his employment with Sahib had never come up.

"What should we do about him?" Mercer asked testily. He remembered Sahib's decision to work with Brand even after his blatant display of disrespect.

Sahib watched him, seeming to read his thoughts.

"You are to treat Brand no differently than before. I will let you know when he is to be brought to me."

Mercer turned to the door.

"Joe," Sahib said. "Send Umar in, please."

Mercer opened the door. Umar waited outside, leaning against the metal skin of the building.

"Sahib wants you," Mercer informed him.

Umar entered and closed the door as Mercer left. Joe passed through the entrance to the compound. Finding his car, he took a seat there as he considered what he had learned about Brand.

Montez was a former employer who tolerated no disloyalty, nor did he suffer fools with loose tongues. Mercer had been relieved to find a position with Sahib's organization. Montez was cruel, but his current squeeze, Selena, was sadistic. Any small amount of mercy in Montez's personality was struck from him by the dark and beautiful Selena's counsel.

Learning Brand was nosing around the operations of his old boss complicated a puzzle that already troubled Mercer. If Montez learned Brand was associated with him, might he not come looking for answers?

Mercer felt his ears grow hot and his breathing shorten as a new dire suspicion grew within him. He withdrew his phone from a pocket and pressed the call button for a contact.

The phone rang twice before it was answered.

"It is early, Joe," Ross greeted him wearily. "I worked late. What's up?"

"How did you vouch for Brand Friday night?"

Mercer ground his teeth at the long silence on the other end of the call.

"Ross?"

"I'm here," the bartender assured him. After another short pause, he said, "I told Beach he worked with you and you were friends."

Mercer was speechless. Ross had dropped his name to get Brand into the Ball.

"Shit!" Mercer cursed loudly, his voice ringing in the close confines of the sedan.

"Goddammit! You used my fucking name!"

"Joe," Ross stammered. "I didn't know..."

Mercer struck the steering wheel. The car shuddered under the blow. He ended the call and threw the phone in the passenger seat.

He was certain Montez would send men to find out more about the man who had crashed their drug distribution meeting. Ross had used his name!

Mercer cranked the engine. The tires spit gravel as he sped away.

33

BRAND PACKED HIS GYM BAG, emptying the locker of his few possessions. He laid the tote and his garment bag, containing his suits, on the bunk. He glanced across the aisle to where Moore was busy securing his own belongings.

"It's been fun," Brand said. "Now we get on with the business of meeting new people and confining them to dark, secure places."

"It's a job," Moore agreed. "I'm headed back home for a much-needed two days off before I am back on the clock."

They gathered their bags from their bunks.

"Come on," Moore said, shouldering his bags. "I'll walk you out."

"It's not going to work, Moore," Brand explained. "I don't swing that way."

"That's not what the word is on the squad bay," Moore laughed.

They met in the center of the aisle. They grasped hands.

"You keep your eyes up," Brand said.

"Watch your back, Contractor," Moore responded. "That piece in your bag is yours, but it could get you killed if there is a relationship change within the department."

"What do you mean by change?" Brand asked in a more sober tone.

"I was sworn in when I joined the agency. The agency pledged itself to me in return. You aren't protected by any formal agreement that could cover you if you make a mistake. Contractors don't last long in this business. You are still a loner in a solitary role. Call on me if I can ever help."

Brand was unsure what to say.

Moore released his hand.

"Come on," he said with a smile. "Let's get out of here before they change their minds."

Brand led Moore to his truck. He had dropped off his rental the previous weekend. They deposited their bags in the bed. Moore took his place in the truck.

"Nice wheels," he joked.

"I knew you would appreciate it," Brand agreed. "You guys in Indiana got flush toilets in what, the mid-eighties?"

"Take me to Hobby, driver, and shut that dirty whore mouth."

Brand started the truck and backed onto the drive. Soon they were on the interstate, headed toward Houston.

Brand entered the entrance to Hobby Airport and dropped Moore at the departure terminal.

They shook hands once again.

"Take care, Moore."

"You too, Brand."

Moore shouldered his bags and was soon lost inside the terminal building.

Brand put the truck in gear and made his way toward the freeway.

He still wasn't sure where he stood with Sahib. Mercer had insisted Sahib was intolerant of independent action. Brand would find out soon enough.

Brand picked up his phone and dialed Mercer. The phone rang several times and went to voicemail.

"It's Brand," he said into the phone. "Give me a call if we are still working together."

He ended the call and laid the phone on the seat beside him. The phone rang immediately. Mercer's name was on the caller ID.

"Hey," he greeted Mercer.

"The prodigal son returns," Mercer said with little humor in his voice. "Are you back for a while, or should we block you out for more vacation time?"

"I'm available for the foreseeable future, as far as I know."

"That's good to hear."

Brand waited as the silence grew. Finally, Mercer spoke again.

"How about a drink?"

Brand hesitated. His last conversation with Mercer was less than cordial. He was suspicious of Mercer's easy dismissal of bad feelings and continued rapport as though nothing had changed between them.

"Why don't I drop by your place in the morning?"

"I'm in a new apartment. Do you want me to pick you up?"

Brand thought about how he would explain the new truck.

"Not necessary. Why did you move?"

"I needed a change. I am living near Montrose now. I'll text you the address and the gate code."

"Cool."

Brand ended the call. Mercer's text arrived as he took the exit near Amy's house. He hoped she would not be angry at the surprise visit.

34

AMY GATHERED THE LAST OF PETE'S CLOTHES and folded them into the little backpack. She hated the summer custody exchange. She would not see her son for two weeks while Justin had him. The three-year-old watched his little TV as she packed for him. Cartoon images flashed on the screen as monkey characters fled from a green puppy with a lolling tongue.

"Pete," she said gently. "Let's get your shoes on. Your dad will be here soon."

Pete kept his eyes on the TV screen as he backed toward his mother, who had collected his shoes from the floor beside the bed. Amy positioned him on the bed and placed the shoes on his feet, fastening the Velcro straps. The cartoon held her son's attention. She didn't have the heart to tell him to ignore the TV while she dressed him. She realized with sadness she wouldn't see Peter for a long time. She wanted the memory of their last conversation to be filled with love, not a scolding.

The doorbell rang.

Amy glanced in the direction of the sound, then patted her son's feet.

"It's Daddy," she announced brightly, zipping the backpack and lifting it from the bed.

Peter's face split into a look of joyful glee as he leapt from the bed and led Amy to the front door. Amy gently pulled Peter to the side as she opened the door. Justin stood there with a judgmental look on his face. He saw Peter and bent over to greet his son.

"Hello, Petey," he said, hugging the boy.

Amy held the backpack as she watched them embrace. She looked past Justin. His Maserati convertible was at the curb, an attractive blonde in sunglasses occupying the passenger seat.

Amy frowned.

Justin saw the frown and straightened from greeting Peter, his eyes on her face.

"I need to talk to you privately," he said in a serious tone. "Come on, Petey. Let's get you situated."

Justin picked up Peter and grabbed his backpack from Amy.

"I'll be right back."

He carried Peter to the car and strapped him into the car seat in the back of the convertible.

"You remember Lynda, Petey? I'll be right back. Mommy and I have to chat for a moment."

Justin returned to the porch.

"Ames," he said, pocketing his sunglasses. "I want custody of Pete. Lynda and I are getting married, and he needs a more stable home to grow up in than he has here."

Amy crossed her arms, her anger growing. She disliked the pet name, and this wasn't the first time he had threatened to file for full custody rights.

"I don't want a daycare raising our son," he continued.

Amy tried to control her emotions. She wanted to give Justin no fodder to use against her in court. She tried to calm herself as she focused on an old pickup pulling up to the curb.

"That's not going to happen, Justin," she warned him in an even but strained voice.

The truck door opened, and Brand got out.

"Shit," she said under her breath.

"What?" Justin asked with a frown at her profanity.

He assumed she was reacting to his custody proposal.

"Pete is young enough to be impressionable. We need to ensure he has positive role models and character-building experiences."

Brand walked past the convertible. Lynda lowered her sunglasses to get a better look at him as he walked around the car toward the sidewalk leading to the house.

"That is a load of crap, Justin," Amy continued, trying to end the conversation. "I don't have time to argue with you about this again. He stays with me."

"You are an unfit mother, Amy. I have proof you are dating a criminal."

"What?" she gasped in shock.

"You were seen leaving here with a man a couple of weeks ago. He turns out to be a client. You could be disbarred."

Brand walked up the sidewalk, stopping at the bottom step of the porch.

"Are you having me followed, Justin?" she asked, anger nearly choking her.

"You can date who you want," he explained evenly. He was enjoying her distress. "I suggest you pick your boyfriends more carefully. From what I have seen in the photos, your new beau seems to be a bit of a bum. Maybe I will end it for you. He doesn't quite measure up to the standards of manhood you are used to."

"Is that right?" Brand asked from behind Justin.

Justin turned in surprise at the voice behind him.

"Brand," Amy begged. "Let me handle this. Justin, this is Carson Brand. Brand, this is my ex, Justin Landry. Brand, can you give us a moment?"

Brand stepped up the stairs, taking Justin's hand in response to the introduction.

"Sure, Amy," he replied affably. To Justin, he said, "Good to meet you."

He looked at Amy as he said, "Mr. Landry is going to be brief anyway. I can wait."

Justin was several inches shorter than Brand. He looked up at Brand in frustration, the difference in height obvious. He glanced at Amy as he attempted to pull his hand from Brand's grip.

"This is not over, Ames," he warned, trying to regain some of his superiority over her. "Let go of my hand, asshole."

"I'd watch my mouth if I were you. We are in the presence of a lady, and I won't tolerate disrespect toward her."

"You won't tolerate..."

His words trailed away as he saw Brand's eyes harden.

Brand released his hand, and Justin turned on his heel.

"He will be back by 6 p.m. Sunday week," Amy warned Justin's back.

"Whatever," Justin said without turning.

Brand and Amy watched silently as Justin started the convertible and drove away, scratching tires.

Brand turned to Amy.

"Sorry to drop in unannounced."

"Again," she reminded him with a half-hearted look of disapproval as she tried to master her emotions at Justin's accusations.

"Again," he admitted with a chuckle.

"Come in," she said, holding the door open. "I could use a drink."

Brand squeezed past her.

"It is Friday night."

She closed the door.

"Have a seat on the sofa. I'll grab you a beer."

"Thanks."

After a few moments, she joined him in the living room, carrying a wine glass filled with red wine and a beer bottle. She handed him the bottle and took her place on the sofa near him. She sipped the wine, looking him over.

"I hear you have been on one of your secret missions the past couple of weeks," she said curiously.

"I just had some personal business to finish."

"And is it finished?"

"I think so," he replied guardedly. "Who told you about my break?"

"Randy and Camille," she replied, watching his reaction closely. "They asked me over to the campaign headquarters and grilled me about you."

"Grilled you?"

"Apparently, they are concerned with your extracurricular activities and asked if I could shed any light on them."

"I see," Brand said thoughtfully as he drank from the bottle.

"I'm worried about you," she admitted, leaning toward him. "I may have gotten you involved with something... I don't know what to call it. I don't trust Camille, and Randy is not the same man I knew in college. There are rumors the campaign is backed by questionable people."

"I've heard that too."

"Maybe it's time to look elsewhere for work. Maybe even get out of town."

Brand looked Amy over closely. He was surprised at the gravity of her advice. Was she getting rid of him? He had heard part of her ex-husband's conversation. A private investigator was watching her. Was he a liability to her?

"I have considered leaving," he admitted mildly. "Is that what you want me to do?"

Amy was surprised at Brand's display of vulnerability in the question. She sipped her wine as she formed a response.

"It isn't about what I want," she finally replied. "There seems to be a storm growing around you. I must admit there is an unusual amount of secrecy to you. Everyone who knows you seems to think so. The general consensus is one of obvious concern and even consternation. Everywhere you go, trouble seems to follow. Maybe it isn't your fault, but it follows you all the same. I think you should separate from the campaign and go your own way."

Brand sat back in dismay. This was straight talk indeed. Amy was an attorney, and she wielded authority now. He set the beer bottle on the coffee table.

"Thanks for the beer. I'd better be going."

Amy placed a hand on his knee.

"Don't go. We are only talking, Brand. I have been wanting to talk with you since the fundraiser."

Brand grunted his dismissal.

"Not about your background or your past—about us."

He looked her in the eye. She had a knack for keeping him off balance.

"Is there an us?" he asked, picking up the bottle.

Amy sat back, satisfied he was not leaving immediately.

"You are here in my house having a drink with me on a Friday night. That's something, isn't it?"

Brand sipped the beer.

"It is," he agreed. He took a moment to think about his presence there.

"What about your ex, Justin?"

Amy winced.

"Isn't it crazy how two people can start out so in love and end up hating one another? I remember when we couldn't bear to be apart. We trusted each other with every secret. That trust bound us. Now all I feel is embarrassment that he knows everything about me and would reveal any of it to anyone to get his way."

"Relationships are the riskiest business anyone can enter into," Brand agreed. He sipped his beer as he thought about his late girlfriend Natalie. He once again felt caution about starting a new relationship. He focused on the present.

Amy watched him with keen interest. She saw her words moved him to deep thought.

What is his story? she mused curiously.

"Have you eaten?" she asked him, lightening the mood.

"I am hungry," he admitted. "How about I take you out?"

"Just dinner?"

"Why?" he asked.

"Because if the movie is bad, I'll have to sit through two hours of it."

"Sure," he said. "I'll drive."

"Is that your truck outside?"

"Yep. She ain't pretty, but she's mine."

"I'll drive," Amy insisted with a smile.

35

CAMILLE OPENED HER EYES as the nightstand glowed with the green hue of her cell phone pulsing silently. Who was calling her in the middle of the night?

She grabbed the phone and read the screen. Rising from the bed, she left the bedroom carefully, not wanting to wake Randy. In the kitchen, she answered the call.

"It's late," she said as her greeting. She listened to the voice on the other side of the call.

"When did he call?"

She waited as the answer came.

"Why are you calling me this late if he called hours ago?"

She straightened as she listened further.

"That's not going to happen," she replied curtly.

She slumped slightly, leaning against the countertop of the kitchen island.

"Alright," she said in resignation. "I understand."

Her body language registered distaste at what she heard next.

"You are in front of the house?"

She moved quickly to the living room and parted the heavy drapes. A car was parked at the curb in front of her house. She could make out the dark silhouette of someone in the driver's seat.

Ending the call, she hurried back to her room, where she pulled a wrap from the chair back and quietly left the bedroom, closing the door behind her. Exiting through the side door, she crept quickly to the front of the house, crossing the yard while glancing around for alert neighbors or late-night passersby.

She opened the passenger door and slipped into the car. The dome light briefly illuminated the driver. Her wrap was thin, as was her nightgown, and he could discern her curves and outline even through the covering garments.

She closed the door, and they sat in darkness.

"There are better places for us to meet," she said in a calm voice, managing to disguise her anger.

Sahib reached out his hand and cupped the back of her neck.

"I needed to see you now, so I came to where you are."

"Randy could wake at any moment," she said without heat. "You said Brand is back. What have you learned about where he has been?"

"Joe tells me our friend appeared at a drug deal in Montrose. I am certain Joe is connected in some way. He has moved into a new apartment, and he has been absent for days now. He called to tell me Brand contacted him this evening and is meeting him at his apartment tomorrow morning."

"You mean this morning," she corrected him with a tinge of annoyance.

"Are you angry with me, Camille?"

His expression hardened at the prospect that she would treat him with anything other than cordiality, no matter the time.

Camille recognized his expression and softened her tone.

"You mentioned Brand was meeting Joe. What is the plan to deal with him?"

"Do you feel we need to 'deal' with him?"

"I think there are a lot of unknowns with him. I agree with you that he is not law enforcement, but his actions warrant caution. I suggest he is more of a threat as a non-policeman than if he were acting in an official capacity. He exhibits a very suspicious interest in our organization and others. Even if he is not a poisonous snake, sometimes it is better to chop off the head before he bites."

Sahib acknowledged her wise counsel. He looked at the outline of her fine profile in the dark. The moonlight cast enough illumination to hint at her beauty. He pulled her toward him and kissed her hungrily, his tongue seeking hers. She returned the kiss, reaching for him and pulling him closer.

It was midmorning when Brand knocked on Mercer's apartment door. It was early enough that he doubted the man was out of bed. Surprisingly, the door opened, and Mercer stood there fully dressed.

"Come in," he urged Brand, looking quickly outside for signs of clandestine activity.

Brand went to the little galley kitchen, lifting an empty cup from the dish rack. He inspected the inside before helping himself to the coffee pot. He leaned against the counter as Mercer joined him and poured himself a cup.

"Thanks," Brand said, lifting the cup in salute.

"Yeah," Joe said. "Help yourself."

They sipped their coffee, occupied with their thoughts. Brand shifted his feet as he prepared to speak.

"Nice place," he observed. "Kind of a sudden move, wasn't it?"

Mercer considered Brand's comment with a flash of a frown, which he quickly attempted to hide.

"I've been thinking about new digs for a while. The time seemed right, so I did it."

Brand sipped his coffee.

"I heard on the news on the way over that an HPD cop killed another unarmed black kid last night. I figured you would be gearing up for the inevitable protests."

"We are the wrong skin color to participate in that one," Mercer said. "There are other security guys who handle that demographic."

Brand waited for clarification. After a moment, he realized there was none forthcoming.

"Am I still working with you guys or not?"

"Sahib told me to treat you as before. Apparently, he wants to keep you around."

"Did I catch you on your way somewhere?" Brand asked, indicating Mercer's being dressed.

"We have a meeting with Randy this morning."

"They know I am back? Word travels fast."

"I knew you would want to know if you were still gainfully employed or not, so I called."

"What time?"

"We need to leave now. I'll drive."

"I'll follow you. I bought a truck."

Mercer gave Brand a look of surprise.

"Handy. Let's go."

He set the cup in the sink and led Brand to the front door.

36

BRAND AND MERCER ENTERED RANDY'S OFFICE. The candidate was at his desk, and Camille sat on the sofa in the corner. The two men took seats in chairs before the desk.

Randy leaned back in his chair.

"Welcome back, Mr. Brand. Where did your travels take you?"

"Thanks," Brand replied. "I prefer to keep my personal life personal."

Randy showed his annoyance.

"The only reason you are still working with my campaign is because Camille has the notion there is something redeeming about you, and we need someone like you here."

Chappell glanced at Camille with a look reflecting disagreement with her opinion.

Brand fought the urge to walk out of the office. He had held few jobs in his life, preferring to work for himself. He secretly believed most self-employed businessmen were such because they were incapable of holding down a job. Whether it was their inability to pass a drug test, background check, or just their inability to show up on time, the malady moved most entrepreneurs to create a job in the only organization that would hire them despite their failings. He considered himself of the same makeup. His issue was dislike and intolerance of criticism from a boss.

Chappell watched Brand as these thoughts presented themselves in a dour expression.

"In the spirit of restarting our relationship," Chappell said, lifting his hand, "I would like to offer my hand to you in exchange for your commitment to me and my campaign, with no future surprises."

Brand pressed the rebellious instincts fighting for prominence to the back of his mind. He stood, accepting Chappell's hand.

"You got it," Brand said.

"Good."

Brand and the candidate released their handshake.

Brand returned to his chair.

"Joe," Chappell said in a brighter voice, "we are hosting an outreach rally to help with the mourning for the youth killed last night. I need you and Brand to attend. The affected neighborhoods are volatile, and we fear our street team may not be safe from frayed emotions. Monitor and report. Intervene only if our people are in danger."

"Understood," Mercer said. "We'll get going."

"Thank you," Chappell said as he stood. "Good to have you back, Mr. Brand."

Brand accepted his thanks with a nod as they left the office.

He followed Mercer to the back door leading to the rear parking lot. Mercer's phone chimed, and he pulled it from his pocket. He tapped the phone as he walked to his car.

"Received the address. I'll text it to you now that you are independently mobile."

He read the text further.

"Meet me there at 8 p.m. this evening. I'm sending you the address now."

Brand's phone chirped, indicating he had received the address.

"I thought we were the wrong demographic for this job," Brand said to Mercer's back.

"I guess I was wrong," Mercer replied dismissively.

"See you there," he called as he walked to his truck.

Brand parked his truck in Houston's Third Ward, not a half-dozen blocks from where he had left Oscar tied up in a second-floor tenement so many weeks before. The neighborhood looked rough. It reminded him of photos he had seen of Detroit or Boston's minority districts. If the campaign considered this a lower-risk neighborhood for Caucasians, he couldn't imagine how dire a risky neighborhood would appear.

He stepped onto the hot pavement of the street and closed the door without locking the truck. He doubted anyone would be interested in the vehicle or any of its contents, but he didn't want to add the expense of replacing a broken window if it were burglarized.

He glanced at the address on his phone. It was difficult matching the texted address with a physical location. The numbers on the buildings were mostly nonexistent. He found a street number here and there. He counted off the addresses before he finally found the place. The building was a three-story tenement that appeared abandoned. He wondered if Mercer had made a mistake.

As it neared the appointed meeting time, he noticed the empty street filling gradually with milling people. Most were Black, and all were angry. The neighborhood buzzed with the heightened emotions of the growing mob.

He looked around carefully. He didn't see Mercer nor anyone from the campaign outreach team. His instincts sounded a nearly imperceptible warning. Something seemed off to him. A sense of pride galvanized his resolve, causing him to move deeper into the neighborhood. He had nothing to fear, he reasoned. He wasn't a cop and posed no threat to anyone there.

He crossed a wide street intersecting the street he walked. To his right, he heard crashing and yelling as a large group of protestors made its way down the street in his direction. He stopped short. Over the din, he heard a voice yell at the crowd.

"There! That white man is a cop! He's looking for his next dead nigger!"

Brand searched the crowd for the speaker as the mob focused on him. He was exposed and alone, facing several hundred angry Black men and women. His more detailed inspection of the crowd identified the speaker.

He recognized Umar by his tattoos and gold tooth. He was yelling and pointing at him. The crowd responded to his encouragement by increasing its speed, closing on the lone white man. The campaign set him up. Mercer set him up. Umar manipulated the crowd. He wanted his revenge.

Brand looked to the right from where he had come. Another mob approached from that direction, blocking the path to his truck. Behind him, the street seemed more open, but additional protestors were gathering there also.

He turned and headed at a sprint toward the smaller crowd. The pursuing mob roared as it raised its pace. Brand was reminded of a pack of hounds, their bloodlust heightened to a fevered pitch at the flight of their prey. The sound of the gaining mob was eerie in Brand's ears. He had never heard anything like it.

The cacophony of voices growled and screamed, charging the very atmosphere with a dreadful energy. The gathering protestors ahead of him grew aware of the approaching mob. At a distance, they had not yet connected the fleeing white man with the angry mob. Brand felt certain they would realize his role sooner rather than later.

He neared the closest group, about a half-dozen young Black men carrying pipes and sticks. He ran headlong into their midst, grabbing a galvanized metal conduit pipe from one of the surprised men. The others cursed him and struck at him as he ran past them carrying the weapon.

Others ahead saw his actions clearly, moving toward him in reaction to his aggressive move. Three men spread wide across the street. They brandished their rude weapons, ready to strike Brand down as he approached.

He continued toward them, gaining speed. As he closed upon them, all three men swung their pipes at his head like players swinging at a slow-pitched softball. He ducked, narrowly avoiding the blows. He struck the man on his right in the sternum. He thought he heard a crack as bones broke inside his victim. Brand spun, catching the man to his left behind the head with a lucky shot. Both men fell to the hot pavement.

Brand was relieved many in the demonstration were flight, not fight, people. He glanced behind him. The larger mob gained frighteningly.

Umar was at the head of the group, leading them and egging them on.

Brand lengthened his stride to a dead sprint. He looked for a barrier he could climb or pass through that would pare down the large mob to a smaller, more manageable group.

The wide road was bordered by an assortment of dingy storefronts and small ramshackle houses. Short chain-link fencing surrounded some of the homes, but he saw nothing that would cause any of the pursuers to break off from the chase.

He was tiring at the high pace. He knew he had little time to gain any type of advantage. He dared not look behind him again, though he could tell by the increased volume and density of the pursuers' collective voice that their numbers had grown.

He approached an intersection and turned right. Ahead, the buildings created a united front of smaller shops and sheer-walled warehouses. He was trapped in a concrete canyon with no escape on either side. Ahead of him lay only a long expanse of level paved street. He had entered a gauntlet.

He heard the mob round the corner with a crashing wave of noise. He dropped the pipe, conserving his strength and increasing his speed.

His breathing was becoming labored, and he was feeling a growing desperation.

Doubt was beginning to weaken him when, just ahead on his left, he saw a narrow opening between two of the concrete buildings. He made for it with the renewed energy of the desperate.

As he entered the narrow alley, he feared it would dead-end, and he would be completely trapped. His heart fell as he entered the space. Ahead of him was a brick wall where another building butted against the other two at his sides.

He stopped short, breathing hard. He drew a sharp breath as he looked to his left. A metal drainpipe was bolted to the concrete wall where it issued from the roof, emptying into a grate just under the spout.

Brand leaped high, grabbing the pipe. He pulled himself upward as the mob's voice filled the narrow space behind him. The sound rasped at him like a spur. With a surge of adrenaline, he climbed the black metal pipe. The mob filled the space behind him as he lamented his slow speed of ascent. The leaders would surely arrive before he was out of arm's reach.

He felt his right foot grasped firmly, pulling his leg away from the pipe and down. He looked down at a narrow sea of angry Black faces. Umar was among them. It was his hand grasping Brand's foot.

"You ain't getting away, white boy," Umar yelled over the crowd.

Brand strained with all his strength, rising a fraction, but Umar's grip held. With a mighty pull, Brand hauled himself up with his arms and left leg. He was able to move only a few inches before he felt Umar's weight pulling him down toward the crowd.

With a sensation akin to panic, Brand felt a lightness behind his eyes as he pulled with his arms. He felt pain as his connective tissue strained with the force of his resistance. His left leg soon hung independent of the pipe. His arms alone bore the full burden of his weight and some 250 pounds of Umar's.

Brand scowled with a growing certainty of the inevitable outcome of the struggle.

Umar looked up with a gleam of victory in his eyes as Brand's left foot crushed his nose and closed his eyes. The foot fell again like a sledgehammer blow on his unprotected face. Umar's grip failed. He struggled blindly to renew his purchase, pulling off Brand's shoe but releasing him to climb out of reach.

Brand was fortunate in many respects, the most favorable being Umar's broad shoulders and powerful build blocked the alcove housing the drainpipe. The mob was so tightly packed no one could move Umar to clear a path for any other pursuers.

Brand cut his bare right foot on the steel bands fastening the pipe to the building, but he managed to clamber the last few feet onto the flat roof.

On the warm gravel of the flat roof, he rolled on his back, breathing in heavy, rasping pulls of air. Although exhausted, he knew he needed to move quickly. His fatigued body betrayed him. He felt weak and sore. His shoulders ached sharply from his exertion on the drainpipe.

Once he got control of his breathing, he rolled onto his stomach and pushed himself onto all fours. He stood with a mighty effort. The yelling of the mob was identifiable as shouted instructions to clear the alleyway and cut off the fugitive's escape.

Brand stumbled to the rear edge of the building. The ground was at least 16 feet below. The weed-covered and junk-laden lot promised all manner of hidden sharp objects awaiting his descent. He sighed resignedly as he lowered himself slowly onto his stomach, easing over the roof edge. If he hung from the roof, he would still have some 10 feet remaining to drop to the overgrown debris field below.

The sun had fallen below the dingy urban horizon, and a scant gray light provided him with limited visibility. The mob might be well on its way around the long row of industrial buildings, running toward him. If they arrived before he escaped, he would be trapped.

His arms shook as he slid his lower body over the edge. His exhausted arms and shoulders hardly slowed his weight shift. The jolt of his dropping body weight dislodged his grip, and he fell helplessly to the darkening ground beneath.

His feet struck the ground heavily. He rolled with the fall, absorbing the energy of the impact, employing a technique he had used in the alley weeks before: a Parachute Landing Fall. He curled his body onto his lower legs, then hips, then shoulders. He felt a sharp pain near his rib cage as he collapsed with the fall.

He raised himself onto his knees; his bones seemed intact. He grabbed the painful area and looked down. A bloodstain spread under his T-shirt. He searched the ground and saw a shard of broken glass rising evilly from the grass. It was pointed and jagged.

He pulled his shirt over his head and examined the wound. It was an ugly puncture, bleeding freely. He twisted his T-shirt into a makeshift pressure bandage and bound it tightly over the cut.

The growing sounds of the riot drew his attention from the injury. He lifted himself to his feet and made for the street outside the fenced area in which he stood. He squeezed through a tall broken gate, attached to the fence by a single hinge and a loose rusty chain secured with a large padlock. He turned right, away from the sounds of the mob. He knew he was headed toward where he had parked his truck. Hopefully, the mob had not split in two directions to surround him.

He wasn't sure how much instruction they would accept from Umar. He knew little about mob mentality, but from what he had learned, strategic planning and execution were not typical behavior. Brand gambled Umar would not expect him to return to the heart of the Ward, preferring to continue toward an established business district where he could easily enlist help.

His tactics paid immediate dividends. He made his way back to the wide street through which he had been pursued. The lane was empty of protestors. The dark windows of the houses may have hidden cowering residents, but none of them revealed themselves as he shambled by, holding his wound gingerly.

He found his truck. The driver's-side door was open, and the seats had been cut. The hood was raised. He saw the battery was missing. He cursed quietly, looking around him.

An older car was parked a short distance from his truck. It was an old enough model that he hoped it had an exterior hood release. He moved quickly to the car and felt around the grille for a release handle. He found none. He tried the driver's-side door. It opened readily. He pulled the hood release under the dash.

He returned to the engine compartment and raised the hood. He tested the tightness of the battery's terminal connectors. The positive side came away easily. He had to twist the negative side a few times before it came free. He pulled the battery and returned to his truck. He dropped the battery into the empty cradle and twisted the cables on as tightly as he could without a wrench. He tried the ignition. The truck started immediately. Brand put the truck in gear and moved onto the roadway.

37

MERCER PUNCHED THE WALL OF THE MANCAVE. Brand was still alive! He was screwed. The man would come looking for him; if nothing else, for answers.

"Sahib, this is bad," he complained.

Umar frowned behind the bandage over his broken nose.

Sahib watched Mercer impassively.

"Do you fear him?" he asked, his tone coloring his words with deprecation.

"Yeah," Mercer said honestly in a loud voice. The strength of his conviction was meant to impart the real hazard Brand posed. He had seen him in action. If he trained with a paramilitary group, he may be quite formidable.

Sahib's face displayed surprise at such candor in Mercer's cowardice.

"And you, Umar? Are you afraid of him?"

Umar glowered at his boss. His jaw worked as he processed his rage.

"He got lucky. It won't work out that way again."

Mercer laughed without mirth.

"From the looks of you, he had a hand in the luck."

"Fuck you, white man!" Umar growled.

"We will not fight one another," Sahib said sternly. "Brand will come here. He will know I am responsible. Umar, tell Lutah and Achmed to come in and stay here at the compound."

Umar nodded.

Mercer watched Sahib.

"Joe, I need you to find Brand and bring him here," Sahib instructed. "Tell him you knew nothing about it. Tell him you were called from the meeting place by a last-minute phone call. Tell him I am here alone, and you will help him exact his revenge."

"And if he doesn't believe I was called away?"

"You know the man better than I do. Is he capable of violence with you?"

"I know he is capable of violence."

"Does he carry a gun?"

"He hasn't since I have known him."

Umar grunted his disgust.

Mercer watched Umar as he considered contacting Brand and lying to him about his role in the plan. Finally, he shrugged and turned on his heel. Without a word, he left the compound.

Brand awoke with a groan. He glanced at the LED display on the clock. It read 1:45 p.m. He stood from the bed and went to the bathroom. When he returned, he sat on the bed, turning on the TV. His mind began working on the events of last night as the television came to life and the drowsy cobwebs of sleep were swept from him. His back ached, as did his taxed muscles and connective tissue.

His thoughts, however, were strong in their clarity of conviction. He had been set up. Sahib had to be behind it, although Mercer and Umar were complicit.

What was unclear to him was the motive. This could not be about his leaving for two weeks. What was clear was that Mercer and Umar had been allied against him, meaning Sahib had his reasons for wanting him dead or incapacitated. Did they expect the mob to kill him or only injure him? Would Sahib escalate his efforts to a more direct attack? Brand knew Umar hated him. Was he a killer?

Mercer remained low on Brand's danger radar. He was hardly a threat hand-to-hand. He appeared to be no more than a devoted employee in Sahib's shadowy organization.

Brand had been underestimated many times in his life, typically to the detriment of those who underestimated him. He did not plan to make the same mistake with Mercer.

His phone lit up with a call. The ringer, as usual, was on silent. Brand retrieved the phone stiffly. The display showed the call was from Mercer. He answered.

"Hey, Joe," he said blandly.

"Hey, Brand. How did things go at the protest last night? Sorry I missed it. I got called away while I was en route. It looked like quite a show from the news stories."

Brand glanced at the TV, where video clips of rioting and looting flashed silently.

"Yeah," he replied. "It was quite a show."

Mercer was silent for a long moment. Finally, he spoke.

"Look. I heard about last night. I want you to know I knew nothing about it. Umar and Sahib were talking about it this morning at the compound. I don't know why they set you up, but I am on your side. We should meet and talk about what we need to do next."

It was Brand's turn to think. He hadn't expected Mercer to call. He certainly didn't expect him to deny everything and try to ally himself with him. The conspiracy against him was more serious than he imagined.

"I am up for breakfast if you are interested," Brand said innocuously.

"I've eaten," Mercer said. "How about we meet at my apartment?"

"Alright," Brand agreed. "I'll grab a bite to eat on the way."

He ended the call, dropping the phone on the bed beside him. It annoyed him that Mercer and Sahib thought him simple enough to buy Mercer's disclaimer. He didn't subscribe to coincidence. He was unlikely to believe that any aspect of the setup was happenstance. He knew Mercer was involved. The phone call did more to confirm his suspicions than to belie them.

Brand stood with a twist to his face. The painkillers were wearing off. He went to the vanity outside the little bathroom. He extracted a pain pill from the brown bottle and filled a glass with water from the tap. He took the pill and went back to bed. He decided to put off his meeting with Mercer and test his theory that Mercer was still complicit.

_____

Mercer called Sahib. His phone conversation with Brand had been nearly three hours prior, and there was no sign of him. Sahib answered the phone on the first ring.

"Well?" he asked simply.

"He said he would come by my apartment more than three hours ago. He hasn't arrived yet. What do you want me to do?"

Sahib was silent as he developed a plan. Finally, he spoke.

"Tell him I just called you, wanting you to come to the compound now because all of my other men are in the field. Tell him I am alone here, and you will be the only man guarding me. Like I said before, bring him here. We will deal with him."

"You want me to call him back?"

"Is there another way of contacting him?"

"You don't think he might perceive the call as a desperate ploy?"

"To call a colleague?" Sahib scoffed. "Of course not. Remember, Joe. You are a friend concerned for his safety. You want to help him."

Mercer was unconvinced.

"I'll try," he said reluctantly.

"You will make this happen," Sahib commanded. "Stop vacillating."

Sahib ended the call abruptly.

Mercer stood from the sofa. He went to the kitchen and popped open a beer. By nature, he wasn't a planner. He was a doer. He wasn't unintelligent by his estimation, but he was not a deep thinker either. Immediate and decisive actions had served him well in his life. Nuance and psychological games weren't his strong suit. He felt a deep reluctance to press Brand. His instincts told him the urging would make Brand suspicious of him.

"Shit," he barked.

He lifted the bottle and drained the contents in one pull.

He set the bottle on the kitchen counter and dialed Brand. The call went to voicemail. Mercer decided to leave a message.

"Hey, Brand," he began with forced confidence. "I just got a call from Sahib. He told me all his guys are in the field, and he wants me to come by and keep an eye on things. Give me a call. This is your chance to talk to him and get to the bottom of what happened last night."

Mercer ended the call and dropped the phone on the counter. A couple of minutes passed before the phone rang. He saw Brand's name on the caller ID. He hesitated a moment, then answered the call.

"Hey, Brand," he greeted him. "I expected you a couple of hours ago. Are you lost?"

He tried to force a tinge of humor into the last part of his greeting.

"Not lost," Brand replied. "I heard your voicemail. I am on my way now. I'll be there in half an hour."

"See you then."

Brand ended the call.

He leaned forward in the cut seat of the old truck. He suspected Sahib was pressuring Mercer to get him to the compound. Brand had no doubt a trap was being set for him. He saw no way around it. Dealing with his opponents head-on had served him well in his life. He held to the practice now.

Mercer was waiting outside the apartment when Brand arrived in his old truck. He pulled up beside Mercer.

"I'll follow you," Brand said.

Mercer moved to his car.

Brand followed Mercer to Sahib's compound. He parked his truck a distance down the street, outside of casual view, and walked to the compound gate, where Mercer waited for him. Past the gate, Brand heard no sounds of activity.

"I'll go in first," Mercer instructed. "You follow a few seconds later."

Brand shook his head.

"We'll go together."

Mercer pursed his lips at Brand's authoritative tone.

"Have it your way," he said with a shrug.

They entered the gate. Brand scanned the compound as they approached the mancave. Nothing moved. The sun was well into its retreat to the west, but the day was still bright and hot.

At the doorway to the mancave, Mercer glanced at Brand before turning the door handle. They entered the wide interior. Sahib stood in the center of the room. Umar and two other men leaned against the bar. Mercer joined the men, leaving Brand alone in the doorway.

"Come in, Mr. Brand," Sahib invited him cordially, no trace of malice darkening his tone.

Brand glanced at Mercer, who avoided his eyes. Umar glared at him from behind his bandaged nose. The other two men were unfamiliar to Brand, although they appeared to be Middle Eastern.

"What do you want?" Brand asked as he again faced Sahib.

"Simply to talk," he replied easily.

"Is that why you had Umar send a mob after me last night, to talk?"

Sahib shook his head, dismissing the act.

"We brought you into the fold. We trusted you. You have occupied your time with very strange activities, disappearing for days on end. What would you do if you were me?"

Brand suspected he had been followed to Camp Bravura. He again glanced at Mercer. The man looked at his feet uncomfortably. Brand pursed his lips with certainty. Mercer had followed him, probably after he dropped him at the hotel that day.

"What I do in my spare time, or on my time for that matter, is none of your business."

"Again, you make assumptions with no understanding of your position here."

Sahib looked at his men. They eased away from the bar, spreading apart, moving to surround Brand.

"Who do you work for, Mr. Brand?"

Brand watched the men move to encircle him. Mercer joined them, taking a place in the cordon.

"What are you scared of?" Brand asked Sahib boldly.

"Do I appear scared to you, Mr. Brand?"

"You are certainly frightened of what I may know about you and your organization."

Brand looked at the men who were now very close. He was surrounded.

"These assholes are beginning to piss me off."

"I think they don't like you either," Sahib said with an amused smile. "Do you work for the ATF or the DEA? Did you think you would find a cache of weapons here?"

Brand recalled Moore's warning and the story of the missing weapons. It surprised him Sahib would volunteer the information.

"I don't know what you are talking about," Brand replied. "Mercer told me you run a terrorist organization. I'm just a guy who listened to his stories about you and your operation. I figured you rigged elections and caused social unrest. I didn't know you trafficked in illegal arms too."

Mercer spat on the floor.

"That is a goddamn lie," he stammered. "I didn't tell him anything. He is bluffing."

Umar pulled a long knife from under his shirt and plunged the blade into Mercer's chest to the hilt.

Brand recoiled from the murder, bumping into Achmed. He and Lutah grabbed Brand by his arms. Mercer fell to the floor, his eyes watering as he died.

Umar looked at Brand hungrily.

Sahib stepped closer, raising a hand toward Umar.

"Joe was weak and an infidel, an unfortunate combination. We know you train with some aspect of law enforcement. I want to know who you work for, Mr. Brand."

Lutah and Achmed increased the pressure of their grip on Brand. He tested their strength subtly with his torso. He felt a sharp pain where his sutures strained against the movement. Umar withdrew the knife from Mercer's chest. Brand heard the sucking sound as the blood groove of the knife relieved the vacuum and the blade drew free of its victim.

Brand tensed as Umar raised his eyes slowly to meet his. In them, Brand saw a cruel hunger. The man was a killer. His expression displayed his bloodlust. His hatred for Brand was about to be fed, and Umar reveled in the prospect.

"This is your last chance to save your own life, Mr. Brand. Who do you work for?" Sahib warned as Umar moved slowly toward him.

"Until yesterday," Brand replied. "I worked for you."

Brand looked Sahib in the eye.

"I quit."

Brand stomped on the top of Lutah's foot. The man released his grip as he fell away, howling in pain. Quickly, Brand brought his free fist around and up. He caught Achmed in the throat, collapsing his larynx. He took a step away from Umar and produced the pistol hidden in his clothes. He trained it on Umar. The latter lowered his head, ready to charge Brand.

Sahib drew a pistol from the back of his belt. Mexican Carry. Brand recalled the term in a flash.

He fired in Brand's direction but wide to avoid hitting his men.

Brand took a snapshot at Sahib. The bullet missed and struck one of the collector cars displayed against the side wall.

Sahib fired two more shots as he ducked. He crouched low behind a sofa as he fled toward the back door.

Umar rushed Brand, taking advantage of his distraction with the leader. The bloody knife preceded him like the bowsprit on the prow of a ship. Lutah struggled to rise, but his injured foot resisted his efforts.

Achmed clutched his throat with one hand, reaching for Brand with the other. Brand was surprised the man was trying to press an attack with a crushed larynx.

Umar swung the knife in a wide arc. Brand blocked the swipe with his pistol. The impact dislodged both the gun and the knife. Both clattered on the stained concrete floor. The impetus of Umar's rushed attack at Brand toppled them both.

Brand twisted his body in the direction of the fall, trying to gain a positional advantage on Umar. The man was skilled. He locked his inner elbow around Brand's right leg and pulled himself atop him. Brand attempted to break their fall with his left hand, but he managed only to reduce the impact slightly. Their combined weight struck the concrete, causing Brand a sharp pain in his shoulder.

Umar struck him in the face with a full swing. Brand saw an explosion of red speckles before his eyes. He pulled his knee up and his right elbow down. The elbow struck home at the base of Umar's broad neck and his muscled shoulder.

The bigger man folded under the pain at the pressure point. Brand followed the elbow with a forehead to Umar's bandaged nose. The big Black man howled as his broken nose cracked beneath the impact. His grip upon Brand weakened as he withdrew to protect his nose. Like a tag-team match, Achmed was on him, sufficiently recovered from the throat blow to attack.

Brand was on his back and had very few options. He struck blindly at Achmed's throat once again. The flat-bladed blow found its mark. Achmed struggled to breathe, falling on his side next to Umar.

Brand saw a pistol grip protruding from Achmed's waistband. He spun around on the floor, punching Achmed in the face as he grabbed the weapon.

Umar reached for Brand's gun hand, blinded by the pain from his broken nose. Brand brushed the hand away and rolled to his feet. With impressive resolve, Umar raised himself to launch a desperate lunge at Brand.

Brand pulled the trigger, the bullet striking Umar in the meaty part of his thigh.

Umar collapsed to the floor, grabbing his leg.

Brand straightened, surveying the positions of the three men. Umar groaned and tried to stem the blood leaking from the bullet wound.

Achmed was motionless. It was uncertain whether he had suffocated or had merely passed out from a lack of oxygen.

Lutah sat passively, holding his foot. His posture assured Brand he was not a threat. His eyes were wide with fear.

Brand's gaze returned to Umar, who now watched him with a combination of pain and hate.

"Damn, Umar," Brand said in a sarcastic voice. "This asshole shot you."

Brand approached the wounded man and kicked him in the face. He moved to the side, where he recovered his pistol and picked up Umar's bloody knife. He moved to the double doors, where he cut off two large lengths of twine from the mini blinds covering the narrow windows. He returned and bound the men, hands behind their backs, one at a time. He cut more twine from other window blinds and tied their ankles, attaching them short to their bound hands.

Upon completing the task, the three men were on their stomachs, their feet in the air, secured to their tied hands.

"You are going to tell me where the guns are hidden," Brand told Umar in a dangerous tone.

Umar's face was a bloody mess, but he managed to project hatred and stubborn rebellion.

Brand knelt to his level.

"I am pretty pissed off right now," he said, grabbing the man's ear and twisting it viciously.

Umar screamed at the sudden excruciating pain.

"Where are the guns hidden?"

Umar's swollen eyes watered, but his jaw was locked firmly in defiance.

"This is going to get really bad," Brand warned him. "I'm going to start punching holes in you with asshole's gun. When I am out of ammo, I will start in on you with the knife. Where are the guns hidden?"

Brand pressed the muzzle against Umar's hamstring.

"Stop!" the wounded man screamed desperately.

"Talk," Brand responded.

"They will kill you!" he cried with outrage.

"Who will?"

"My people," Umar growled. He sprayed bloody spit on the floor as he yelled at his tormentor.

"If you don't tell me where the guns are, you will not live to help them do it."

Brand grabbed a handful of Umar's hair and twisted his face toward him. He looked into Umar's eyes.

"Last chance," he warned in a low voice.

He tensed to pull the trigger.

"They are across the yard under the shed, buried."

"Which shed?"

"The middle one with the wood crates under it."

Brand rose, moving to the window. He parted the blinds, seeing the shed across the compound.

He returned, checking each of the men's bindings, ensuring they were secure before stepping outside. He pulled the phone out of his pocket and thumbed through his contacts until he came to Moore's number. He pressed the call button and waited.

"That didn't last long," Moore greeted him. "People will talk."

"Funny," Brand noted without humor. "I found your guns. They are here in Houston, buried in a shed in a fenced compound. How quickly can you get someone here to recover the weapons?"

"What?" Moore stammered, trying to catch up.

"I'm texting you the address now. You need to get cops over here before these guys get free. I'll send you a pic of the buried cache of guns."

"I'll handle it," Moore said uncertainly. "You need to wait there until we arrive."

"Not going to happen, my friend. I have work to do."

"Brand..."

Brand ended the call, then texted Moore the address and a photo of the shed with the wooden crates.

He returned to his captives. He wiped his prints from the knife and the pistol, placing both outside the door to the mancave. He heard sirens as he left the compound. He loped along the street until he arrived at his truck. He felt moisture on the back of his shirt. He twisted around. There was a spreading bloodstain where his sutures had separated during the struggle.

He cranked the truck and drove away.

38

RANDY CHAPPELL SAT ON THE SOFA in Camille's living room. His cell phone was at his ear as he watched Camille swim laps in the pool. He played with the buttons of his lounge cardigan as he listened to the speaker on the other end of the call.

"I don't know much about that, Detective."

He listened again.

"He is one of our principal donors, yes, but we are not chummy, if that's what you mean."

A long pause grew as he listened to the speaker on the other end of the call.

"I'm going to end this call. I think my attorney should be involved if I am to say anything more."

Chappell leaned forward on the edge of the sofa as he listened to the response.

"Is that a threat, Detective? I am a United States congressional candidate. I would act with more respect if I were you."

Pause.

"Yes. That was a threat, sir."

Chappell ended the call and tossed the phone on the sofa beside him. His brow furrowed as he watched Camille ascend the pool stairs, grabbing a towel from a nearby chaise lounge. She toweled her hair, then her body, as she walked to the doors. As she entered, she saw the look on Chappell's face.

"What is it?"

"Sahib's men have been arrested. Joe is dead, and Brand is nowhere to be found."

Chappell was surprised at her reaction. She seemed to receive the news as a physical blow. She stretched her hand to the sofa as if to steady herself. She swallowed as she gathered her composure. When she finally spoke, her voice carried a calm demeanor her body was struggling to achieve.

"Arrested? On what charge?"

Chappell decided to pass on commenting on his observation of her discomfiture.

"I'm not getting a whole lot of details from the police, but they are being held for murder and weapons charges."

"Good God," she exclaimed, wrapping her hair in the towel. "I need to get dressed. I'll get moving to get ahead of this before the press is in full gear."

"Are we screwed?" Chappell asked despondently.

Camille was once more controlled and measured.

"Let's take a wait-and-see attitude for now. Murder and weapons charges brought against employees of our chief donor is not a small thing, but maybe it isn't as bad as it sounds right now."

"The detective on the phone talked to me like I was involved."

"That is their way. You are not involved in anything illegal. They are just beating the bushes for information."

"Camille!" he said with heat. "How do murder and weapons charges work out as 'not as bad as it seems'?"

Camille held him with a grave look.

"Because, Randy, if it is as bad as it seems, then your run for Congress is over. Get a grip on yourself and let me work."

Chappell winced under her words. He gave his attention to his hands, as though the implication of guilt stained them.

Camille watched his acquiescence absently as she formulated a plan of action. She turned, leaving Chappell alone.

It was just before noon when Camille parked her car in front of the attorney's office. The legal firm, Coughlan, Reed, and Simmons, was one of the preeminent law firms in Houston. The historical three-story stone office building housing the firm stood on a busy downtown corner.

Camille entered a lavish front office. The hushed atmosphere of the heavily paneled lobby instilled a sense of awe upon anyone who entered. She halted before the receptionist's desk, removing her sunglasses impatiently.

"May I..." the receptionist began before Camille interrupted her.

"Tell Bob Reed Camille Long is here to see him."

"Mr. Reed is in..."

"Tell him to cancel the meeting, and I will see him immediately!"

The girl frowned at Camille's tone. She touched her thin headset and pressed a spot on the phone display.

"Yes, Mr. Reed. There is a Camille Long here who says you are to cancel your current meeting and speak with her immediately."

Camille frowned at the impudent tone.

As she listened to the response on the headset, the girl looked up at Camille with unwelcome surprise. She touched the headset and smiled meekly.

"He will see you now," she said, her voice thin with fear and doubt. She hoped she still had her job when the demanding woman left after the meeting.

Camille moved to Reed's office with a rapid step, although not rapidly enough to indicate desperation or necessity. Her gait was one of authority and purpose.

Bob Reed, a balding man in his early forties, stood as she entered. A younger man in an expensive suit held the door as Camille entered. He closed the door as he left.

"Good morning, Ms. Long," Reed said, extending a hand.

Camille ignored it as she took a seat in the chair in front of his desk.

"Where are we on this?" she asked without preamble.

Reed sat, withdrawing a page of handwritten notes from a folio atop his desk.

"Mr. Farhad's men are in custody, arrested for murder and federal charges including weapons smuggling, weapons sales, and obstruction of justice," Reed began. Without pause, he continued. "One of the men confessed to the murder of a Joseph Mercer. The subordinate claims Mr. Farhad knew nothing about any of this, and he and the other men acted without his knowledge on both the killing and the weapons."

"Is the DA buying it?" Camille asked, leaning against the chair-back cushion.

Reed shrugged.

"They have a confession on both charges. The man who confessed to the murder, Umar Johnson, whose real name is LaMonte Johnson, had blood spatter on his clothing, and the murder weapon belongs to him. I believe the only reason Mr. Farhad hasn't been brought in yet is because of the confession and the preponderance of circumstantial evidence. The investigation is only just beginning. These things take time."

"This is extremely bad for our campaign. What are your thoughts, Bob?"

"I agree," he said with raised eyebrows. "Involved or not, Mr. Farhad's corporation owns the property where all of this occurred. We will, of course, block any unofficial speculation within the media outlets with threats of libel and slander action if necessary. You are the expert on handling this on the mean streets of electioneering. We can't be of much help there."

"Have you been contacted by Sahib or anyone in the organization?"

Reed shrugged.

"I don't know any more than what I have shared with you, Ms. Long."

Camille stood, smoothing her skirt.

Reed watched her silently. As she turned to leave, he stopped her abruptly.

"I almost forgot to give this to you," he explained, withdrawing a white envelope from the top drawer of his desk. "It was dropped off by courier this morning."

Camille returned to Reed's desk front.

"What is this?"

"I didn't read it," he explained simply. "It was sealed with instructions that only you should read the contents."

Camille took the envelope and dropped it into her purse, turning once more. She left the offices and returned to her car. She started the motor, allowing the air conditioner to keep her comfortable as she read the letter.

'Camille,

Mr. Brand must be brought to the camp within twenty-four hours.

He is armed and distrustful. Ensure he arrives without either advantage.

I leave the details to your considerable talents.

Sahib

Camille reread the note, turning the page over, looking for more of an explanation regarding the request.

What did Brand have to do with this? Why was he armed? How was she supposed to get him to the camp?

"Shit," she uttered, putting the car in gear.

39

BRAND DROVE TOWARD THE CAMPAIGN headquarters, his jaw set in a stubborn expression. He was convinced Chappell was involved in the continued efforts to harm him. He was going to confront the candidate and get to the bottom of this.

Kilgore had been blowing up his phone since his departure from Sahib's compound the night before. Apparently, word traveled fast in Fed World. In his voicemails, the DEA agent's tone was demanding and threatening. Each message offered no information regarding what he wanted to discuss, only a firm command to call him ASAP.

Brand was uninterested in talking to the agent. He ignored the calls. Instead, he ate a late dinner and retreated for a quiet night in a seedy motel near downtown. He switched his phone to silent after dinner, finally turning it back on as he drove toward the campaign office.

The phone rang. This time, he answered.

"I'm here," he said impatiently.

"I need you to come into the office for a conversation about last night," Kilgore said, annoyance prominent in his tone.

"I don't need a conversation about last night," Brand said flatly.

"You are a witness to a murder, based on the evidence at the scene and your phone call with an ATF agent. You are not a cop. Get your ass here now."

Brand gripped the wheel until his knuckles went white. He was unsure what his options were.

"Brand," Kilgore said in a milder tone. "I can't protect you in this if you don't work with me. I need to see you now."

"Protect me?" Brand said incredulously. "Protect me from what?"

"Arrest and prosecution."

"What?" Brand blurted in disbelief. "Are you telling me I'm a fugitive?"

"Not yet," Kilgore soothed him. "We need to get this thing sorted while there is still time for you to tell your side of the story."

Brand hesitated as his mind worked.

"Alright. I'm on my way."

Brand hung up on Kilgore, cursing under his breath.

The phone rang immediately. He saw Amy's name on the display. He answered.

"Hey, Amy."

"Brand, are you okay?"

"Peachy. What's up?"

"I heard Joe was murdered, and Sahib's men are in jail?"

"I heard that too," he replied vaguely.

"What do you mean, you heard it?" she asked. "The word is you were there."

"Who said that?"

Amy paused.

"Sahib's men told the police you were there. They said you instigated the whole thing."

Brand thought about it for a moment. Finally, he replied.

"That's not what happened, Amy. Joe lured me to the compound. Sahib's men killed him and came after me."

"Oh my God," she exclaimed.

Brand waited, but she said nothing more.

"Are you okay?" he asked with slight alarm.

"I don't know," she replied weakly. "I brought you into this. If they are after you, they may want me too."

"Why would they want you? Aren't you and Chappell close?"

"I told you at the fundraiser this isn't about political candidates. There is big money at stake here. I'm afraid. Can you come by?"

"Amy, I..."

"Brand, I really need you. I'm frightened of what they might do to me. Can you come by, please?"

The last was spoken through growing sobs.

"I will," he promised. "I have to make a stop, then I'll come right over."

"Brand, don't make me wait here alone."

"I'll get there as soon as I can," he promised. "I have to take care of one thing first. I'm sorry. I can't avoid it."

"Please hurry, Brand."

"Lock your doors. I'll call you when I'm on my way."

She ended the call.

Brand set the phone on the seat beside him. He adjusted his route, heading for Kilgore's office.

40

KILGORE MET BRAND JUST INSIDE THE ENTRANCE to the federal building. The agent drew him to the side of the wide lobby.

"I need your keys," he urged, putting out his hand.

"Why?"

"Just do it, please."

Brand reached into his pocket and produced the car keys. He dropped them in Kilgore's palm. The agent glanced at two agents waiting at a distance. They approached in a business-like fashion. Kilgore tossed them the keys, and they left the lobby through the front doors.

"Follow me," Kilgore instructed Brand.

Uniformed security guided Brand through the metal detectors. He was frisked, after which he followed Kilgore to the elevator bank.

"What's going on, Kilgore?" he asked warily. "They still have my phone."

"Keep your mouth shut and follow me," Kilgore commanded.

They rode the elevator in silence, exiting on the floor where Kilgore worked. The agent led him to his office and pointed at a chair.

"Have a seat."

Brand obeyed.

Kilgore took his seat behind the desk.

"Why don't you walk me through the events leading up to your arriving at Sahib's compound?"

"Am I under arrest?"

"You're not in cuffs, are you?"

"That's not an answer."

"You aren't answering my question either. Talk to me, Brand. Tell me about what happened that brought you to the compound."

Brand tried to organize his thoughts. His memories were scattered from the considerable stress he had been under: his work with the Kinetic Team, the setup at the demonstration, the trap at Sahib's, and the murder. He was unsure where to start, so he decided to provide Kilgore with a summary. He had been interrogated enough times to know more questions would follow, requiring him to repeat everything he had just said. The fewer the details initially, the better things would go.

"After the night I went to the Golden Stallion, everything changed with the campaign and me. I don't know what happened to trigger the attacks on me, but something did.

"The next week I was away at Bravura. When I returned to the campaign, Chappell asked me a lot of questions about who I worked for and what I did in my time away. I told them it was none of their business.

"Later, Mercer, the dead guy, asked me to meet him at an address to work the protests. I got there, but Mercer never arrived. I went looking for him and was attacked by a group of angry protesters. They chased me until I managed to get away. I cut myself during the escape and had to go to the doctor. They sewed me up, and I checked into a motel and slept it off.

"The next morning, I got a call from Mercer apologizing for the foul-up and asking if I wanted to meet. I asked him about the protests. I told him it looked like a setup to me. He said he knew nothing about it. He said he had been called away en route to the protest site. He offered to walk me into the compound to confront Sahib about it. He told me Sahib was alone. His bodyguards were supposed to be in the field.

"We showed up, and Sahib was there, but so were three of his goons. One of them was Umar, the guy I met earlier. I didn't recognize the two others. Umar stabbed Mercer with a big knife. He was coming for me next, but I managed to get free and got hold of a gun from one of the two guys holding me. In the struggle, Umar got shot. I tied them up and was able to discover Sahib had a cache of weapons on the grounds.

"I called an ATF agent I met at Bravura and told him about the weapons. I'm sure you know who I mean. I left the compound and laid low until I took your call today."

"That's it?"

"That's it."

"Why didn't you stay until the cops arrived?"

"My stitches were bleeding, and I didn't want to wait around while you guys worked everything out. I didn't feel up to being grilled for hours. I figured we would get together at some point."

"This is not a get-together," Kilgore explained sarcastically.

"Don't play with me," Brand warned. "You know what I mean."

The two agents to whom Kilgore had given the keys entered the office.

"Nothing," one of them said.

"Brand," Kilgore asked, "where is your weapon?"

"It wasn't in the truck?" Brand asked innocently.

"Don't play with me," Kilgore warned, using Brand's own words.

"I stopped off on the way and locked my stuff in a bus station locker."

Kilgore shook his head. Brand seemed to have a habit of hiding things in bus station lockers. It might be prudent to remember that.

"Where's the locker key?"

Brand hesitated. Finally, he said, "Under the seat, driver's side, tucked in the upholstery fold."

Kilgore waved to the agents.

"Go."

After the agents left, Kilgore looked at Brand.

"Why did you secure your belongings before you came here?"

"I don't trust you, Kilgore. You placed me in danger with no regard for my safety. I don't know where I fit in your world. I plan to be cautious until I know."

Kilgore leaned back in his chair. He studied Brand for a long moment before he spoke.

"I like you, Brand," he began slowly. "I have followed your exploits since San Antonio. You have been able to accomplish things no one could. Your luck never seems to run out. I think maybe it is more than luck. I decided to bring you into my team in an unofficial way. I sent you to Bravura to fill in the holes in your skill set. The Golden Stallion op was a test—a test you passed with flying colors."

"If you say so," Brand disagreed. "What about Agent Spencer? He rides my ass like a stepfather."

"He's a good man. He is not wise to my plans for you. Maybe he sees you as a threat. Maybe he is envious of your position as a contractor; you get the fun without the responsibility. I'm only guessing about Spencer, but he's not the issue.

"Your getting involved with this campaign on your own, and the activities you have been involved with, pushed your activation date forward before I had a chance to gain final clearance for you with the organization. We need to secure you and your equipment until we get you up and running."

"Does it occur to you I am involved in something pretty big here?" Brand asked.

"It is beginning to look like that."

"What's going on then?"

"I truly don't know what is up. Our purview is limited to the mission of our organization. Joint task forces require planning and authority from higher up. That's why Moore didn't talk to you about the campaign when you asked him."

Brand's suspicions were confirmed.

"Yes," Kilgore admitted. "Agent Moore and I had a detailed conversation."

"So, now what?"

"Once we recover your weapon, you are free to go. I need you to keep in touch with me."

Kilgore knocked on his desk.

"You answer the phone when I call, understood?"

Brand nodded.

"Where is my phone?"

"It will be waiting for you at security."

"I guess you guys went through it."

"Yep."

Brand waited at the federal building for two more hours before his phone and gym bag were returned to him. Kilgore allowed him to keep the truck, and he climbed into the hot cab as his phone cycled on. When it was fully powered up, a multitude of pings and beeps announced he had missed several calls and texts. He checked the voicemail log. He had received two calls from Amy. He played the messages.

"Brand," Amy's frightened recorded voice said, "There is someone outside at the curb. I don't know the car, and I can't see the driver. Are you on your way? Please get here."

Brand played the next message.

"Brand, they are getting out of the car and coming to the door."

Her voice was a panicked whisper.

"They are at the door."

He heard a knock in the background of the recording.

"They are banging on my door! Go away," she screamed. She had apparently moved the phone away from her mouth as she called to whomever was behind the door.

He heard a loud crash. He heard Amy scream and the deep voices of at least two men. He could not make out anything distinct being said. He heard crashing and banging as the intruders struggled to trap Amy. He heard the phone hit the floor, then voices. Someone picked up the phone and spoke with a Middle Eastern accent.

"Come to the compound west of Houston if you want to see the woman alive. Come alone and unarmed."

The call ended.

Brand looked at the timestamp. The calls had been placed half an hour earlier.

Brand remembered Moore's description of the terrorist camp. He doubted he was going to a school campus where he would visit like a parent called to the principal's office. With no gun and no surprise, he was walking into another trap.

His concern for Amy hampered his thoughts with an urgency that could prove deadly if he allowed his fears for her to dominate his actions. He struggled to pace himself. He had to determine how to gain an advantage.

An idea occurred to him. He started the truck and left the federal building.

41

IT WAS MID-AFTERNOON WHEN CAMILLE returned to the campaign office. She had been only marginally successful in heading off the news. Two of the major networks were already leading with initial information from unvetted sources.

Her interviews and press releases were being received with doubt in media circles. The growing drama was too seductive for them to run any type of grounding story. The news cycle was quicker than her ability to buffer the story.

None of this was a surprise. The sensational headlines would run. The rumors would fly. Hopefully, with the right spin and the assistance of friendly media, in time she would gain control of the narrative.

With a last look at her phone, she left her car and entered the back door of the campaign office. Sahib had not called, and he wasn't returning her numerous attempts to reach him.

She entered the headquarters' large campaign space. The usual sounds of bubbly giddiness from volunteers were reduced to a muted buzz of hushed voices as she moved among the desks and flyers. As more of the staff noticed her, the office grew silent. They watched her as she made her way to Randy's office.

She wanted to say something to reassure them, but she suspected nothing she could say would blunt the sensational rumors they had heard.

Instead, she continued without making eye contact with anyone in the crowded room.

When she entered, Chappell was standing behind his desk. It was apparent from his strained expression and his nervous shifting from foot to foot that he was at his wit's end.

"My God," he exclaimed in a harsh whisper. "Where the hell have you been the last twenty-four hours?"

"Sit down, Randy. We need to talk."

"You think?" he replied in exasperation.

Camille sat in one of the chairs in front of Chappell's desk. The candidate remained standing, his stiff posture registering the defiance he felt.

"The media is leading with this story everywhere," she explained. "It has gone national. We have to ride it out for a few days until the momentum slows and we can get our side out there."

"I thought that's what you've been doing," he complained in a louder voice.

"Stay calm, Randy. This is clickbait at present. The media lives on ratings, just like we do. Our play is to keep a low profile and disseminate limited information until an attempt at journalism kicks back in. At that point, we can shape the narrative."

Chappell watched her, motionless for a moment. Finally, his mouth parted in an angry smile.

"That is your plan, Ms. Campaign Manager? Wait and see how the press spins this? Since when is a good offense not the best defense? I am not a marketing genius, but I do know human nature dictates people will always insert a negative into an unknown. If we don't get our side of the story out, we will lose support. A drop in the polls is like an infection. It gets worse before it gets better—and getting better is a pretty optimistic stretch."

"You are right," she agreed. "You are not a marketing genius. You also seem to know almost nothing about how a story cycle gestates and matures. What is your plan? Are you going to jump in front of a microphone and deny, deny, deny? You may as well jump in front of a speeding bus. The result will be the same."

Chappell restrained himself with a mighty effort. His career was breaking apart as he stood there listening to Camille insult him and offer impotent solutions to his approaching demise. He took two deep breaths to calm himself.

"What, specifically, is our course of action as you see it, Ms. Long?"

"Are you willing to listen to an idea other than the one you are committed to?"

Chappell sat in his chair behind the desk, making a show of ratcheting down his heightened emotions.

"I'll listen to anything that sounds reasonable."

Camille crossed her legs as she formed her thoughts into words he would hear.

"Randy, we are not in control of this issue today. We will not be in control of it for a few days. The story will have to reach an initial climax before anyone will want to hear our side. Once that happens, journalists will contact us to help them formulate a complete story. When that happens, we regain control.

"In the meantime, we must perform our due diligence. We need to know what happened in Sahib's facility."

"I had my doubts about Sahib from the moment you introduced us," Chappell interjected curtly. "There are other sources of funding."

"I was not the one who introduced you to Sahib, Randy," she retorted, anger sharpening her tone. She closed her eyes to calm herself.

"This is not productive," she said in a more controlled voice. "If you need a reminder, here it is. His organization is a heavy hitter within our party. He funds every one of our national elections to one extent or another. Do you really think your Texas Native PAC could have come close to his contributions?"

Chappell didn't reply.

"No," she said, answering her own question. "It couldn't. You are here and in the lead because of Sahib's organization. You would do well to remember that over the next couple of days."

Camille paused. Chappell's expression reminded her of an upset little boy. His helpless look touched her.

She rose, laying her purse on the chair. She rounded the desk and knelt next to his chair. She raked the back of his neck lightly with her nails.

"My love," she said softly. "If a president can be accused of cheating on the First Lady in the Oval Office, get impeached, and have all the details exposed, and still win a second term, why can't we get past this?"

Chappell looked into her eyes. He considered her words.

"Leaders in Congress spent millions of taxpayer dollars and wasted years of legislative sessions trying to unseat a sitting president. The facts were public, and the participants were exposed. Every one of them was re-elected. The public is long on trust and short on memory. This too shall pass. Trust me."

Chappell looked at her gratefully. He felt a growing embarrassment at his earlier exhibition of panic.

"I'm sorry, Camille. Truly I am. Thank you for being patient with me."

Camille smiled. She canted her head to look more fully into his face.

"We are in this together, my love. I won't let anything happen to you."

Chappell's relaxed posture stiffened as they heard a commotion outside the office. Camille stood as the door burst open.

Carson Brand stood in the doorway. His face was bruised, and there was blood on his shirt. He closed the door with a violence that shook the wall.

Chappell opened his mouth to protest.

"Shut up, Chappell. Camille, take a seat. We are going to have a talk about your involvement in a plan to kill me."

"What are you talking about?" Chappell asked.

"I said shut up."

Brand took a step toward the desk. Chappell and Camille retreated as far as they were able. The back wall arrested their escape. Brand waited for Camille to obey his order to take a seat. She realized this and moved between Chappell and the desk as she made her way to the sofa in the corner. She sat carefully on the edge of one of the cushions.

"Ever since I walked into your campaign, people have been trying to kill me. Does this sound like business as usual to you, Chappell?"

The candidate said nothing in return. He seemed oblivious to Brand's claims.

"No," Brand continued. "It doesn't. Now, Amy Landry has been kidnapped, and I have been told to show up at a terrorist camp outside of town or she will be killed. Do you know anything about any of this?"

"I most certainly do not," Chappell replied firmly. "Amy has been kidnapped?"

Brand ignored his question.

"How about you, smart girl? Are you involved in this mess?"

"I am just learning about any of this from you now. I am sorry, but I am having trouble believing your claims."

"Look at me, Camille. Does it look like I am making this up?"

"You are right. You look like hell, but that doesn't support any of your claims."

"My claims!" Brand repeated bitterly. "Do you know Joe Mercer was murdered yesterday?"

"Of course, we heard about it."

"I was there when one of Sahib's goons knifed him. The same guy came after me. I was lucky to survive it. Now they want to finish the job."

Brand turned suddenly and flung the door open.

A large crowd had gathered at the doorway. They retreated in fright. Troy Doell was near the front, his mouth open, his Adam's apple sliding slowly up and down as he swallowed.

"Do you want me to call the police?" he asked meekly.

Chappell cleared his throat.

Brand looked at him.

"Do we need to call the police, Mr. Brand?"

"I'm not sure you want that kind of attention, Chappell."

Camille waved a hand toward the door.

"Troy," she said. "Get everyone back to their seats. We will work this out peacefully."

Troy hesitated.

"Back to your workplaces," Camille urged firmly but without heat. "We'll bring you all up to speed after our meeting with Mr. Brand."

The crowd dispersed, and Troy drew the door closed silently.

Camille rose from the sofa.

"May I stand?"

Brand didn't react. He merely watched her, intent on finding the truth behind her words.

Camille approached him. Her voice lowered to a soothing register. Brand was struck with the impression of a snake hissing, "Trust in me."

"Think about what you are saying, Brand. This is a campaign office. Randy is a candidate for U.S. Congress. We receive campaign donations from many people and organizations. We can't vet every one of them. The news of the murder and the weapons charges has shaken us to our core. We had no idea. The media fallout has been unprecedented. Everything we have worked toward is at risk."

She was directly before Brand, nearly touching him.

"I am heartbroken you have been in danger and now are under threat. We need to notify the police about Amy. We want to help if we can."

She reached for one of his hands.

"You have to know we had nothing to do with any of this."

Brand pulled his hand from her grasp. He placed his hands on his hips. She was convincing. He was not yet certain she was telling him the truth, but he was beginning to doubt his suspicions about her and Chappell.

He shook his head wearily.

"We can't contact the police. My instructions were to come alone."

"Where are you supposed to go?" Camille asked.

"A compound a few miles south and west of Houston. I understand it used to be a terrorist camp."

"What?" Chappell asked, bewildered by his words.

"I know," Brand agreed. "I didn't believe it either, but it's true."

"So, it is Sahib's men who told you to go to this compound?"

"I don't know whose men they are exactly," Brand began.

"So, you can't be sure it is Sahib behind this?" she asked.

"Sahib pulled a gun and shot at me yesterday," Brand informed her, his anger growing at her efforts to exonerate her donor. "I'm pretty sure he is behind this."

Chappell made a disbelieving noise as he struggled to keep up.

"Let me go with you, Brand," Camille offered.

"That," Chappell blurted, "is completely out of the question. The man pulled a gun and shot at another human being. This is way too dangerous. We have to notify the authorities immediately."

He grabbed the phone on his desk. Brand reached the desk in a stride and slammed his hand over Chappell's.

"You won't do anything that could get Amy killed," he warned menacingly. "Camille seems to have a close relationship with the man, seeing as she spends his money like it is her own. Maybe she can talk sense into him."

"Camille," Chappell pleaded. "Don't do this. You don't know what Sahib is capable of."

"I know Sahib," she explained. "I will be safe. I know I can defuse all of this before it gets worse."

She moved to the candidate.

"Remember," she said soothingly. "Trust me."

Chappell clamped his teeth over his protests, knowing they would be pointless.

Camille went to the chair near the door, collecting her purse.

"Let's go," she said to Brand.

42

CAMILLE PARKED THE CAR IN THE LOT BEFORE the first building inside the perimeter fence of the terrorist compound. They had been waved through by the civilian guards at the entry gate. They faced no opposition as they neared the main building.

The grounds were sparsely appointed with yellowed grass and a few oak trees scattered about the compound. The lawn was well mowed but lacked any type of formal landscaping. Behind the first building were several white structures. Paved roads wound between them, and cars were parked before each in small caliche parking lots.

Camille parked her car among the half dozen cars and dark vans in the front parking area. They stepped out of the car and walked toward the front door.

Brand opened the door and peered inside. He saw only an unoccupied reception area containing a desk and shelving filled with informational pamphlets and knickknacks. He entered and searched the room but saw no one. He listened but heard no sound of anyone inside. Brand beckoned to Camille, who stood just outside the open front door. She entered, closing the door behind her.

Again, he listened cautiously. He heard nothing to indicate they were other than alone in the building. They made their way slowly down the central hallway leading from the reception area toward the back of the building. Brand checked each office as they progressed. All were empty.

The last had a large double-door entry. The doors were open as he stopped to look within.

At the far end of the room, atop a raised platform, Sahib sat behind a long, ornate table. Sahib was dressed in what Brand imagined was traditional clothing for a man from the Middle East. A long conference table filled the middle of the room.

Amy sat at the far end of the table on the left side. He saw no one other than the two.

"Come in," Sahib invited him from his seat. "The Imam will join us momentarily."

Brand entered. Sahib sat straighter in surprise as Camille entered close behind.

"Camille, why have you come?" he asked urgently.

Camille moved casually toward Sahib.

"Brand asked me to come along and see if I can talk sense into you. Is that a possibility?"

Sahib stroked his chin, a smile growing under his trim beard. Before he could respond, a side door opened. He smiled as he rose.

An older man in full traditional dress entered, followed by a dozen similarly dressed men. The older man walked around to Brand's side of the table and approached him with an extended hand.

"Mr. Brand. My name is Imam Abu Mazoorah Al Shahan. Welcome to our education facility."

Brand accepted the Imam's hand. For a moment, they were face to face as the Imam scrutinized him. The Imam released his hand and looked at his palm curiously.

"Interesting," he said, turning to Sahib. "I still live after the encounter. Mr. Brand seems to be no more than a mortal man."

The Imam turned his back on Brand and went to the table on the dais. He sat in the central chair and rested a hand on the table. Sahib took his seat. The Imam raised the other hand elegantly.

"Mr. Brand, why are you here?"

"I'm here to get Amy. You already know the answer to that question. Why have you brought me here?"

"I hoped we might speak together. Please approach. It tires me to raise my voice. Shall we speak civilly as men?"

Brand looked around at the dozen men before he moved forward along the right side of the long conference table. He glanced at Amy. She seemed to be unharmed, although her expression showed fear. He noticed something beneath the look. What was she hiding? He couldn't be sure. He was certain, however, that she showed no relief at his arrival.

His eyes again went to the dozen men who had positioned themselves at uniform intervals along the walls behind and to each side of the Imam. They were younger than the Imam, their faces stony and menacing. Brand guessed they were the Imam's personal guards, perhaps terrorist soldiers.

"You admire my men," the Imam observed with pride. "Have you ever heard of Al-Quds, Mr. Brand?"

Brand shifted his weight impatiently.

"Al-Quds is the elite branch of our military might. These men are my personal security. I trust you will behave until our business is concluded, yes?"

Brand waited silently as Camille returned to his side. Sahib watched her with interest. Amy paid little attention to anything other than a spot on the conference table, where her eyes remained focused.

Brand began to speak.

"What is our business, Mr. ...?"

"Enough," Sahib interjected hotly. "This is not a civil conversation. This man threatens everything we have worked for, oh glorious Imam."

To Brand, he pointed and yelled.

"Who do you work for? Why have you infiltrated my organization? Talk or die!"

Brand's anger flared as Sahib ran his mouth behind the protection of greater numbers. He wanted to get at him like a pit bull in a ring. When he replied, his voice was low and raspy as he mastered his anger.

"I don't work for anyone, as I have told you again and again. I was brought to you by Mercer. What I do in my spare time is my business, but I am not a cop or any kind of agent."

Camille stepped forward.

"Why was there a cache of weapons at your compound, Sahib?" she asked pointedly. "Why did your men murder Joe Mercer? What have you been working for that required the harm or even the death of this man?"

Sahib dismissed her with a wave of his hand.

"This does not concern you, woman. This concerns the council. This is a matter for true believers, not infidels, and certainly not a woman."

Camille sputtered as anger and indignation constricted her words.

"There will be silence," the Imam commanded. He pointed to one of his guardsmen.

"I will not tolerate your insults," Camille raged when she was finally able to speak.

The guardsman moved rapidly toward Camille. He dropped her with a backhand blow.

Brand didn't react to the attack on Camille until the blow was on the way. He slowed Camille's fall to the floor with his right hand. He grabbed the retreating Al-Quds warrior by his keffiyeh and yanked him backward. The guard's head cracked on the concrete floor, thinly covered by a dark wood laminate.

Brand saw to Camille, who moaned as she stood with unsteady balance, her hand to her face where the blow had struck.

Brand was growing impatient with the meeting and the mood of casual caution toward him as a foe. The terrorists were confident in their numbers and apparently in their faith. He wasn't interested in debating their cause or listening to more about how he was an infidel and should be eliminated. He had heard about the Muslim hatred for Christians. He wasn't spiritual as a rule, but he identified as a Christian when pressed.

The remaining guards produced arms from their clothing. Brand faced a myriad of small arms, from pistols to Uzis, all of them trained on him.

The Imam lifted a hand, two fingers extended in a gesture of restraint.

"I apologize for Sahib's petulance. He is still angry you gained the upper hand in your last meeting."

"He can have another try if he wants to," Brand offered with a grand wave of his hand. "And any of your thugs who want to slap a woman around again can do so at their own peril."

"Mr. Brand," the Imam said with a hint of sympathy. "You will not leave here alive. The courtesy I extended you was only to learn more about my enemies. You have admitted you are alone. You will not be missed when you are gone."

Brand glanced around him as he listened to the Imam's decree of death. He was exposed. Camille was also a concern, being directly in the line of fire. He looked at Amy. She had lifted her eyes from the table and now watched him impassively. Her expression again gave him pause. Was she drugged? His questions about Amy were fleeting as guards moved toward him and Camille.

Camille had recovered enough to recognize what was happening.

"I am a high-profile political player. You will not get away with this. I work for powerful people. They know I am here!"

As the guards captured Brand and Camille in a rush, the Imam spoke.

"Who do you think the powerful people you speak of work for, woman?"

Brand and Camille were swept up by the guards and led out to the back of the building. They walked, surrounded by their captors, to the back of the property where a concrete-block building with a flat roof sat in the middle of a field. Metal pipes protruded from the roof. A huge plastic cistern sat beside the structure. Brand concluded the squat building was a pump house.

They were brought inside through a steel door. Inside, the air was cool and humid. Brand smelled water. In the center of the room was a perfectly round hole in the concrete foundation. The walls were bare except for the back wall, where an array of large valves and metal pipes were affixed to the cinder blocks.

As the door was closed, the two prisoners and the dozen captors were tightly packed inside the small room. By keeping a safe distance from the large hole in the center, the occupants were packed shoulder to shoulder and belly to back.

Brand peered over the edge of the concrete rim but could make out no details as to the depth of the hole nor what it contained. As one, the captors pressed the two prisoners toward the hole.

Camille cried out as she leaned against the pressing guards. Brand felt strong hands pushing him toward the hole. He glanced at Camille. She was ahead of him, dangerously near the edge. Another look into the group of captors showed him a glimpse of several weapons, holstered to free the captors' hands for the grim work ahead.

Brand twisted his body, but the guards were ready for him. They clutched his shoulders firmly. He allowed his body weight to fall. They did not anticipate his dropping to the floor.

They reacted quickly, but the tight quarters hindered them. They recovered and renewed their grasp on Brand, but not before he had grabbed a nearby Uzi belted to one of the guards.

He lifted the muzzle and pulled the trigger. He had never fired an Uzi before, and the rapid spray of bullets surprised him. He panned the shots in a tight semicircle, carefully avoiding shooting in Camille's direction.

The bullets found several of the guards, dropping them as they cried out and groaned in pain. Brand punched one of the guards restraining

Camille, hoping he could help release her. She looked at him with helpless terror as two of her captors threw her into the abyss.

She screamed as she fell. The splash followed a long while after she disappeared into the hole. Brand realized the hole was deep. He kicked at one of the captors who had thrown her in. The man caught the blow on his left shoulder blade. He tipped slowly as he tried to catch his balance. He disappeared into the hole, falling silently.

While the man fell, the others reached for their weapons. Brand was able to shoot three other men before they brought their arms to bear.

The close quarters rendered aiming impossible. They fired wildly in Brand's direction, striking other captors. Brand pulled the dying man from whom he had borrowed the Uzi around as a human shield. Bullets struck the man deeply. Brand felt a bullet pass through the man and strike him with only enough force to break the skin. Brand grabbed a pistol from the floor and returned fire rapidly at the shooters. He struck two men hard, center mass.

A bright light illuminated the room as someone managed to open the door to the pump house. The survivors and those only slightly wounded made for the safety of the outside. Brand counted eight men lying in pools of blood on the floor. Four had escaped—no, three. He had forgotten about the man who had fallen into the hole.

Brand moved to the edge.

"Camille," he called. "Can you hear me?"

He heard no answer.

"Camille!" he yelled, louder this time. "Are you okay?"

He thought he heard a voice. The sound was dim, and he suspected his imagination was playing tricks on him to allay his fears. He heard the voice again, this time stronger.

"Brand," Camille called to him. "I am okay. It's dark, and I can't see, but I think the man is dead. Get me out of here!"

"Can you touch the bottom?"

She didn't answer immediately. Finally, she responded.

"No, I went down a few feet. There is no bottom."

"Can you find a handhold on the walls? There is no way the entire well is concrete."

He waited as she checked the wall.

"Yes," she replied. "I can hold on to the wall, but the rocks are smooth, and there isn't much grip."

"I need you to stay calm, Camille," he called to her, placing as much confidence in his words as he could. "I have to get out of here and find a rope or something I can use to get to you. Can you do that for me?"

Her voice was barely audible with the depth of the well and her fear, but he heard her answer.

"Yes."

"I'll be right back."

He peered into the hole, trying to gauge the distance to the bottom. He estimated the depth to be around 50 feet or so. He searched around the floor until he found a pistol with rounds remaining in the magazine.

He stepped to the open door, peering outside. He jerked his head back behind cover, expecting a hail of bullets. None came. He heard only birds and cicadas in the few trees growing nearby.

He risked a longer look around the exterior of the pump house. Distant movement drew his attention. The last of the men had reached the back door of the main building where he and Camille had been captured. The fleeing Al-Quds disappeared through the door and into the building.

Al-Quds warriors did not impress him as much as they did the Imam.

Brand searched outside the pump house for something with which to rescue Camille from the well. He found nothing.

He ran to the nearest building. It appeared to be a schoolhouse filled with cowering young men and well-dressed faculty members. He saw nothing helpful. He returned to the heat outside and ran to the next building.

This was a residence hall filled with small sleeping quarters containing two small beds and two chests of drawers in each.

The next building was a dining hall. He found a large spool with a fire hose wrapped around it. He grabbed the coupler at the wall connection and twisted. The brass fitting was torqued tightly. He inspected the fitting for retaining pins or snap rings to no avail.

He jumped over the buffet line and entered the kitchen area behind it. He found a butcher knife in a knife block.

He returned to the fire hose spool and cut through the heavy nylon-braided hose. The knife was sharp but not ideal for the job. His hand ached by the time he severed the hose from the coupler.

He pulled the hose off the spool, slinging it over his shoulder with a mighty effort. The hose was heavy; he estimated its weight at more than a hundred pounds.

He departed the dining hall and returned to the pump house as quickly as the heavy load would allow. Moving one of the bodies aside, he dropped the hose on the floor.

He leaned over the dark hole.

"Camille," he called, out of breath. "Are you still with me?"

She answered immediately, her voice quavering with relief.

"Yes. I'm still here."

"I'm going to drop this hose to you. I need you to find a way to tie it around your waist. You will need to keep your hands free to help. I need you to climb as I pull."

"I'll try."

He lowered the severed end of the hose slowly into the hole, unwinding the rough coil with difficulty. Finally, he reached the end of the hose connected to the brass nozzle. He hoped to use the fixture as an initial handgrip when he pulled. He leaned against the dangling weight with a grunt.

"Can you reach the hose?" he asked in a strained voice.

"It is just above me," she replied. "I can just reach it, but I can't tie it around me."

"Shit," he said under strain.

"What, Brand?"

"Grab the end of the hose. I'll haul you up. I need you to hang on tight."

"I've got it."

He felt her weight added to the heft of the dangling hose. He was certain the combined weight was more than two hundred pounds. It was a lot of weight to haul hand over hand for fifty feet.

He looked around him. His eyes locked onto the valves and pipes on the back wall. He hoped he could pull enough hose to reach the wall.

He pulled with all his strength. With a mighty effort, the hose rose two feet. He got his feet under him once more and hauled on the hose. He pulled another three feet.

He glanced at the pipes. His eyes burned with sweat. He repositioned his feet and pulled again. He groaned heavily with the effort he was exerting. He was nearing the pipes. If he could manage to wrap the hose around one of them, he could conserve some of the energy he was using to maintain a hold on the heavy hanging weight. He pulled again. He nearly fell as the hose lost some of its weight resistance.

"Hey!" he yelled with alarm, thinking she had lost her hold on the hose. He listened but didn't hear the splash of her falling body.

"It's okay," she said brightly. "I'm standing on a narrow shelf. Give me some slack, and I can tie off the hose."

He sighed with relief. He was unsure whether he could have started over and pulled the same distance again. He gave her some slack. He felt vibrations as she tied the hose.

"It's wet on this ledge," she said. "It's blood. Oh my God. The man must have struck his head on this ledge on the way down."

"Are you tied off?" Brand asked her with a strained voice. Even without her added weight, he was still supporting nearly a hundred pounds.

"Yes. I'll try to climb as you pull."

He hauled on the hose once again. Her climbing helped with her weight and took some of the hose's weight. Brand was able to draw several feet with the first pull. His next tug gave him enough slack to wrap the hose around one of the large metal pipes. He used both hands to pull the down end of the hose as he drew the upper end toward him. In this way, he gathered hose length below him on the floor until he tired. The pipe allowed him to rest for a moment without holding the weight.

Within minutes, Camille's hands grasped the top edge of the concrete hole. Brand hauled on the hose with the last of his strength as she clambered onto the foundation. She surveyed the bloody carnage around her with wide eyes. Her clothes were wet, and her face was bruised from the blow she had received or from the impact of hitting the water in the well.

"Are they dead?" she asked as she stood, untying the hose from her waist.

"Yeah," Brand replied wearily. "Come on. We need to find Amy."

They felt a warm gratitude for the hot afternoon sun and the open country around them. Their situation could have ended much worse.

At the back door of the main building, Brand pulled the pistol from his waistband. Camille looked at the gun curiously. She had heard the stories about Brand, but seeing him like this was a novel experience for her. She moved closer to him as they entered the building. He glanced at her. She returned the look. He recognized her need for safety.

"Stay behind me," he instructed quietly.

They arrived at the conference hall. It was empty, as were the hallway and adjoining rooms.

"Where is everyone?" Camille asked no one in particular.

"Let's see if we can get to your car."

As they entered the reception room, Brand pushed Camille to the floor as a flurry of gunshots sounded from behind the doorway leading to the restroom hall.

Brand leaped behind the reception desk and trained his pistol on the near corner of the entryway. A dark-haired head eased into view as one of the Al-Quds guards peeked around the corner. Brand shot a neat hole in his forehead, and the man fell to the floor.

Camille moved to stand. Brand pressed her back to the floor.

"Wait," he commanded in a whisper.

A second guard leaped through the doorway, firing wildly toward Brand and Camille. The rounds impacted the wall behind the desk. Brand exposed only his shooting arm and an eye around the desk, double-tapping the man center mass. The wounded man moved to fire once more, and Brand shot him between the eyes.

Brand rose, checking the gun for remaining ammunition.

Camille stood slowly. Her ears rang from the gunfire, and she felt light-headed at the sight of the two dead men.

"My God. What is going on?"

Brand moved to the restroom hallway and checked for additional foes. As he suspected, the hall was empty. He doubted the second man would have rushed into the open alone. If he had help, others or another would have attacked him.

"Get in the bathroom," he instructed.

"What..."

"Do it!"

His voice was an urgent whisper once more.

"Someone is outside."

Camille moved as instructed, locking herself in one of the restrooms and dropping flat on the tiled floor.

Brand looked between the mini blinds and the corner of the window frame. He saw nothing other than grass and the sidewalk. He waited. There! A foot came into view as someone crept along the sidewalk.

Brand yanked the blinds open enough to aim, shooting the third guard through the window. Breaking glass showered the ground below the window. The guard grabbed at the wound in his neck, spewing blood on the sidewalk. He fell onto the grass and lay still.

Brand heard a noise from the rear of the building. Someone had entered the back door. He sidled toward the hallway leading to the rear of the building. He aimed the pistol and waited. A slight figure appeared. It was Amy.

She saw him and smiled a tearful welcome as she recognized him. She hurried down the hallway and fell into his arms. She shuddered as she buried her face in his chest.

"Thank God you are alive," she said, her voice muffled by his shirt.

Brand pressed her gently away from him so he could look at her.

"Where is Sahib and the Imam?"

"I think they ran," she said, her face wet with tears.

"Why did they let you go?"

"They just left me. I went to look for you, then I heard shooting. I came back, and here you are. Where is Camille?"

"She's in the bathroom."

Amy looked at him with a bewildered expression.

"Hiding," he explained. "Come on."

He turned toward the reception area.

"I told you to leave," Amy said in an even tone. "You should have listened."

As Brand turned, he heard a shot, and his back burned high up near his right shoulder. He fell to the floor. Turning his head, he saw Amy, a pistol in her hand.

"I'm sorry, Brand. Our cause is just."

Amy lifted the pistol. She handled the weapon awkwardly.

"Justin had the sense to leave when I warned him."

He raised the pistol in his throbbing hand and shot her in the chest. Amy fell to the floor with a cry.

The pistol fell from his numb hand and clattered on the floor beside him. His vision dimmed as he felt his body grow light. Camille knelt beside him, pressing her hands to the wound.

"Brand," she cried desperately. "There is a lot of blood. Were you shot twice?"

"One is busted stitches," he explained weakly as he lost consciousness.

43

BRAND OPENED HIS EYES SLOWLY. His head swam, and he felt light as a cloud. The pain in his back was no more than a minor ache. He looked around as his vision cleared. He was in a hospital room.

Kilgore stood near his bed, watching him with a keen eye.

Brand tried to sit up. Bad idea. The pain pierced the morphine screen, and he fell back onto the pillow with a groan.

"He lives," Kilgore announced unnecessarily.

"I can't believe I got shot in the back again," Brand complained with a grimace.

"That's what you get for sticking your nose into ATF business," another voice declared from outside Brand's limited view.

He turned his head. Moore stood there, his hands in his pockets.

"Hey, Moore," Brand greeted his old training partner. "Fancy seeing you here. Now who's churning up talk?"

"You rest easy, old friend," Moore said. "You just uncovered a huge plot to take control of our government. You deserve a vacation."

"What are you talking about?" Brand asked vacantly.

"Are you lucid enough that I won't have to do this again later?" Moore asked with manufactured impatience.

"I'm fine," Brand assured him. "Tell me."

"When we raided this camp before, we found no weapons nor any sign the facility was being used for terrorist activities. Remember, we don't attack schools.

"When you found the weapons in the Houston compound, we were able to trace the serial numbers and confirm they were the same weapons we were looking for. Farhad is one of the leaders of IOA. He handles the day-to-day running of the operation."

"Farhad?" Brand asked.

"Sahib," Moore explained. "Anyway, IOA is the chief donor for Randy Chappell's campaign, as well as a score of others over the years. IOA places these candidates.

"Farhad's kinetic team is the radical activist arm of the organization. They gin up violence among peaceful protesters. IOA funds the efforts, bringing outside forces into the protests to commit violent acts and press the demonstrators to break the law.

"You got too deep into the organization to live. Joe Mercer was killed for the same reason. We haven't apprehended Farhad or the Imam, but they won't get far. They certainly can't get out of the country."

"What about Amy Landry? Why did she shoot me?"

"We're still digging into Amy. Looks like she was involved. She probably knew Farhad for years. Farhad most likely converted her."

"I thought she liked me," Brand said doubtfully.

"Brand, she shot you because she was a part of the organization."

"But she isn't... sorry, wasn't Muslim," Brand said, confused.

"She was a convert. Many in IOA are as Western Caucasian as you and me, buddy."

"And Camille?"

Moore shrugged.

"She is guilty of poor judgment only, as far as we can tell. She was loyal to a key donor. No crime in boning who you like."

Kilgore cleared his throat to remind the two he was still in the room.

"The implications will rock our political system for years to come," Kilgore predicted. "Investigations are being launched against Chappell and several other candidates, as well as a half dozen sitting congressmen and women, for their ties to the terrorist group. The assassination of Speaker Cole was carried out by the same group. He threatened to expose the whole thing, and they couldn't allow it."

Kilgore buttoned his suit coat.

"We'll leave you to rest, Brand. I'll be in touch."

Kilgore left the room.

Moore moved to Brand's side.

"You're a tough bastard. I'm glad you lived through this one. I'll look you up next time I'm in town."

Moore patted Brand's shoulder, then left.

Brand sighed as his thoughts whirled.

His doubts were interrupted as he sensed someone at the door. He looked toward it. Camille leaned against the doorframe. Her shiner was less obvious. He guessed it was part healing and part makeup. She wore slacks and a buttoned shirt closed just enough to please Brand.

"How are you feeling, Brand?" she asked.

"Sore. You?"

She touched her bruised face.

"Sore."

She sat on the bed next to him.

"Thank you for saving my life back there. I owe you so much. I guess you heard about Randy and the campaign."

Brand nodded.

"What are you going to do now?" he asked.

"I don't know," she replied candidly. "It's too late in the season to pick up another campaign gig. My name will probably be mud after all of this comes out."

She looked at him with a smile.

"Maybe I'll find some big strong man who can look out for me and marry him."

"Good luck with that," Brand said.

"The doctor says the bullet hit bone and did minimal damage, so you'll be out of here in a few days. What's next for you?"

"I think I might head home for a while."

"San Antonio?"

"Yeah," he replied. "I'm not that fond of Houston anymore."

"That is a common opinion here. Maybe I'll look you up in San Antone."

"It's San Antonio."

"Sorry, Mr. Sensitive."

"Thanks for going with me to the compound. I guess you couldn't know what they were really up to."

Camille looked into his eyes.

"Is that gratitude?" she asked with a smile.

"If you hadn't gone, I might have bled out before anyone came."

"You're welcome."

They sat in silence, not knowing what else to say.

Camille stood and smoothed her slacks.

"Good luck, Carson Brand," she said sadly. "Look me up sometime."

She left the room as Brand struggled with a reply.

EPILOGUE

BRAND ENTERED THE DOUBLE GLASS DOORS decorated with a cartoon dog holding a cocktail. He heard the jukebox playing a heartbreaking country song. As usual, the bar was packed with the regular happy-hour crowd. He recognized many of the patrons.

Rod Dog's Saloon was unchanged. He had been gone only a few months, but he was surprised that a piece of his old life was still there. So much had happened since his last drink at the watering hole.

Karen, the bartender, spotted him and shuffled through the narrow access space in the bar top. She clapped her hands and laughed as she grabbed him in a friendly embrace.

He returned the hug and kissed her on the mouth.

"Hey," she warned. "You're still in the friend zone, mister."

"How about a double bourbon rocks?"

"Coming up."

He found a seat at the bar. He returned the regard of the few regulars who greeted him. Karen set the drink before him on a bar napkin.

"Where have you been?" she asked, looking him in the eye.

"Maybe I'll tell you the story after a few more of these," he replied wearily. "It's good to be back."

Karen smiled and moved to take drink orders.

Brand sipped his bourbon. The bite of the drink and the familiar surroundings of his longtime watering hole transported him. His thoughts darkened with memories of Bert, Natalie, and even Christina. He had seen so much death in the past few months. He downed the drink, motioning to Karen for a refill.

She brought a newly filled glass, collecting the empty.

Brand looked across the bar. He saw the ghost of his late best friend, Bert, in a chair chatting up one of the women at the bar.

Brand felt his throat constrict as his eyes burned with tears he wouldn't free. The image of Bert tore at him.

In his reverie, Brand watched as Bert turned from his latest conquest and looked fully at him. His friend lifted his drink in salute.

Brand watched, motionless with a deep melancholy.

Bert lowered the drink and smiled.

Brand sipped from his glass, struggling with emotions he could not thwart. He looked back at his friend. The pleasant memory was gone. In his place was a woman talking to her companion, a professional-looking man in a suit.

Brand emptied his glass and gestured to Karen for a refill.

She smiled, adroitly pouring another with a heavy pour. She replaced the empty once again.

"You look thinner," she observed as she collected the moist bar napkin beneath it.

"I guess I am," he agreed faintly.

"Are you back for a while?"

"Not sure," he replied honestly.

Karen had known him for many years. She had never known Brand to be a social creature. He was always private about his life and his troubles. She sensed he was troubled now but had no idea how to talk with him about it. Instead, she smiled at him.

"It's good to have you back. Holler if you need something."

Brand lifted his glass to her in thanks.

"I will."

She moved away to fill more orders.

Brand sipped the bourbon, beginning to feel the growing comfort of a warm buzz. He sensed someone take the seat beside him at the bar. He glanced to his right.

The newcomer was Agent Kilgore, dressed in jeans and a button-down shirt. Karen appeared before him.

"What can I get you?" she asked with a smile.

"Whatever he's having will do."

Karen's expression froze for a moment as she silently questioned who the newcomer was.

"Coming up," she said, moving away to fill the drink order.

"This place has a good vibe," Kilgore noted. "I can see why you come here."

"I like it," Brand agreed.

He spun his glass slowly, watching the ice melt and mix with the booze in slow eddies.

Karen returned, placing a bar napkin before Kilgore. She set the glass on the napkin. She looked at Brand, checking on his drink status.

Brand smiled and shook his head. Karen moved away.

"How's your back?" the agent asked, sipping from the highball glass with a sour expression.

"It's a little sore. The doctor ordered bed rest for a couple of weeks."

Kilgore lifted the glass again.

"Not a bourbon man," Brand remarked, watching as the agent squinted as he pulled another sip from the glass.

"Not really," Kilgore admitted. "I guess it is an acquired taste."

"Nobody drinks it because they are okay with it. Bourbon is a commitment, a relationship. If you love it, you stay with it. If not, you stay away from it."

Kilgore considered the observation silently for a moment. Finally, he turned a fraction toward Brand.

"I came by to give you an update. We captured Sahib and his boss, the Imam. They were boarding a private jet at one of the small private airports near Houston. The Iranian embassy is raising three shades of hell over the incident. The camp has been shut down until the investigation is completed."

Brand kept his attention on his drink.

"As for you," Kilgore continued, "you are officially on the team now. You can carry a gun and help us catch bad guys. Even your buddy, Agent Spencer, has accepted that you are an official contractor. Congratulations."

"Thanks," Brand said with a glance in Kilgore's direction.

"You're welcome," Kilgore returned, draining his cocktail with a sour face. "When you are finished with your bed rest and convalescence, I need you to report to our field office downtown. We need to get you to work ASAP. I'll text you the address and phone number."

Brand considered Kilgore for a long moment.

"I appreciate your pulling my ass out of that jail cell. I'll take a week or so, then I'll be there."

"Good," Kilgore said as he stood. He reached for his wallet.

"I got it," Brand said. "You can get the next one."

"Thanks," Kilgore said. "See you in a week or so."

With that, he left, leaving Brand alone with his thoughts.

Karen returned with a fresh drink.

"Friend of yours?"

Brand considered her for a moment.

"Not really. Just a colleague."

"You have colleagues now?" Karen asked with a friendly smile. "Since when are you a corporate guy?"

Instead of waiting for an answer, she moved away to help a customer.

As she cleared his view, his gaze drifted across the bar.

A dark-haired woman sat alone near the far wall.

Brand froze.

Christina.

She smiled.

His first thought was that the bourbon had finally caught up with him. He looked away and rubbed a hand across his face. When he looked back, she was still there.

Slowly, he rose from the barstool.

She stood as he approached.

For a moment, neither spoke.

Then they embraced.

"I was told you were dead," Brand said.

"A lot of people were."

He pulled back and stared at her.

"I looked for you."

"I know."

Brand shook his head in disbelief.

"I can't believe you're here."

Christina smiled sadly.

"Neither can I."

"Are you hungry?" she asked.

"Starved."

"Then let's get out of here."

Brand dropped several bills onto the bar and followed her toward the door.

Karen caught his eye and smiled.

He waved.

Outside, Christina led him toward the side lot beside the bar.

"My car's over here."

Brand followed.

They reached a black Mercedes coupe parked near the edge of the lot.

"Nice car," he observed.

Four large men stepped from the darkness.

Brand stopped.

Christina stepped away from him.

"I'm sorry, Carson."

The regret in her voice was unmistakable.

"I had no choice."

The men closed on him from every direction.

Brand stared at Christina as they seized his arms.

"What the hell is this?"

She didn't answer.

The men forced him toward a waiting black SUV.

The rear door slammed.

The engine roared.

The SUV spit gravel and accelerated into the night.

The last thing Brand saw through the tinted glass was Christina standing motionless beside the Mercedes.

Continue the Carson Brand Series

Carson Brand survived cartel violence, political corruption, and the deadly machinery operating behind public power.

But his worst fight is still ahead.

Reasonable Sin

Wounded. Hunted. Stripped of his memory.

Brand arrives in a small Texas town with no clear past, no allies, and armed men closing in from every direction. As cartel operatives, mercenaries, and federal agents tighten the net around him, Brand must uncover who he really is before the truth gets him killed.

Fast-paced, violent, and relentless, Reasonable Sin pushes Carson Brand deeper into the hidden world of betrayal, survival, and conspiracy.

Continue the series now:

REASONABLE SIN, A CARSON BRAND ACTION THRILLER

ABOUT THE AUTHOR

CRAIG RAINEY IS AN AMERICAN ACTOR, SCREENWRITER, MUSICIAN, AND AUTHOR KNOWN FOR CREATING GRITTY, CINEMATIC STORIES ROOTED IN HIDDEN POWER, FRONTIER VIOLENCE, CONSPIRACY, AND SURVIVAL. A TEXAS NATIVE WITH FAMILY ROOTS TRACING BACK TO THE ORIGINAL STEPHEN F. AUSTIN SETTLERS, RAINEY DRAWS HEAVILY FROM A LIFETIME OF REAL-WORLD EXPERIENCE THAT INCLUDES MILITARY SERVICE, RANCH WORK IN SOUTH TEXAS, CONSTRUCTION, AND DECADES SPENT STUDYING THE DARKER MACHINERY OPERATING BENEATH MODERN AMERICAN LIFE.

RAINEY IS THE CREATOR OF THE CARSON BRAND SERIES, A GROWING COLLECTION OF GROUNDED CONSPIRACY THRILLERS BLENDING CARTEL VIOLENCE, POLITICAL CORRUPTION, COVERT POWER STRUCTURES, AND LONE-MAN SURVIVAL AGAINST SYSTEMS LARGER THAN HIMSELF. HIS WESTERN FICTION, INCLUDING MASSACRE AT

CRAIG RAINEY

AGUA CALIENTE AND HOODOO WAR, EXPLORES THEMES OF REVENGE, FAMILY LEGACY, AND THE BRUTAL REALITIES OF FRONTIER JUSTICE IN THE AMERICAN WEST.

AS A SCREENWRITER, RAINEY HAS EARNED MULTIPLE AWARDS AND OFFICIAL SELECTIONS, INCLUDING BEST SCREENPLAY (2023, 2024), BEST NARRATIVE PERIOD PIECE, AND BEST BREAKOUT WRITER FOR HIS SCREENPLAY ADAPTATION OF MASSACRE AT AGUA CALIENTE. IN 2024, HE WON BEST ACTOR FOR HIS PORTRAYAL OF WALKER IN THE WESTERN FILM THE OLDEST POSSE. HIS WORK CONTINUES TO ATTRACT INDUSTRY ATTENTION FOR ITS CINEMATIC REALISM, EMOTIONALLY CHARGED STORYTELLING, AND ATMOSPHERIC PORTRAYAL OF VIOLENCE, POWER, AND SURVIVAL.

RAINEY CONTINUES TO WRITE AND DEVELOP NEW NOVELS, SCREENPLAYS, AND FILM PROJECTS FROM TEXAS.